HOME FOR WOUNDED HEARTS

ASHLEY FARLEY

Leisure Time Books
a division of
ahb publishing

ALSO BY ASHLEY FARLEY

Nell and Lady
Sweet Tea Tuesdays
Saving Ben

Sweeney Sisters Series
Saturdays at Sweeney's
Tangle of Strings
Boots and Bedlam
Lowcountry Stranger
Her Sister's Shoes

Magnolia Series
Beyond the Garden
Magnolia Nights

Adventures of Scotties
Breaking the Story
Merry Mary

For those struggling with addiction, homelessness, and domestic abuse

FAITH

*F*aith raised her glass of champagne for a toast. She rarely indulged in luxuries like the expensive bottle of Veuve Clicquot, but achieving one's life goals called for a celebration. Never mind that it took losing her mother to Alzheimer's and killing her ex-husband in self-defense to identify those goals.

"Tomorrow's the big day. Each of you have played a vital role in seeing this dream come to fruition, and I thank you from the bottom of my heart." She clinked glasses with each of her dinner companions in turn, first with her current husband, Mike, on her right and then their guests seated across from them—Dr. Robin Bowman, her staff psychologist; and Dr. Moses Ingram, her personal therapist and close friend.

She sipped her champagne and licked her lips. "But I have to admit, I'm scared to death."

Mike placed a hand on her shoulder and squeezed. "You're gonna do great, babe. You've come a long way from the battered housewife who stumbled into my emergency room with a broken nose to the founder and director of a women's shelter. This project has been yours from conception. And you should be damn proud of yourself."

"Conception," Faith said, swirling the champagne around in her glass. "That's an interesting choice of words considering the circumstances. I conceived this child, and I've been carrying it around for nine months, but now that I'm giving birth to it, like any mother of a newborn, I'm worried I'll fail."

Placing an arm on the table, Moses leaned toward her. "It's only natural for you to have reservations. You're worried you'll fail, because you've put your whole heart into this endeavor, and you want so desperately to succeed. Let that worry be the fuel that drives you. You have much to offer. You are one strong lady, Faith Neilson. Now it's time for you to share the strength with others."

Moses's patience and reassurance had gotten her through the worst of days, and she trusted him explicitly. She sucked in an unsteady breath and held her head high. "You're right. I can do this."

"That's the fighting spirit." He placed his massive hand over hers. To say Moses was a big man was an understatement. At six and a half feet and three hundred pounds, he was a giant, although a gentle one. His formidable presence alone made her feel safe.

"Why don't we discuss your concerns?" Robin said. "I know it would help me to go over everything one last time."

Faith studied the woman's flawless caramel skin and warm hazel eyes. Back in January, when Moses had first introduced Faith to Robin, she'd felt an instant connection based on their mutual desire to help women in need. During the months that followed, as they'd worked together to put everything in place at the home, their professional bond had morphed into friendship.

"That's a great idea." Faith lifted her fork. "But let's eat while we talk. I intended this dinner to be a celebration." She stared down at her ahi tuna steak. "Mike, you've outdone yourself again."

Moses forked off a bite of tuna, closing his eyes as he savored the fish. "That is some kinda good, my friend. You know your way around a grill like no other."

Once they'd all taken several bites of food, Robin said, "As far as I'm concerned, we've done everything by the book. We have more than ample liability insurance. Our attorneys have filed the appropriate documentation. We've gotten the necessary certifications and passed all the required inspections."

Moses chimed in, "I agree. We've elected a dedicated group of strong professionals to our board of directors, and we're continuing to make progress with corporate sponsorships and grant solicitations. We've developed a strategic plan, and the website's in the works."

"And let's not forget about the residents themselves," Mike said. Not only was he a member of the board of directors, he'd also agreed to be the doctor on call for the shelter. "You've defined your admission guidelines and intake process, and you're already providing shelter for five residents. You're on your way."

"About that," Faith said, setting her fork down and wiping her mouth. "I'm not so sure that taking in residents before we officially opened for business was such a good idea."

"I disagree," Robin said. "These women are good fits for our program, and they need our help. We couldn't very well turn them down. And this soft opening has allowed us the opportunity to work out a few kinks in our program."

Faith knew all too well what it was like to be on the run with nowhere to hide. She cautioned herself against second-guessing her decisions. If she wanted to be a strong leader, she needed to portray self-confidence. "No, of course we couldn't. We've been ready for residents for weeks. It wouldn't be right to turn these women away because we hadn't officially cut the ribbon."

As they finished dinner, they talked on about legalities and formalities. Faith waited until she served homemade banana pudding for dessert, her mama's recipe, before broaching the subject of money.

"Our finances are my primary concern. Mike and Moses, I'm grateful for all the money you've raised. If the cost of renovating the Humphrey estate hadn't exceeded projections, our accounts would be in much better shape. I don't see how we'll survive the first year without state funding."

"I'm confident the funding will come through." Moses placed his napkin beside his empty plate and sat back in his chair. "If not, there are plenty of sources we can tap. Let me worry about the money, Faith."

"Ha. That's easier said than done. I'm an accountant, remember?" Faith had been the accountant for her family's seafood business for years, some years more profitable than others.

The front door slammed shut and Faith's nine-year-old daughter, Bitsy, entered the room. She went straight to Moses and wrapped her arms around his neck from behind.

Moses patted her hand. "Hey there, you. Where've you been?"

"At my friend Chloe's house, studying for a math test."

Robin said, "Your French braids look great, Bitsy. I really like your hair like that."

Bitsy ran her hand down one of her braids. "Thanks. Chloe braided it for me."

Faith smiled at her daughter. "Say goodnight, sweetheart. It's time for you to get ready for bed."

Bitsy dropped her arms from around Moses's neck. "But Mo-om . . . I haven't seen Moses in like, forever."

"Don't *but Mom* me, young lady. We have an early day tomorrow."

Moses winked at Bitsy. "I'll see you at the opening ceremony. We'll have a nice chat then."

"Whatever." Bitsy rolled her eyes with a show of adolescent attitude and stomped off to her bedroom.

"Sorry," Mike said, pushing back from the table. "I'll go talk to her."

"Our little Bitsy's growing up," Moses said with a snicker. "She was only about six when I first met her. Timid little thing. For someone who suffered so much at such a young age, she's come through like a champ. She's a survivor, Faith. Like you."

"Let's hope I survive the tumultuous teenage years," Faith muttered.

"Bitsy's an angel compared to my teenagers," Robin said.

"That's not true at all. Your boys are two of the finest young men I've ever met." Faith had met Robin's fifteen- and seventeen-year-olds on several occasions. Not only did they excel in academics and athletics, they possessed gentlemanly manners and doted on their mother. "How do you do it, Robin? You make having a high-pressured career and being a single parent look easy."

"Believe me, it's far from easy. We have our share of challenges. But, with an alcoholic for a father, they learned from a very early age to be resourceful and to look out for one another. And for me. They are not unlike Bitsy in that regard. Having a turbulent childhood makes for a stronger adult. I've spent enough time with your daughter these past few months to tell she has her priorities in order. Even the finest kids cop attitudes from time to time." Robin wiped away the tear that was making its way slowly down her cheek. "And speaking of our children, I should get home to mine, to see what crisis du jour awaits me."

The threesome rose from the table and gathered up the plates, taking them to the kitchen. When Moses and Robin offered to help with the dishes, Faith shooed them away from the sink. "I can knock these out in no time. I want the two of you to go home. You need to be bright-eyed and bushy-tailed in the morning, so you can pick me up off the ground when I faint."

They shared a laugh as Faith walked them to the door.

"You're gonna do great," Moses said, bending down to kiss her

ASHLEY FARLEY

cheek. "You have angels watching over you. One very important angel, in fact. Lovie would be so proud of what you've accomplished."

Faith nodded, smiling, but she didn't trust herself to speak. She stood at the door, watching her friends drive off in their separate cars. Mike joined her in the doorway a few minutes later.

"Do you think all this is happening too soon after Mama's death?" Faith asked, staring out into the dark night. "It's not even been a year. I feel ready to climb Mount Everest one minute and I want to crawl in my bed and hide from the world the next."

"You're processing your grief," Mike said, wrapping his arms around her. "But I daresay that having the shelter to focus on has helped you get through the worst of it." He brushed her hair aside and kissed the nape of her neck. "Go to bed. You have a big day ahead of you. I'll clean up the kitchen and be right in."

Faith closed and locked the door, leaning against it for support. She'd shared happy times these past few years with Mike and Bitsy in their cozy one-story home with its lovely view of the inlet. But her memories of those happy times were overshadowed by the devastating event that had taken place twelve months ago. She moved down the hall to the spot three feet in front of her bedroom where she'd shot her ex-husband at point-blank range. Mike had thrown away the carpet and had the house professionally cleaned, but the image of Curtis lying in a pool of his own blood was forever etched in her mind.

A judge had sentenced Curtis to twenty years for the torture he'd put his wife and daughter through. She'd been mortified when he'd been released early, on early parole, last spring. Faith's body froze as she remembered when the stalking began. Purchasing a gun had been the hardest decision she'd ever made.

Faith thanked the Lord every day that Bitsy had been at a friend's swimming party at the time of the shooting. But her mother had been napping in the guest room when Curtis forced

6

his way in the front door, and Lovie suffered a stroke that day from which she never recovered. As Faith sat beside her dying mother's hospital bed, she'd vowed to spend the rest of her life helping women in crisis. And now that dream was about to come true.

2

FAITH

*B*utterflies batted around in Faith's stomach the following morning as she faced the small crowd of family, friends, and townsfolk gathered for the ribbon-cutting ceremony. As with most waterfront properties, the side of the home facing the inlet was considered the front. But Faith had opted to hold the ceremony under the porte cochère, at the driveway entrance out back, in case they had rain. She needn't have worried. The weather was ideal with clear skies and warm temperatures, as one might expect for late April in the Lowcountry.

Shoulders back and head held high, she welcomed her guests. "Good morning! And thank you for joining us for this monumental occasion."

She wore a simple pale-blue sleeveless dress with a floral scarf at her neck, and courtesy of one of their new residents, a new hairstyle—shoulder-length layers and streaks of blonde that added shine and life to her brunette locks and made her appear considerably younger than her forty-six years.

Faith continued, "Our community, our beloved town of Prospect, is long overdue a women's shelter. There was a time, not that long ago, when I was trapped in an abusive marriage. My sisters rescued me from my home." She smiled at her older sisters in the front row—Sam with her crop of messy blonde hair who'd always been her rock, and Jackie who looked as sophisticated as ever in a St. John tweed suit, four-inch heels, and square designer sunglasses. Faith's face grew serious again. "But . . . by offering me a place to hide, they put the rest of our family in grave danger. At the time, the nearest shelter was forty miles away, which presented a challenge for me with a six-year-old daughter and a truck that barely ran."

She paused to take a deep breath. "Our mission for this shelter is to mend broken hearts. In addition to women suffering from physical abuse, we welcome those who are homeless, dealing with addiction, or coping with grief over the loss of a loved one. When necessary, our staff psychiatrist, Dr. Robin Bowman, known to our residents as Dr. Robin, will refer our patients to other facilities for more specialized care. We currently have five rooms with ten beds, five of which have been filled for over a week now. You may be wondering why we've admitted residents before our official opening. In Dr. Robin's own words, 'These women are good fits for our program, and they need our help. We couldn't very well turn them down.' I'm excited to announce that plans are in the works for an annex offering ten more rooms for a total of twenty beds.

"Our goal is to be as self-sufficient as possible. We will eat from the land and the sea. We will share the responsibilities of fishing our waters, growing our produce, and preparing our meals. We'll live like pioneers, bonding together as a family working side by side. We are fortunate to have the multitalented Emilee Early on staff. Her duties are many as house mother. She is receptionist, meal planner, and special events coordinator. And she will live on property should any of our residents need assistance during the night."

When Faith extended her arm to Emilee in the front row, the

house mother turned to face the crowd. With her small stature that radiated energy, she'd dressed for the occasion in a rainbow-colored tunic and white leggings with her dark bob smoothed back by a hot pink headband. As she waved, Emilee flashed the lopsided smile that had initially drawn Faith to her. Emilee never talked much about herself, except to say she'd gotten married too young, divorced within a few years, and never had children. Faith knew Emilee was devoted to her aging mother, the reason she'd returned to the area from Savannah in recent years.

The breeze blew a wisp of Faith's hair in her face, and she tucked it behind her ear. "There are many people responsible for making this day possible. At the top of the list is Mayor Harmon and the City of Prospect for donating the Humphrey estate to our cause. The property has been uninhabited for the past ten years when the last remaining Humphrey heir died and bequeathed the property to the city." She gestured at the two-story, porch-wrapped lowcountry-style house behind her. "The home is lovely now, but when it fell into our hands last fall, it needed an enormous amount of work. My husband, Mike, an emergency room doctor at Creekside Regional Hospital, and my dear friend and locally renowned psychiatrist, Dr. Moses Ingram, worked tirelessly to procure funding from local citizens and corporations for the renovations."

The crowd erupted in cheers and someone near the back chanted, "Go, Big Mo!" A former University of Georgia line-backer and Heisman Trophy candidate, Moses stood out as a big celebrity in their small town.

"Another generous soul is with us today, not in body but in spirit. Most of you knew my late mother, Lovie Sweeney, who recently passed away from Alzheimer's disease. Mama greeted every stranger with a smile and was always first in line to offer a helping hand to those in need. Based on the sizable gift made from her estate, we are dedicating the home in her honor." She turned to the gray-haired gentleman to her right. "So, without further ado, I'd like to invite Mayor Harmon to cut the ribbon and officially declare Lovie's Home for Wounded Hearts open for business."

As she handed the mayor the large scissors, Faith noticed a woman wearing a red quilted raincoat and knitted toboggan—despite the cloudless sky and eighty-degree temperature—and dragging a tattered suitcase through the thick St. Augustine grass as she paced in large circles near the back of the crowd.

Faith motioned to Moses, who was standing behind her, to move in close. Cupping her hand over her mouth, she whispered, "There's a woman at the back of the crowd who looks lost, like she might need our help. Will you check on her, please."

From his six-and-a-half-foot vantage point, Moses spotted the woman over the top of the crowd. "I see her," he said, stepping away from Faith and nudging his way through the mass of people.

The mayor cut the ribbon, the attendees applauded, and Faith called out, "You're all invited to join us on the front porch for refreshments. The view of the marsh and inlet beyond is stunning. As you tour the complex, be sure to peruse the fascinating memorabilia—framed letters and newspaper articles as well as a number of black and white photographs—exhibited in the grand hallway for more information about the prominent Humphrey family who built this estate and helped establish our town."

Faith turned to her daughter and enveloped her in a warm embrace. "We did it, Bitsy. We've been through a lot together, but we survived."

Bitsy returned her hug. "Yes, we did, Mama."

Mike gathered them up in his arms. "I'm so proud of both of you."

Faith kissed her husband's rosy cheek. "Thank you, sweetheart. We wouldn't have made it without your support."

His blue eyes twinkled as he touched his finger to the tip of her nose. "You made all this happen, Faith Neilson. Your road has been long and winding, but your journey has brought you here, to this magnificent place where you'll be able to make a difference in so many women's lives."

Mike kissed the top of each of their heads before turning them loose. "As much as I'd love to stay, I'm due at the hospital, and this munchkin needs to get to school." He smiled at his stepdaughter. He treated Bitsy better than her real father ever had, and she loved him dearly in return. "I won't be home for dinner. We're short-staffed and I have to work overtime. I'll see you in the morning."

"Can we eat here, Mama?" Bitsy pressed her hands together in pleading formation. "Please."

"Of course, sweetheart," Faith said, knowing how much her daughter loved to explore the property and have the residents dote on her. She gave Bitsy's brown ponytail a playful yank.

Faith watched her husband and child walk off arm in arm across the circular gravel driveway to the parking area near the utility sheds where Mike had left his truck before entering the house. An expansive center hallway with heavy paned doors on both ends offered visitors a view of the inlet upon arrival. Natural grasscloth wallpaper in the grayish-green color of the marsh adorned the walls and a Turkish Oriental in pale tones of blue softened the dark random-width oak floors and curving mahogany staircase. The grand hallway was the hub of activity where Emilee could usually be found at the Queen Anne receptionist's desk just inside the front door, greeting guests with a smile and a corny joke that relieved tension and made them laugh.

Friends and acquaintances offered Faith their congratulations as she made her way through the crowded hallway. She was nearing the other end when she felt a hand on her shoulder. She turned to face Caroline Becker whom she hadn't seen in years. She was pretty as ever, toned and tan and blonde, but the light that had once shined from within her was gone.

"Caroline! Welcome to Lovie's Home. I'm so glad you came."

A soft smile tugged at the corners of Caroline's lips. "Congratulations on your remarkable achievement. I'm familiar with the property. You have one of the loveliest marsh views in the Lowcountry."

Faith looked through the opened door at the sun sparkling off the inlet creek beyond. "I agree. My hope is the residents will find peace in the beauty of the estate."

"I'm sure they will. I know I have." She cast a nervous glance around her. "I was wondering . . . well, I've never done anything like this before, but I'd like to volunteer here. If you're even looking for volunteers. When you mentioned eating off the land, I thought maybe I could help. Gardening is a hobby of mine."

Faith wondered about Caroline's inspiration for wanting to volunteer at the shelter, if it was in some way related to her son's death four years ago. Regardless, she was grateful for her offer.

"Would you be willing to spearhead the gardening project? We've staked off the area, but that's as far as we've gotten. It's a major undertaking. Unfortunately, we can't afford to hire a professional. I don't want to pressure you. You may not be interested in such a big time commitment."

Caroline bobbed her head up and down. "I'm definitely interested."

Faith smiled. "That's great news! If you can stick around for a while, we can talk more after the other guests leave."

"I'd like that," Caroline said. "If you'll point me in the right direction, I'll take a look at your proposed plot while I wait."

Taking Caroline by the elbow, Faith steered her to the entrance to the dining room. "Go straight through here to the kitchen and out the back door. You can't miss it."

She waited until Caroline had disappeared into the kitchen before going outside to the wide, columned porch where she stood and watched her guests mingling among themselves while they nibbled on finger foods and sipped punch around the banquet tables on the lawn below. Tears of pride welled in her eyes as she thought about all she'd accomplished.

Jackie and Sam broke off from the crowd and made their way toward her. "You're not getting all sappy on us are you." A smirk played on Jackie's red-painted lips as she fished a Kleenex out of her bag.

"Who me? Sappy? Never." Faith took the tissue and blotted her eyes.

"Yeah, right," Sam said. "You haven't stopped crying since Mama died last summer."

"I admit it," Faith said. "I loved our mama and I miss her like crazy."

"At least you're in the right place to mend your wounded heart." Sam placed her arm around Faith in a half hug. "I'm going to head out, kiddo. You did an excellent job today. You get the honors of speaking to the crowd when we reopen the market in June," she said of their seafood market that had tragically burned to the ground the previous May.

"No thanks." Faith's gaze shifted to their older sister. "Jackie's the public speaker in the family."

"Don't look at me." Jackie's hands flew up in defense. She'd never had a stomach for the seafood business. "I have my own business to run. Speaking of which, I've gotta hit the highway. I have a meeting in Charleston in an hour."

"Thanks for being here today," Faith said, kissing the air beside her sister's cheek. "And thanks for all you've done. The house looks amazing."

"It does, doesn't it?" Jackie spun on her heels and admired the interior of the house through the open door behind them. "I have a few more odds and ends to donate. I'll bring them home when I come this weekend."

"But you've already given us so much," Faith argued. Owning a design firm based out of Charleston, Jackie had played a major role in remodeling the ramshackle estate. She'd donated many pieces of furniture, either castoffs from clients or items she'd ordered that hadn't worked out.

"It's for a good cause, and I can use the tax deduction." Jackie took hold of Sam's arm. "Come on. I'll walk you out."

After her sisters had been swallowed up by the throng of people in the hallway, Faith turned her attention to her other guests. She spoke with members of the community, many who were merchants eager to contribute their wares to the home. The owner of the local mom-and-pop hardware store offered to donate crab traps, casting nets, and fishing rods. The gardening store manager promised several flats of vegetable plants and herbs, and the woman who ran the home goods store donated a hammock.

"You have the perfect place to hang it, between those two trees right there," she said, pointing at two live oaks down by the water.

Most of the food platters were empty and the last guests were leaving by the time Faith noticed Moses sitting in the rockers at the end of the porch with the woman in the red raincoat. When she moved toward them, Moses stood to greet her. "Faith, I'd like you to meet our new friend, Molly Maguire."

Faith smiled down at the visitor who was about forty years old and wore multiple layers of clothes under the red raincoat—a long, gray knit skirt over faded jeans and a flannel shirt and crew neck sweater beneath a puffer vest. "Welcome to Lovie's Home."

Molly nodded in greeting.

"She heard about us from friends in Charleston. Isn't that right, Molly?"

"Yessiree. A shelter for women in fancy digs like these, you better bet all my homeless friends are talking about it. I didn't know it was opening day, though. I would've waited till tomorrow if I'd known so many people were gonna be here. Is it true that anyone can come here?"

"You have to fill out some forms," Faith said. "And we have

rules you have to follow. As long as you have some form of identification—"

Molly chewed on this a minute. "Will an expired driver's license work? That's all I got."

"We'll discuss logistics later," Moses said. "Molly tells me she's hungry. Why don't you sit with her while I get her some refreshments?" As he strode off, he winked at Faith, signaling to her that he considered Molly a flight risk.

Faith dropped to the empty rocking chair beside Molly. "What brings you here today?"

The weathered skin on Molly's face puckered when her cracked lips parted in a smile, revealing a missing canine tooth. "I came to get myself a new life," she said, her blue eyes shining bright.

The woman's childlike enthusiasm warmed Faith's heart. "Then I'd say you came to the right place. Why don't you start by telling me about your old life, so I know what you're looking for in a new one?"

"Ain't much to tell," Molly said, clenching and unclenching the fabric of her skirt. "I've been living on the streets of Charleston for the past seven years. I don't got much, 'cept the clothes on my back and what's in here." She touched the handle of the tattered suitcase parked on the wooden floor beside her dirty sneakers.

Faith shifted in her seat to face Molly. "I can't imagine how difficult that's been for you."

Molly brushed a hank of greasy brown hair out of her face with the back of a calloused hand. "It ain't so bad, really. I like being outdoors, communing with nature."

"Do you mind if I ask how you got to be . . . um . . ."

"It's okay to say homeless, Miss Faith. It ain't a dirty word. I don't much like to talk about my past, though. Nothing good happened to me back then that's worth remembering."

Robin returned with a cup of fruit punch and a small plate piled high with finger sandwiches, chunks of ripe cantaloupe, and deviled eggs. "Moses was called away on a patient emergency. He asked me to deliver this to Molly." She handed their guest the plate. "Welcome to Lovie's Home. I'm Robin Bowman, but the residents all call me Dr. Robin."

Molly smiled up at her as she stuffed a deviled egg into her mouth.

"I understand you're from Charleston," Robin said, taking a seat in the rocker on the other side of Molly. "Did you have trouble getting here?"

As Molly devoured the food, speaking with her mouth full and spitting crumbs, she told Robin and Faith about her experience hitchhiking from Charleston to Prospect. "I thumbed a ride with a trucker, a real nice man carrying a load to Walmart. Been a long time since I've ridden in a motor vehicle. Them some crazy drivers out there. Nearly scared the tar outta me."

Faith smiled. "Well, you're here now. That's the important thing. When you're finished eating, I'll take you inside and show you your room."

Molly shook her head with vehemence. "Oh no, Miss Faith. I'm afraid to go inside."

Faith frowned. "Afraid of what, Molly?"

A guarded expression fell over Molly's face. "Just afraid. Since I been living on the streets, I've only slept in a shelter a handful of times. And only on the coldest nights."

"Where are you planning to sleep, then?" Robin asked.

Molly's eyes darted around the porch. "Out here somewhere. I got me a mat. I'll just cuddle up next to the house. I won't be a bother to no one."

She met Robin's gaze over the top of Molly's head. "I'm afraid that's against our regulations. We have certain security measures in place for the safety of our residents." Faith paused, buying time as she determined the best way to handle the situation. "You came to us for help in starting a new life. In order for us to help you get past your fears, you have to trust us. I have one of my

17

favorite rooms available." She pointed at the side of the house above her head. "A corner room with big windows overlooking the inlet. How about if I show you the room, and introduce you to the other occupant, a real nice resident named Tilda Watson, and then you can decide if you'd like to stay?"

In a skeptical voice, Molly said, "I guess there ain't no harm in looking at the room. But I ain't making no promises."

"I understand."

As they were helping Molly gather her things, Robin whispered to Faith, "Are you seriously considering putting her in the same room with Tilda?"

"I have a hunch about this," Faith said. "Tilda has told us nothing about herself except that she's seventy-five years old. Molly might be just the right person to get through to Tilda."

"Or she might send Tilda over the edge for good."

3

MOLLY

*G*ripping the handle of her suitcase, Molly tripped up the sweeping staircase alongside Faith with Dr. Robin following closely behind them. She took in the ginormous rooms with their tall ceilings, dark floorboards, and walls of windows. She would normally be quaking in her boots in such a place, but the soft greens and cool blues on the furniture and rugs, the colors of the outdoors, made her feel oddly at home.

"This house sure is pretty," Molly said. "I wasn't expecting it to be so big."

Faith smiled. "With over twenty thousand square feet, we definitely have plenty of room. It was built as a summer home in 1920 by the Humphrey family from upstate South Carolina. They invited their wealthy friends down for elaborate house parties on the weekends. Can you imagine what that must have been like in the roaring twenties?"

Molly envisioned beautiful ladies wearing fringed dresses and smoking cigarettes in long holders. "Like *The Great Gatsby*."

Faith glanced over at her. "Do you like to read, Molly?"

"Yes'm. The public library is my favorite place, cool in the summer and warm in the winter, with rows and rows of wonderful books to read."

"So you do go inside sometimes?" Faith asked.

"I ain't afraid of the library none. They have several doors and plenty of people around. Besides, since I don't have a permanent address, they won't let me have a library card to check out books."

"We'll add that to your list of goals for your new life," Faith said. "In the meantime, we have lots of books here that you can read."

They reached the top of the stairs, turned right, and walked to the very end of the hallway. Faith knocked on the door. "Tilda, this is Faith. May I come in? I have someone I'd like you to meet."

A muffled yes came from within. Faith opened the door and they entered the room. A woman much older than Molly with short hair, a mixture of gray and black, and smooth skin sat reading a book in a comfortable chair by a fireplace. After years of huddling around burning wood in metal trash cans, Molly could spot a fake fire a mile away.

"Good gracious, Tilda, it's stuffy in here." Faith crossed the room to the fireplace and turned off the gas logs. "It's springtime in the South. Why on earth do you have the fire on?"

"I got chilled earlier," Tilda said, closing the book and placing it in her lap.

Faith moved to the windows and threw open the middle of the three. Turning to face them, she said, "Tilda, I'd like you to meet our newest resident, Molly Maguire."

Molly smiled and wiggled her fingers at Tilda, who dismissed her with a quick once-over.

"Molly's going to be your new roommate," Dr. Robin said. "That is, *if* she decides to stay with us."

Faith spread her arms wide. "See, Molly. With all this natural light, it's just like being outside."

Tilda stood, smoothing out her gray linen slacks. "Do I have a say in the matter?"

"I'm afraid not," Faith said.

"Then you'll need to do something about that," Tilda said, eyeballing Molly's suitcase. "It smells to high heaven."

"We'll worry about that later," Faith said, shooting Tilda a warning look.

Tightening her grip on her suitcase, Molly inspected the room more closely. She gestured at the pair of iron beds with soft pillows and fluffy white comforters. "*If* I decide to stay, which one would be mine?"

"The one by the window," Tilda said. "I'm afraid of heights. And of people breaking in. And lightning during thunderstorms."

Molly narrowed her eyes at the persnickety woman. Fraidy cat like her wouldn't last a day on the streets. "Fine by me," she said. "Being by the window is like being outdoors."

Molly shifted her gaze to the closed door between the beds. "What's in there?"

"The bathroom." Robin opened the door for Molly to see inside. "This is the only room with its own bathroom. The rest of the residents have to share the hall bath."

"Do the doors have locks?" Molly asked.

"For the safety of our patients, we've removed the locks from all the doors," Robin said. "But we have strict rules about protecting one another's privacy. We're a family here, Molly. No one wants to harm you. We've got your back."

Faith came to stand beside her. "What do you think? Will you give us a try? Shall we get the paperwork started?"

Molly scratched the back of her neck. "I don't know, Miss Faith. It's nice and all, but I'm not sure I'm ready."

"I understand," Faith said. "And I want you to be comfortable with your decision. Since you're already here, why not have a hot shower and a meal? We can even provide you with some clean clothes. If you still want to leave after lunch, I'll see what I can do about locating you a ride back to Charleston."

Molly was tempted. She hadn't had a real shower in years. Maybe even a decade.

Robin stepped inside the bathroom. "There's a white robe on the back of the door. After your shower, we'll take your clothes downstairs to the laundry." She produced a plastic Ziploc bag from the medicine cabinet. "You'll find everything you need in here—shampoo, soap, toothbrush, and toothpaste."

"All right," Molly said with a tone of uncertainty. She wasn't yet ready to trust Tilda. "But I don't want to be left here alone. Will one of you stay in the room while I'm in the shower?" She looked back and forth between Faith and Robin.

Faith smiled. "I'll be happy to. You take all the time you need. I'll wait right here until you're finished."

Molly wheeled her suitcase into the bathroom and closed the door. Lowering the toilet seat, she sat down with her elbows propped on her knees, studying the room with its sparkling white tiles and glassed-in shower. She debated the safety of getting naked in a strange bathroom with only Miss Faith, a woman she'd known for an hour, to protect her from kooky Tilda. The desire to be clean won her over and she finally gave in.

After several minutes of fiddling with the controls to get the temperature right, she peeled off her filthy clothes and stepped into the shower, the warm water running like liquid velvet across her skin. She lathered the soap, scrubbing her skin with a cloth, and then washed and rinsed her hair three times. When she got out, she dried herself with a fuzzy towel and slipped into the white terrycloth robe. As she was brushing her teeth, she caught a glimpse of her glowing skin, pink and plump, in the mirror. She'd taken the first steps toward a new life. And despite her apprehension, more than anything, she wanted to see it through.

When Molly emerged from the bathroom, Faith was alone in

the room, standing at the window with a sad expression on her face. Molly cleared her throat, and Faith turned to face her.

"How was your shower? You certainly look refreshed."

"You have no idea, Miss Faith. I ain't felt this good in years."

"And that's only the beginning. Robin and Tilda have gone downstairs to help with the lunch preparations." She held her hand out toward the door. "Shall we head down to the basement. We'll put a load of wash in and take a peek in our thrift closet. Many of our generous townsfolk have donated a wide variety of apparel and other goods. I'm sure we can find some things to fit you."

Molly wasn't keen on the idea of going underground, and as they left the room, she walked on Faith's heels down the hall to the elevator. When the elevator doors closed, locking them in, she white-knuckled the handle of her suitcase and sucked in a breath, holding it all the way down. Much to her relief, the basement was only partially buried with above-ground windows and a door leading to the outside. In the laundry room, Faith instructed Molly to unzip her suitcase and dump the contents into the supersize washing machine like the kind they have at the laundromat.

Faith added liquid detergent and turned on the machine. "Now then, let's see what we can find for you in our thrift closet." She opened a door leading to the adjacent room.

Molly remained glued to her spot in front of the washing machine. "I can't leave my belongings unattended, Miss Faith."

"No one will bother your things, Molly. But if it makes you feel better, I'll leave the door open." Faith stepped across the threshold into the other room. "See, we'll be able to keep an eye on the machine from here."

Molly sighed—the day was a day for firsts—and reluctantly followed her into the closet. Floor-to-ceiling shelves, packed with folded pants and shirts, lined one wall of the large closet while dresses and coats hung from metal racks opposite.

"I thought I remembered seeing this in here." Faith tugged a suitcase the same size as Molly's free of the bottom shelf, brushed off the dust, and rolled it over to her. "I hope you're planning to stay, and won't need this until you're ready to venture into your new life, but it's all yours whenever you decide to go."

Molly pressed a trembling hand to her chest. "Do you mean it, Miss Faith? Can I really have it?"

"Of course you can." She set the suitcase on the worktable in the center of the room. "Now, let's find some things to go in it." She faced the shelves. "Most of the apparel is divided by type. Underwear. Pants. Tops. Sleepwear."

"I haven't worn a bra and panties in years," Molly said with a sheepish grin.

Gesturing at the shelves, Faith said, "Then by all means, help yourself."

Molly approached the shelves with caution. She carefully selected a bra she thought might fit, even though she had no clue about her size, and a Fruit of the Loom package of six cotton briefs.

Faith took the things from her and placed them in her new suitcase. "With your slender figure, I'm guessing you're a size six." She pulled assorted items from the shelves, dumping them on the table. "You'll get dirty doing chores, so be sure to pick out several outfits. It's a good idea to try everything on. I'll give you some privacy." She exited the room via a different door.

Panic gripped Molly's chest when the door closed with a loud click. But the sight of the washing machine in the laundry room and the sound of the water swooshing around inside the metal drum slowed her racing heart. As she reached for the table to steady herself, her hand came into contact with the soft cotton fabric of a pair of pajamas. The thought of sleeping in those comfy pajamas in the bed upstairs with the fluffy white comforter chased away her fears, and suddenly, the possibility of a new life became more real.

She untied the robe, letting it fall to the floor, and stepped into a new pair of panties and fastened on the bra. For the next twenty minutes, she tried on clothes—pants and shirts and shorts —admiring herself in the mirror behind the door. She couldn't remember the last time she'd had so much fun. By the time Faith returned, she'd set aside several pairs of pants with a hodgepodge of tops, including the outfit she was wearing—a pair of dark denim jeans and a black gingham cotton blouse.

"If this is too much, I can put some things back," Molly said gesturing at her pile of clothes.

"It's not too much at all. You'll need these things in your new life." Faith gave her shoulder a squeeze. "Are you ready to go upstairs for lunch?"

Molly looked from the washing machine to the exit door out in the hallway. "I don't know, Miss Faith. Someone could come right through that door and take my belongings." Even though she never turned away free food, she added, "I'm not really that hungry anyway."

"Nobody will mess with your laundry, Molly. Come on upstairs and meet some of the other residents."

Molly remained silent, her face pinched in determination.

"Then I'll have someone bring you a sandwich. Do you have any dietary restrictions?"

The thought of food made her stomach growl. "No'm, I'll eat anything you put in front of me."

Following Faith out into the hall, she watched her disappear up a flight of stairs. The sounds of pots clanging and women chatting drifted down from the kitchen above. She longed to be a part of such gay-sounding camaraderie, but she doubted that a street bum like her would ever fit in.

She returned to the laundry room, and pulling a chair up in front of the washing machine, she watched her laundry spin around and around inside. Ten minutes later, a wisp of a girl with a streak of blue in her white-blonde hair that matched her romper came scurrying down the stairs. Molly pushed her chair out of the way and stood with her back to the washing machine, protecting her laundry.

"Here's your lunch." The girl handed Molly a paper plate with a sandwich, sweet potato chips, and fruit salad on it. "I'm Rosalie. Rosalie Morton."

"Rosalie," Molly repeated, admiring the way the name rolled off her tongue. "I'm Molly Maguire. I'm here to get a new life. What're you in for?"

Rosalie giggled. "This isn't a prison, although sometimes it feels like one. My mama kicked me out of the house. Can't say I blame her. I've gotten fired from every job I've had since I graduated from high school two years ago. We don't have money for college, which is fine since I suck at school, anyway. So, I'm here to figure out my life. I want to be a hairstylist. I'm pretty good already." She lifted a strand of Molly's limp brown hair. "You could use a cut and a dye job. Will you let me experiment on you?"

Molly swatted her hand away. "No thanks. I ain't interested in having blue hair."

"Blue isn't for everyone." She spun Mollie around as she inspected her hair. "But blonde streaks might look nice. I did Faith's hair. She looks positively glam, don't you think?"

While Molly liked the idea of a new hairstyle, especially one as pretty as Faith's, she'd already encountered enough new changes for one day. "Let me think about it."

"Whatever." Rosalie shrugged and spun on the heels of her wedge shoes.

Molly transferred her clothes to the dryer, and while she waited for them to dry, she savored the ham and cheese sandwich on fresh wheat bread. Once her laundry was folded neatly in her new suitcase, she traipsed back up the two flights of stairs to her room. She swung her suitcase onto the bed and stretched out with her legs on top of it. Closing her eyes, she took pleasure in the comfortable mattress and soft pillow. She was dozing off when she was startled awake by a presence looming over her. She cracked an eyelid to see Tilda staring down at her.

"What're you doing in my room?" Tilda asked.

Molly propped herself up on her elbows. "I'm your new roommate, remember?"

Tilda frowned, as though she didn't remember. "Why are you sleeping with your suitcase?"

"When you live on the streets, you have to protect your things, else someone will run off with them."

"This isn't the streets. And you don't need to worry about me stealing your belongings. I assure you, we don't have the same taste." Tilda crossed her arms over her chest. "I should be the one guarding my possessions from the likes of you."

Leave it to Molly to get stuck with a roommate like Tilda. She was just like them rich ladies who lived in the harbor-front mansions in Charleston who looked down their noses at Molly when they passed on the street.

Molly swung her feet over the side of the bed. "Look, lady, I ain't no thief."

"And neither am I," Tilda said with a fixed stare.

Standing face-to-face, Molly saw fear in her new roommate's eyes. So they had something in common after all. "Do you mind me asking why you're here? I mean, you seem so put together with your fancy talk and expensive clothes. Did your husband beat you or something?"

"My husband is dead, not that it's any of your business. And no, he did not beat me." Tilda turned her back on Molly, retreating to her chair by the fireplace.

Suddenly the walls began to close in on Molly. "I hope you don't mind if I push my bed closer to the window. I feel kinda claustrophobic."

"It's your bed to do with however you wish," Tilda said lifting her book from the table beside her.

Molly planted her hands on the metal side rails. As she pushed the bed several inches toward the window, a mouse shot out from a small hole in the wall and scuttled across the floor.

Spotting the mouse, Tilda leaped to her feet and onto the chair, squealing like a little girl.

Molly chased the mouse around the room and into the corner by the door. "It won't hurt you none. It's just a tiny little mouse." She held the mouse up by its tail.

"Get rid of it!" Tilda shrieked. "Flush it down the toilet or something."

Molly stuffed the mouse in its hole and blocked it in with her shoe while she dragged the bed back across the floor. "Now then," she said when the bed was back in place in front of the hole. "He won't be bothering us anymore."

"Until he finds another hole to escape from," Tilda said, teetering on the chair and gripping her book to her chest.

Molly went to the window and stood looking out across the lawn at blue skies and marshlands. She'd embarked on this journey, and scared as she was, she planned to see it through for better or worse. Life on the streets was hard. She was tired of digging through trash cans and begging for change. She trusted Miss Faith and Dr. Robin. Oddly enough, she felt safe in the corner room of this enormous house. If she could make friends with crackpots on the streets, she could find a way to get along with her roommate.

Turning away from the window, she opened her suitcase on her bed and unpacked her clothes into the bureau on her side of the room. When she finished, she stored the suitcase in the room's one closet and went to stand in front of Tilda, who was seated in her chair, knees drawn to her chest and feet off the ground. "I'm sorry if I scared you with the mouse," she said in a soft voice.

"I'll have nightmares for weeks because of you, thank you very much."

4

CAROLINE

*C*aroline walked along the edge of the marsh to the dock and sat down against a piling with her legs out in front of her. For the past several years, she'd come here, weather permitting, three of four times a week. She'd ridden her bicycle from home, walking it around the chained No Trespassing sign at the entrance to the long gravel driveway. She usually brought a sandwich with her and a women's fiction novel by one of her many favorite authors. With a blanket spread out in the shade of a tree, she'd escaped for hours into the world of fiction where the characters always had happy endings. She had no ties to the Humphrey estate. There were no memories here to haunt her. She could force her mind to go blank and her body numb.

A shadow appeared on the dock in front of her and she looked up to find Faith standing nearby, gazing out at the inlet. "You would think I'd grow tired of looking out over the water, but I never do," Faith said.

Caroline inched her way up the piling to her feet. "I know what you mean. The salt air has special healing powers, which makes this an ideal spot for Lovie's Home." While the marsh and the trees and the water hadn't *healed* Caroline, the setting made her misery more tolerable.

"We are very blessed. Let's just hope we can keep this boat afloat," Faith said with a faraway look on her face.

"Are you having financial trouble already?" Caroline asked.

"Nothing we can't handle. I hope. We just need to figure a few things out." She shifted her gaze to Caroline. "What did you think of the location for our garden?"

"You've chosen a good spot with ample sunlight. It helps to be near your toolshed. I would suggest building raised beds for better drainage. What're you thinking of growing?"

"Herbs and vegetables mostly. I asked Cook, our cook, to come up with a list. The normal stuff like tomatoes and peppers and green beans. Alfred, the manager at Prospect Home and Garden, has offered to donate several flats of plants."

"That's very generous of him," Caroline said. "I would suggest getting started immediately. It's already late in the growing season."

"We're talking about an untold number of volunteer hours, Caroline. That may be more than you bargained for."

"I have nothing but time on my hands. And I can't think of a better way I'd like to spend it. I've built garden boxes before, and I'm happy to donate the necessary materials. In fact . . ." Caroline chewed on her bottom lip in thought. "I may very well have everything I need in my garage. If I start working on the boxes first thing in the morning, I can have them ready for soil and plants in a couple of days."

Relief washed over Faith's face. "You're a godsend. Once Cook finalizes her list, I'll call it in to Alfred along with an order for a load of whatever kind of soil you think we need. We've started a compost pile behind the shed, and there are plenty of gardening tools, wheelbarrows, and watering hoses inside."

"Whatever you're lacking, I'm sure I have at home," Caroline said.

The women turned together and started walking back toward the house.

"How many residents should I assign to the project?" Faith asked.

"Two should be plenty. Any more than that, and we'll trip over one another." They reached the kitchen door where Caroline had left her bike. "I'll see you bright and early in the morning."

As she pedaled off down the driveway, Faith called after her, "Thanks again, Caroline."

For the first time in years, her life had purpose, and she planned out the project in her head as she rode her bike the long way home—along Creekside Drive past the marina and down Main Street. Dreading her return to an empty house, she stalled for time by circling the blocks in her picturesque neighborhood, admiring the manicured lawns and fresh flower boxes. When she finally turned onto her street, she was surprised to find her husband's car in the driveway. Troy seldom arrived home from work before dinner. And usually it was much later than that.

Parking her bicycle in the garage, she entered the house through the kitchen door. Troy was propped against the granite countertop with his carry-on rolling suitcase at his feet. Her skin prickled in alarm. He was an accountant with a local firm. He never traveled for work.

She went to the sink to wash her hands. "You didn't tell me you were going on a trip."

"It's not a trip, Caroline. I've been offered a job with a firm in Portland, Oregon."

She shook the excess water off her hands and dried them with a dish towel. "Is that some kind of joke, Troy? If so, I don't think it's funny."

He gave his balding head a solemn shake. "I would never joke about such a matter. I've already packed the rest of my things in the car. I'm driving across the country. I start work on Monday."

Pushing off the counter, he took her by the shoulders, turning her body to face him. "Tragedy either brings couples closer together or it destroys the marriage. In our case, it's the latter. We're like zombies, you and me, walking around in a daze. We don't know how to help each other. We're only dragging each other down."

Tears spilled over her eyelids and slid down her cheeks. "How could you do this?" She shoved him away. "You never even bothered to tell me you were interviewing for jobs."

He ran his fingers through his thinning hair. "Because I knew you'd try to stop me, and because I love you so much, I would've let you. And then we'd be stuck here, suffocating in our grief. The house is yours to do with how you see fit, although I hope you'll consider selling it and starting over somewhere new."

"I can't sell it. I can't leave the memories."

Troy's shoulders slumped as he exhaled loudly. "You'll always have the memories in your heart, Caro. But being here with all his things is like living in a haunted house. It's been four years and you're showing no signs of moving on with your life."

She threw her hands in the air. "So now it's all my fault."

He hung his head. "I've tried everything to get through to you, but you've pushed me away at every turn."

"Don't I even get a say in our future?"

"You have plenty of say in *your* future," Troy said. "But you need to go for counseling, Caroline. It's the only way you're going to save yourself."

Troy had been in therapy for years, and he'd begged her to seek counseling as well. But she didn't see how talking to a stranger about her innermost feelings would help.

He lifted the handle on his suitcase. "My attorney will be in touch about the divorce." He kissed the top of her forehead and left the house through the kitchen door, vanishing from her life as abruptly as their son had four years ago.

Collapsing onto the nearest barstool, she stared out the

window into her backyard. How could she possibly leave her garden? Since Cory's death, bit by bit, she'd converted every square inch of her lawn into a bountiful garden of flowers and vegetables and herbs. Bringing plants to life and nurturing them while they grew was the only happiness she knew.

She sat at the kitchen counter until the world outside her window grew black. The more she thought back over the past year, the more she realized their breakup had been inevitable. But she'd denied it like she'd denied everything else in her life. Troy was right. She couldn't help him, because she couldn't help herself. If only she would die, she could be reunited with her only child.

Several months back, Troy had pressed her to put her family farm on the market. Now she understood why. She'd received a couple of offers, and even though she hadn't visited the farm once since the accident, she couldn't bring herself to sell it. Winding Creek Farm, a hundred and twenty acres of fields and forest on the inlet just outside of town, had been in her family for three generations.

She felt like crying, but the tears wouldn't come. Her stomach growled, but the thought of food made her nauseous. Even a glass of white wine had no appeal. She was dead inside. By leaving, Troy had pulled the plug on her life support.

She sat with her elbows on the table, chin in hand, and eyes on the oven's digital clock. When nine o'clock finally rolled around, she got up from the barstool and went upstairs to bed. She passed Cory's room and was on her way to her own bedroom when she heard him call out, "Hey, Mom! Can you help me with my homework?"

She retraced her steps and stood inside his doorway. She envisioned him lying on his belly on his bed, surrounded by textbooks, looking up at her with his mischievous smile as he brushed an errant hunk of sandy hair out of his eyes. A shelf extended the length of wall above his bed, showcasing his collection of baseball trophies. He'd been accepted to college on a baseball scholarship. He had a bright future ahead of him. Until the tragic accident that claimed his life. An accident on the ATV that Troy had bought for him against her wishes.

Troy's words echoed in her mind. *Being here with all his things is like living in a haunted house.*

Caroline knew this to be true. She spent her days outside— either working in her yard or exploring the Humphrey estate or riding her bike ten miles for a walk on the beach. Her outdoor activities kept her mind occupied. It was at night, when she returned home, that the ghosts came out.

Closing the door to Cory's room, she hurried down the hall to the master bedroom. After washing her face and brushing her teeth, she changed into her gown and climbed into bed. Retrieving her current novel from the bedside table, she opened to the bookmarked page, but she was too distracted to read. She turned out the light, slid deep beneath the covers, and closed her eyes. But her demons prevented her from sleeping. She was plagued by flashbacks—the accident, the traumatic days following Cory's death, his funeral—and memories of the sorrowful years since. Voices, happy and sad, filled her head—the sounds of children's laughter and adults arguing.

Hours later, when she could take it no more, she got out of bed and slipped on her robe. She went to the kitchen for a cup of chamomile tea. But as she roamed the house with her tea, she couldn't escape the demons. She thought her mind might explode by the time she returned to her bedroom. She removed her large suitcase from the walk-in closet in the hall and packed it with underwear, toiletries, and a wide assortment of clothes from jeans to shorts to tops and lightweight jackets. It was three o'clock in the morning, the night pitch-dark without the light of the moon, when she stored her suitcase in the cargo area of her small SUV. She attached her bicycle to the rack on the rear of the car and backed out of the driveway. She drove east to Charleston and then south on Highway 17. She made it all the way to Beaufort before her mind cleared enough for her to think straight. She accepted the fact that she'd been stuck in a time warp for the past four years. She couldn't run away from her pain and sorrow like Troy. In order for her to move on with her life, she would first have to face the past. If only she knew how to go about doing that.

She made a sudden U-turn in the middle of the dark highway and headed back toward Prospect.

5

FAITH

aith, leaving her husband and daughter asleep, sneaked out of the house before sunrise on Tuesday morning to get an early start at her office. Mike was on day shifts this week, which meant he could drop Bitsy off at school on his way to the hospital. If only he worked nine-to-five all the time. He was the oldest doc on his staff, and though he often talked about starting his own medical practice or partnering with one of the area's two successful groups of family doctors, he thrived on the frenzied pace of the emergency room and wasn't yet ready to give it up.

Faith spent several hours at her desk poring over her accounts. She'd been the accountant for her family's seafood business for years. She understood balance sheets, and no matter how many times she ran the numbers, she arrived at the same dismal projection. She expected to receive word any day from her application for state funding. It wouldn't solve all their financial problems, but it would be a welcome start.

She emerged from her office to find Emilee already at work. Faith came from a family of highly efficient, highly effective women, but Emilee's organizational skills and ability to network with people raised the bar. Faith slept better at night knowing the house mother was tucked away in the old maid's quarters above the kitchen, on call 24/7 for whatever needs arose.

"You're here early," Faith said.

"Just trying to get caught up with some work." A mischievous smile crept onto Emilee's lip. "Did you hear the one about—"

Faith cut her eyes at Emilee. "I don't have time for jokes, Em. I need to schedule an emergency board meeting for this afternoon or tomorrow morning. Can you make the calls for me, please?"

Emilee dropped the smile and her expression grew serious. "Certainly," she said, reaching for a pen and notepad. "How should I explain the urgency?"

"Tell them it's a matter of finances," Faith said and walked away before Emilee could interrogate her further.

She took her clipboard to the solarium where she posted chore assignments for the week on a large calendar whiteboard, positioned on a wooden easel. The process was arduous. The residents complained if she failed to fairly rotate the less popular chores—toilet cleaning, window washing, and weed pulling. And she tried to accommodate those residents who had preferences for special tasks and projects. She wanted her residents to venture outside of their comfort zones, to try new experiences that might lead to a hobby or career opportunity down the road.

Faith looked up to find Molly in the doorway, her eyes darting about as she took in the room. "Good morning, Molly," she said, setting down her red marker. "Did you sleep well last night?"

"Like I hadn't slept in years. Am I allowed to enter this room?"

Faith extended her arm. "By all means. You are free to enjoy any of our common areas."

Moving to the center of the room, Molly held her arms out by her sides as she spun around in circles. "It's like the outside came inside."

Three of the room's walls housed the original hand-blown,

floor-to-ceiling mullioned windows. The ceiling was painted robin's egg blue, and a short-pile carpet the color of grass covered the black and white marble floor. Wicker sofas and chairs, lacquered a dark shade of teal, boasted cushions with tropical leaves in shades of blues and greens.

"It does have that outdoorsy feel," Faith said as she, too, admired the room.

Molly went to stand in front of the bookshelves on the one windowless wall adjacent to the main room. "You weren't kidding when you said you had a lot of books."

Faith joined her in front of the bookshelves. "We have a wide assortment in here and in the bookcases in the parlor. Mysteries, romances, and classics, and a fair number of self-help books as well." She removed a copy of Hemingway's *The Sun Also Rises* from the shelf and opened it to the back cover. "Each book has an index card. To check out the book, just sign your name on the card and leave it on Emilee's desk."

Molly took the book from her and gripped it to her chest. "Do you mean it, really? I can take the books to my room and read them in bed at night?"

Faith couldn't help but smile at the woman's excitement over something most people take for granted. "You absolutely can. We only ask that you treat them with kindness and return them to Emilee when you're finished."

"Oh, yes ma'am. I'll be very careful with them." She returned the book to the shelf. "I'm feeling antsy, Miss Faith, with too much time on my hands. Is there something I can do to help out around here?"

"Funny you should mention it. I was just going over the week's chore assignments." She walked Molly over to the whiteboard and explained how to read it. "It's important for our days to have structure. Immediately following breakfast, we'll divide into rotating groups to tackle our indoor chores. When you finish, you'll report to Caroline in the backyard for a special project. As much as you love the outdoors, I thought you might enjoy helping her plant our vegetable and herb gardens."

Molly's face lit up like a child's at Christmas. "I'd love that. This is like being at summer camp."

"Some aspects of life here are very much like summer camp. This afternoon, my nephew will begin his Salt Life program. For the next two weeks, he'll be here every day at three to teach us how to fish, crab, and scavenge for clams and oysters. All of the residents are required to attend these clinics. Today, he'll be showing us how to bait and set a crab trap."

"That sounds like so much fun," Molly said, bouncing a little on her toes.

"I applaud your enthusiasm, Molly, but I caution you about getting too excited. It's not all fun. In addition to your chores, you're required to see Robin three times a week for therapy. Your first session is after lunch today. And, every afternoon before dinner, we gather in the parlor for group therapy, which is also facilitated by Robin. We can't forget your primary reason for being here, and that's to . . ." Faith pointed a finger at Molly, an indication for her to finish the sentence.

"Get me a new life," Molly said, grinning from ear to ear.

"Exactly." She rested a hand on Molly's back. "Now, let's go see if we can help Cook with breakfast." As they walked together through the parlor, Faith asked, "How're you and Tilda getting along?"

"Fine. I don't let her bother me none. What's she in for, anyway? Insomnia? I'm guessing she didn't sleep more than an hour last night."

"I'm not at liberty to discuss that," Faith said. "It's up to Tilda to tell you if she chooses."

Molly shrugged. "I asked her, but she wouldn't say."

They entered the dining room where three of the residents were already seated at the table. Rosalie, whose bubbly personality made her a joy to have around and who had already made great strides in therapy during her five days at the home. Timid Sheila Thomas, whose list of phobias was long. Sheila reminded Faith of a lost puppy. If her first two days at Lovie's were any indication, she would be with them for a very long time. And then there was Barb Simpson who had misled them about her alcoholism when she arrived two days ago. Barb needed a proper detoxing, more than Faith's staff was equipped to handle, and would be leaving them after breakfast for a rehab facility in Charleston.

"Speaking of your roommate," Faith said. "Where is Tilda? It's almost time for breakfast."

"She's upstairs washing out her silk nightgown in the bathroom sink." Molly left Faith and wandered over to the buffet where pitchers of juices and milk were available for self-serve.

Faith continued on to the kitchen where Cook was garnishing plates of eggs Benedict with sprigs of dill and parsley. Her real name was Alberta—Bertie for short—but everyone just called her Cook. "I've told you a thousand times we don't have the budget for fancy foods," Faith said. "This is not a luxury resort."

Cook cut her dark eyes at Faith. "You gotta chicken coop full of hens laying eggs out back, Miss Faith. I made my own sauce, and instead of English muffins, I baked my own bread. I used half the bacon I would on a normal breakfast platter." She planted her hands on her wide hips. "And, for your information, I take pride in my work, whether I'm cooking for a women's shelter or a five-star luxury resort."

"I'm sorry, Cook," Faith said, kissing the chef's rosy cheek. "I didn't mean to come down so hard on you. I've got budget on the brain this morning. I was just in the office going over the accounts. But don't forget some of our residents still need to learn basic cooking skills."

"I haven't forgotten." Cook inclined her head at the striking brunette standing at the counter beside the stove. "I just introduced Louise to her first onion."

Louise looked up from her work, her lovely face shiny with onion tears. The young woman had come straight to them from rehab. Several years ago, she'd begun abusing drugs and alcohol to relieve the stress of her career as an investment banker. When she'd lost her job, her parents had insisted she commit herself to a rehabilitation program. Even after five weeks in rehab, she was not yet ready to live on her own. To further complicate matters, in her late twenties, she was faced with finding a new low-pressure career. She had been the first in the initial group of residents to arrive five days ago.

"What's the onion for, anyway?" Faith asked Louise.

"I'm making turkey chili for lunch," she answered proudly.

Faith lifted the lid on the commercial soup pot on the stove. "That smells delicious." She was lowering the lid when she caught a glimpse of a rolling suitcase beside the back door. "Whose suitcase?"

Cook followed her gaze. "Your new gardener's. She left it there this morning when she got here at the crack of dawn. She mumbled something about needing a place to stay for a few days. She seemed upset, but I didn't ask any questions. That's Dr. Robin's job."

Her suspicions had been correct. Something was going on in Caroline's life other than a burning need to volunteer at a women's shelter. "I better go see what that's about." Faith exited the house through the back door and walked the short distance to where Caroline was using a circular saw to cut lumber for the frame of her raised beds. Caroline set down her saw when she saw Faith coming toward her.

"I'm impressed, Caroline. You're the only woman I know who can use a skill saw. Careful, though. I might decide to hire you as my full-time handywoman."

"As it turns out, I might be looking for a more permanent position. At least a place to crash for a few days." Caroline bit down on her lower lip to stop it from quivering. "Do you by any chance have an extra sofa?"

"I can do better than that. I can offer you a bed in a room. But first you have to tell me what's going on."

Caroline wiped a damp strand of hair off her forehead with the back of her gloved hand. "My husband left me. Out of the blue, he packed his things and moved to Portland, Oregon. He never even told me he was interviewing for a job."

Faith had to work hard to hide her surprise. Caroline and Troy had been through so much. How could he up and leave her like that? "When did this happen?"

"Last night," Caroline said, wiping at her eyes. "He was waiting for me when I got home from here."

"Surely he didn't sell your house out from underneath you without giving you a chance to find somewhere else to live."

"On no! It's nothing like that. He gave me the house, but I can't stay there, Faith. It was bad enough without Cory. But now . . . alone . . . I didn't sleep at all last night."

When she began crying in earnest, Faith drew her near. "You're not alone, Caroline. You are welcome here, at Lovie's Home, for as long as you need to stay. Have you gone for professional counseling?"

"No, but I should have. I know that now. It cost me my marriage. I thought we were doing okay. We weren't exactly happy. But we lost our son. I don't expect to ever be happy again. I just need to find a way to get through the days, until I can be with Cory again." She sobbed into Faith's shoulder. "If I weren't a Christian, I would have already taken my life."

Faith felt a powerful ache in her chest for this poor woman, and she realized that her own face was covered in tears. "People *do* get over losing their children, Caroline. Maybe your life will never be the same, but you can, you will, find happiness again. We can help you, but only if you let us. Are you willing to try?"

"I think so," she said in a weak voice.

"There now," Faith said, stroking her hair. "You're gonna get through this." She held Caroline tight until her crying finally subsided and she pulled away.

"We take baby steps around here," Faith said with a smile. "And the first one for you is eating breakfast."

Caroline used her shirttail to wipe her eyes and nose. "Thanks, but I'm not really hungry."

"Residents are not allowed to skip meals." She looped her arm through Caroline's. "Come on. I'll introduce you to your new roommate. Rosalie's only twenty years old, but I have a sneaking suspicion the two of you need each other."

In the dining room, Faith addressed the other residents and Emilee. "I'd like to introduce our newest resident, Caroline Becker."

"Welcome, Caroline," the table said in unison.

"She'll be rooming with Rosalie." Faith sought out their youngest resident. "Can I count on you to show Caroline to your room after breakfast?"

"Yes, ma'am," Rosalie said in an energetic tone.

"I've appointed Caroline in charge of planting our vegetable and herb garden. We're blessed to have someone with her knowledge and experience."

The residents applauded.

Faith motioned Caroline to a vacant chair beside Louise and took a seat at the head of the table, opposite Emilee at the other end. "Now then, I believe it's Tilda's turn to say grace."

Everyone bowed their heads and waited for Tilda to offer the blessing. When no one spoke, Faith cracked an eyelid, raising her head when she realized Tilda wasn't at the table. "Where is she?"

"Look!" Molly cried, pointing across the grand hallway to the parlor. "It's raining inside!"

Faith pushed abruptly back from the table and dashed across the hall with the residents on her heels. She stared at the stream of water dripping from the ceiling. "That's coming from your bathroom, Molly."

She raced up the stairs to Tilda's room, and breaking her own rule, she burst through the door without knocking. Tilda was reading by the fireplace, seemingly oblivious to the water running over the sides of the sink and flooding the bathroom floor.

Faith's concern for the older woman escalated. From her chair, Tilda had an unobstructed line of sight into the bathroom. If she was that unaware of a flood taking place right before her eyes, did she pose a threat for more serious accidents for herself and others around her?

6

MOLLY

*A*fter breakfast, Molly joined a crew of two other women to clean the upstairs. When they finished scouring the bathrooms, they moved on to vacuuming and dusting the bedrooms and hallway. After seven years of focusing solely on her own survival needs, Molly found that working with other women to fulfill a common goal gave her a sense of purpose.

When the household work was done, she went outside to the garden. She'd had mixed emotions about the garden lady when they met at breakfast. Caroline didn't have much to say, and her face appeared to be set in a permanent scowl. Grumpy types didn't bother Molly so much. She certainly had her share of surly moods. But she'd learned the hard way that it was good to give people their space when they weren't feeling their best.

Caroline, seemingly surprised to see Molly, looked up from wrestling with a roll of wire mesh. Her clothes were soaking wet and rivers of sweat ran down her face. But she seemed less tense than she'd been during breakfast. Like Molly, the outdoors agreed with her.

"I'm supposed to help you," Molly said. "What do you want me to do?"

"Let's see." She glanced around at her project in progress, as if searching for something for Molly to do. "Why don't you hold this hardware cloth in place while I staple it to the wooden frame."

"What's it for? The cloth, I mean."

"It helps keep the weeds out."

They got down on their knees together and Caroline stretched the wire mesh over the sides of the wooden frame. "Now, hold it tight here"—she showed Molly where to put her hands—"while I staple it."

But when Caroline came at the wire mesh with her gun, shooting three consecutive staples in the wood, Molly shrieked and quickly drew her hands back. "Good Lord in heaven. That's a loud noise."

"Sorry." Caroline sat back on her haunches, wiping the sweat out of her eyes with her forearm. "This is really a one-person job, anyway. I've dug an outline in the grass where the frame will go." She pointed at a nearby pile of yard tools. "Why don't you grab a shovel and start digging up the grass. We need to work quickly. A truck from the hardware store will be arriving soon with a load of soil."

"Yes, ma'am," Molly said, getting to her feet. Choosing a pointed shovel from the pile of tools, she went to the center of the outlined box and rammed it into the ground.

"You'll have more success with a flat shovel." Caroline took the pointed shovel from Molly and replaced it with a flat shovel from the pile. "Here, let me show you. Start at one end of the rectangle, along the line I've already created. Dig the shovel into the ground and peel away the top layer of grass and dirt, like so." She demonstrated three times before handing Molly the shovel. "Now, you give it a try."

It took Molly twice as long to scoop up the same amount of grass. "That's the idea," Caroline said. "But try to pick up the pace. We really must hurry."

Caroline had made it look so easy, but Molly was able to dig up only small patches of grass. After Caroline finished stapling the wire mesh to the frame, she grabbed another shovel and went to work at the opposite end. Out of the corner of her eye, Molly watched Caroline digging and tossing her way toward her. The gardener's damp T-shirt clung to her lean upper body revealing taut bicep and shoulder muscles. On the outside, Caroline was the picture of health with golden skin and sun-streaked hair. But her eyes, so deep blue like the ocean, spoke of a sadness Molly could relate to. *What is your story, lady?* she wondered, but she was too intimidated by her to ask.

The sound of a truck horn interrupted Molly's thoughts. "I'm almost done," Caroline said without looking up. "Go meet the driver and ask him to bring his load of dirt over here."

"Yes'm." Molly dashed across the lawn, waving her arms to get the driver's attention. He rolled down his window, and she pointed at Caroline. "We need the dirt over there where she's working."

He navigated his truck across the lawn, dumped his load of soil inside Caroline's wooden rectangle, dropped several flats of plants on the ground, and drove off again within minutes. For the next hour, Caroline and Molly transported wheelbarrows full of compost from the pile behind the shed to the garden. Molly's energy soon ran out, and she stretched out on the ground, admiring the flats of tender plants while Caroline mixed the compost into the soil with a dirt rake.

"What kind of plants are these?" Molly asked.

"Vegetables and herbs. They should have plastic labels." Caroline straightened, stretching her back. "You don't know much about gardening, do you?"

"Not planting. But I'm an expert at watching flowers grow." Molly loved it in the spring and the fall when the city of Charleston replanted the flower beds in Waterfront Park where she spent most of her days. And nights too depending on which policemen were on patrol.

"Would you like for me to speak to Faith about having you transferred to another project? I need someone who doesn't mind hard work."

Molly jumped up off the ground. "Oh, no ma'am. Please don't do that. She'll kick me back out on the streets if she thinks I'm not pulling my weight. I was just taking a little break. I'll do better. I promise."

Caroline appeared taken aback. "I didn't mean to upset you. I thought maybe you weren't enjoying the work."

"Oh, no ma'am. I love being outside."

Caroline softened. "I'm sorry if I was too hard on you. I'm used to working alone. Let's take a break. It's almost time for lunch, anyway. We'll try again later."

"I can't help you anymore today," Molly said. "I have a session with Dr. Robin after lunch, and then we have our Salt Life program with Miss Faith's nephew at four."

Caroline's brow wrinkled. "What's a Salt Life program?"

"I'm not entirely sure. Miss Faith said something about him teaching us to fish and crab. That's all I know."

Molly jumped back, startled, at the loud clanging of a cast-iron farm bell. "I wasn't expecting that. What's it mean? Is the house on fire or something?"

"That's the signal for lunch," Caroline said and started off toward the house.

As she traipsed after her, a long-ago memory came to Molly's mind of a different bell on a different farm. She rarely thought about the past. She'd been too young to remember the good old days back on the farm with her family. She'd buried the memories from her older years deep in her mind where they couldn't cause her any more pain.

She was ravenous by the time she'd changed into clean clothes and sat down at the table for lunch. When Faith asked her to say grace, she bowed her head and said, "Thank you, Lord, for the food, friendship, and shelter. In that order."

When she opened her eyes, everyone was smiling at her, including Caroline.

After a delicious lunch of turkey chili, fruit salad, and warm cheese biscuits, Molly walked down the hall to Dr. Robin's office at the front of the house. Robin rose from behind her desk to greet her. "Welcome, Molly. Please come in. Have a seat wherever you'd like."

Robin came from behind the desk and waited for Molly to choose between the sofa and the two chairs on either side. The rug and walls were gray, and the furniture was upholstered in a velvety fabric the color of the sky on a crisp fall day. On the wall above the sofa, a painting with splashes of every color in the rainbow added a spot of cheerfulness.

Molly sat ramrod straight at the edge of the sofa with her clasped hands between her thighs. She'd never been in a shrink's office before, and she wasn't exactly sure what was expected of her.

"You're looking well," Robin said, taking a seat in the chair nearest her. "How're you settling into indoor living?"

"It's only been one day, Dr. Robin. But so far, so good. Everyone seems real nice here. My roommate's a little strange. It freaks me out the way she piddles around the room at all hours of the night, but I'm not worried about her stealing my stuff or anything like that."

"Theft should be the least of your concerns," Robin said with a chuckle. She settled back in her chair with her notepad in her lap and her legs crossed. "Tell me about yourself."

Molly shrugged. "Not much to tell about a homeless person."

"Well then, why don't you start by telling me how you became homeless."

"The normal way folks become homeless. I lost my job and

my apartment. That was seven years ago. But once you're down, it ain't so easy to get back up."

Robin jotted something on her notepad. "Do you have any family?"

"No'm. I had a fiancé once. For about a second. He died in a trucking accident before we could get married."

"I imagine that was hard for you."

Molly shrugged. "Happened a long time ago." She ran her hand across the arm of the chair, feeling the soft fabric against her palm. "I have a sister too. But I ain't seen her since our parents died in a house fire and we were sent to separate foster homes."

Robin's eyes narrowed. "I'm so sorry. How old were you at the time?"

"I was ten and my sister eight. I'll never forgive myself for letting Penny down. I begged the social worker to keep us together. But she didn't care what I thought. I was just a little girl."

"Have you ever tried to find your sister?"

Molly looked away. "With all due respect, I don't much feel like talking about this. The past is in the past. I prefer to live in the here and now."

"I'm not interested in talking about your past. At least not today. I want to get to know you better and determine the best way to help you obtain the new life you came here to find. Locating any long-lost family is the obvious first step."

"Oh. Right. That makes sense." It stood to reason they would want to locate any family that might be able to offer Molly a home. "My heart hasn't been whole since the day Penny and I were separated. Don't get me wrong, Dr. Robin. I want nothing more than to be reunited with my sister. But I don't want to be a burden to her. I'd rather figure out my new life before I try to contact her."

"All right then," Robin said, her jaw set in determination.

"We'll have to figure out a different approach. You'll need a job and a place to live. What types of things are you good at?"

"I've been homeless most of my adult life. Surviving is the only thing I know how to do." Molly wrapped her arms around herself and lowered her head. "It's hopeless. I should never have come here."

Robin reached for Molly's hand. "Don't get discouraged, Molly. As you said, it's only been one day. Faith and I will work with you to find a job and a place to live. But I'd also like to help you find peace of mind. You've experienced a considerable amount of heartache in your lifetime."

You don't know the half of it, Molly thought.

Robin asked, "Do you think being homeless was a coping mechanism, your way of running from the past?"

Molly stared out the window at Caroline who was back in her garden raking at the dirt as though her life depended on it. Molly wondered if gardening was Caroline's way of running from the past. "Can we be finished for today, Dr. Robin?"

Robin consulted the crystal clock on her desk. "I don't see why not. I wouldn't want to overdo it on your first day, and it's almost time for the Salt Life program." She got up and walked Molly to the door. "Have you ever been fishing?"

Molly's face brightened. "All the time. Fishing is one thing I'm good at."

"Then why don't you head down to the dock early and see if you can help Faith's nephew set up. Jamie's a nice young man. I think you're going to like him."

Eager to be outdoors again, Molly practically skipped through the grand hallway, out the front door, and down to the water-front. A young man she assumed was Jamie was removing fishing poles from a storage shed near the dock. Robin had forgotten to mention that Faith's nephew was a hunk with dark wavy hair and stormy gray eyes. When he noticed Molly watching him, she flashed a hand at him. "Hi! I'm Molly."

"And I'm Jamie. I'd shake your hand if mine weren't so full."
He held up the rods as evidence.

"Can I help?" she asked.

"Sure! There are two more rods in the shed, if you don't mind grabbing those."

Molly retrieved the rods from the shed and followed him to the end of the short dock. "Miss Faith said you were going to show us how to bait and set crab traps. Do we get to go fishing today too?"

"That's the plan, as long as everyone shows up on time."

She looked up the hill as the other residents emerged from the house. "Here they come now." Molly counted four. They were all there except Caroline.

Jamie waited for everyone to gather on the dock before clapping his hands for attention and introducing himself. He scanned the group, his eyes settling on his aunt near the back. "Faith has two other nephews, but I'm her favorite."

The residents laughed, and Faith called out, "Shh! That's supposed to be our little secret."

Jamie continued, "If you're from around these parts, you know that my family has run the local seafood business for decades. Our building was destroyed by fire last May. We're rebuilding now, and scheduled to reopen on June first. I've been fishing these waters all my life, and I jumped at the chance when Faith asked me to share my knowledge with you. I think of all this"—he spread his arms wide at the inlet—"as the Salt Life, like the brand those four watermen from Florida have developed in recent years. I'm sure you've seen their logo on car decals. In fact . . ." He lifted a brown shopping bag from the dock beside him. "I just happen to have some extra hats if anybody wants one." He removed a stack of hats in pastel colors with a fish and the Salt Life logo on them. He handed the stack to Rosalie, the resident nearest him, to pass around. "There should be enough for everyone to have one.

"Now let's get started. First thing we're going to do is bait and set three crab traps. I use dead fish heads and leave my traps in the water for a minimum of twenty-four hours. I happen to know firsthand that this is a hot spot for crabs. When I come back tomorrow, I'll bring my steamer and gas burner, and we'll cook ourselves a mess of crabs for dinner."

Everyone erupted in cheers. The residents watched closely as he stuffed the fish heads into the bait compartment, tied a float to the rope on top, and tossed the trap into the water near the dock. "It's that simple. Now it's your turn. Why don't you divide into two groups." Stepping aside, he supervised the eager participants as they baited the traps and dropped them into the water. Once they'd finished, Jamie said, "Since we have plenty of time left, I brought along some chicken necks if anyone would like to try string crabbing, or I have plenty of rods if you'd prefer fishing."

Molly waited her turn for Jamie's attention. When he finally came to her, she told him she wanted to fish. She'd caught hundreds of fish off the dock at Waterfront Park with her trusted cane pole, but she'd never used a rod with a reel. To her embarrassment and disappointment, she created a rat's nest of fishing line on her first cast. Recognizing her distress, Jamie sat down on the dock beside her and tried patiently to teach her to cast. When subsequent attempts yielded similar results, he patted her on the head and told her to keep practicing. Frustrated, she returned her rod to the shed, and feeling dejected, she went up to the house to her room. She could do nothing right in this strange new world. Her dream of getting a new life was just that—a dream.

7

CAROLINE

*C*aroline hid behind the garden shack when she noticed the other residents heading toward the dock. When Molly had mentioned that Faith's nephew would be on-site to teach the residents how to fish and crab, Caroline said a silent prayer that it would be one of Jackie's boys, Cooper or Sean, and not Sam's son. But her heart had missed a beat when she saw Jamie Sweeney driving down the driveway in his silver pickup truck an hour ago. She'd come here to get away from her memories. Seeing Jamie, even from afar, had fast-tracked her back to that catastrophic New Year's Day four years ago.

She waited until all the residents had left the house before going to the kitchen for her suitcase. Unsure of where to go, she went in search of Emilee, who directed her to the room at the top of the stairs. The room, on the small size, offered a closet she would have to share with Rosalie, and a bed, nightstand, and dresser for each of them. Positioned in front of a single large window were two club chairs upholstered in a navy-and-white striped fabric that made Caroline think of Nantucket, even though she'd never been there.

She left her suitcase by the bed and went to the window

where she had an unobstructed view of the dock. Jamie's hands were animated as he spoke to the women. From what she could tell, he'd changed quite a bit since she'd last seen him. His shoulders were broader, his face fuller. He'd already graduated from college. He'd become a man.

Opening her suitcase on the bed, she located her toiletry case and her robe and went down the hall to the bathroom, which housed three toilets, two showers, and three sinks. She had a flashback of her years living in a sorority house at Clemson as she removed her shampoo and conditioner from her toiletry case and placed it in one of the empty cubbies built into the wall opposite the sink.

She stayed in the shower longer than usual, relishing the hot water that soothed her aching muscles. She towel-dried her hair, slipped on her robe, and returned to her room. After unpacking her clothes into the empty dresser, she stretched out on the bed with her cell phone. She hadn't looked at her phone all day and half expected to find a text from Troy saying he'd made a mistake and didn't want a divorce after all. But there were no text or voice messages from anyone. The realization that no one needed or wanted to talk to her landed like a ten-ton weight in the middle of her chest. Her parents and only child were dead. Her husband had left her. And her only sibling lived in Montana. They'd never been close, and Caroline hadn't spoken to her sister since the day she'd called to express her condolences when Cory died. She closed her eyes tight, willing herself not to cry. She'd shed enough tears to last a lifetime. *You've been awake for thirty-two hours straight,* she reminded herself. Exhaustion exacerbated her already-raw emotions.

She fell into a restless sleep and was prodded awake an hour later by Rosalie. "Better get dressed, roomie. Group starts in thirty minutes and Dr. Robin doesn't like it when we're late."

Caroline sat up, rubbing the sleep from her eyes. "How was the Salt Life program?"

"Awesome. Jamie taught us how to catch crabs with a piece of string and chicken neck. String crabbing he calls it. We caught a whole bucketful, if you can believe that." Rosalie plopped down uncomfortably close to Caroline. "He's totally hot. Too bad he has a girlfriend."

"Jamie has a girlfriend? Is it serious?" Caroline asked, inching away from Rosalie.

Rosalie shrugged. "I think so. But she's in New York, studying to become a chef."

Good for Jamie, Caroline thought. He would get married and give Sam a slew of grandkids.

"So." Rosalie shifted on the bed to face Caroline, tucking her foot beneath her leg. "You seem like a nice lady. I bet you're a great mom. How old are your kids?"

"My only son was killed in an ATV accident four years ago. He would've been a couple of years older than you."

Rosalie's hand flew to her mouth. Her fingernails were painted teal with white daisies on them. "I'm so, so, so, sorry," she said. "My mom kicked me out of the house. She's probably hoping something like that will happen to me."

"Don't say that, Rosalie," Caroline said in a stern voice. She couldn't imagine any mother would ever have reason to wish her child dead. "I'm sure your mama loves you very much. I bet she had a reason to kick you out of the house."

Rosalie hung her head. "She did. I was drinking too much and using drugs, not to mention staying out all night and bringing boys home. Being here has helped me realize what a brat I've been to her."

"Sometimes parents have to make tough decisions that are in the best interest of the child, even though the child may not see it that way. They call it tough love. I'm sure it wasn't easy for your mom."

Caroline was beginning to understand why Faith had put her

in the room with this young girl. *Who knows? Maybe we do need each other.*

"So, tell me what group is like," Caroline said, going to the dresser for a clean pair of jeans and her favorite pink tee.

"Oh, you know, it's just a bunch of people talking about their problems. It's not really my thing," Rosalie said, but when they met with the group twenty minutes later, she was the one doing most of the talking.

Caroline was surprised by the positive tone of the discussion. Dr. Robin explained that, during every group session, each resident was asked to share something they'd learned about themselves that day. It was obvious how hard these women were working to sort out their problems and better their lives. Caroline sat back and listened, observing each of the residents closely when it was her turn to share. Louise, the beautiful young woman whose hand trembled when she lifted her disposable coffee cup to her lips. Sheila, whose eyes darted around the room. Tilda, who crossed and uncrossed her legs, constantly shifting in her seat. And Molly, whose bright disposition from earlier in the day appeared to have waned.

Caroline couldn't help but wonder if she was somehow responsible for deflating Molly's mood. When it was her turn to tell the group what she'd learned about herself that day, she looked at Molly and said, "I need to have more patience. It's unfair of me to take my problems out on those around me."

Molly's lips parted in a thin smile that quickly faded. Something was definitely troubling her. Molly—whether she was of simple mind or fighting spirit or both—didn't seem the type to let life get her down. After all, she'd survived living on the streets for seven years.

Caroline made a point of sitting next to Molly during dinner, but her attempts at making conversation failed. Molly picked at her meatloaf in silence, excused herself as soon as everyone had finished eating, and hurried off to her room.

Caroline had kitchen cleanup duty. After all the pots were scrubbed and the dishes put away, she selected a Susan Mallery novel from the bookshelves in the parlor and took it upstairs to bed.

She fell asleep with the book open on her chest, and slept the best she had since Cory died. She woke before six on Wednesday morning feeling refreshed and ready to plant her garden. She was making her bed when she caught a glimpse of a familiar-looking figure out on the dock. She went to the window, and, on closer inspection, saw that Molly was yanking monofilament line out of a fishing reel in an effort to untangle a rat's nest.

Smiling to herself, Caroline left the room quietly so as not to disturb a sleeping Rosalie. She stopped by the kitchen for two cups of coffee on her way outside.

"Need some help with that?" she asked Molly as she approached the end of the dock.

Molly held the rod out to her. "I give up. I've tried a dozen times. I just can't do it."

Caroline set the coffee cups on top of a piling and took the rod from Molly. "You don't seem like the type to give up," she said easing the line out of the reel.

"It's not just the stupid fishing rod. It's everything. I can't do anything right. I'm not cut out for the real world. After breakfast, I'm gonna ask Faith to find me a ride back to Charleston. I'll live out my days on the street."

Caroline finished untangling the rat's nest and set the rod down. "You've only been here two days, Molly," she said, handing her one of the coffees. "It's only natural that everything seems foreign to you and for you to feel overwhelmed. You're having a bunch of new stuff thrown at you at once. You're not going to be good at everything. No one is good at everything. Give it some time. Figure out what you like to do the most and then work at it." Caroline saw tears glistening in Molly's eyes. "About yesterday. When we were working together in the garden, I apologize for my short temper. I wasn't myself."

"I don't blame you for being angry," Molly said with a sniffle. "I stink at gardening."

"That's totally not true." Caroline nudged her. "And I'm going to let you prove it to me this morning when we do our planting."

Molly stared past Caroline at the rod on the dock beside her. "I don't get it. I catch fish like nobody's business with a cane pole."

"Then why aren't you fishing with a cane pole, silly?" Caroline got to her feet and went to the storage shed for a cane pole. "What're you using for bait?" she asked Molly when she handed her the pole.

"Jamie built us a live bait well." Molly got on her knees and hefted a homemade cage full of minnows out of the water. Dipping her hand in the cage, she removed a wiggling minnow and inserted the hook in its lip like a professional. She lowered the minnow to the water, and within seconds, she got a bite. She pulled the line in and, grabbing the net beside her, scooped up the nice-size croaker.

"Yay, Molly! You did it. If I were you, I'd stick to the cane pole."

Molly beamed. "I think maybe you're right."

———

After breakfast, Caroline was called for her first therapy session with Dr. Robin who asked her a gazillion questions she refused to answer. She'd told Faith she was willing to try counseling, but now that she was seated in front of the therapist, she resented the invasion of privacy. She didn't know it would be this hard. She wanted to forget about her problems, not dwell on them.

Finally, out of frustration, she blurted, "Why can't we just leave the past in the past?"

"Is that what you're doing, Caroline?" Robin asked. "Because I'm pretty sure you wouldn't be here if that past wasn't still haunting you."

They sat in an awkward silence for several long minutes before Robin told her their time was up. "Think about what I said, and we'll talk more tomorrow."

Caroline hurried out to the garden where she discovered that Molly had already planted all of the herbs. Much to her surprise, she'd even spaced them the appropriate distance apart.

"Great job, Molly," Caroline said, inspecting her work. "I'm impressed. Did anyone help you?"

"Nope," she said, shaking her head. "I googled how on the computer in the main room. Does this mean I proved myself to you?"

"It absolutely does." She dragged the flats of vegetable plants close to them. "Are you ready to plant the veggies?"

"You betcha." She lifted a plant out of the plastic tray. "Come here you cute little"—she paused to read the plant tag—"green pepper plant. Shouldn't we plant all the same type together?"

"That's correct," Caroline said.

She got a kick out of watching Molly work. She handled the plants gingerly and talked tenderly to them as she placed them in the ground and tamped dirt around their roots. Caroline planted three for Molly's one, but she felt certain the extra special treatment would make Molly's vegetables more fruitful.

8

FAITH

$\mathcal{T}$he emergency board meeting lasted more than two hours, but Faith was pleased with the results. She appointed one member to follow up on her request for state funding. Three members volunteered to reach out to influential citizens around the state requesting financial and verbal support. And they voted unanimously to temporarily halt plans for the new dormitory building on hold. Faith felt an obligation to her donors and her residents to make Lovie's Home a success. Growing too quickly without appropriate financing could have a negative impact on their future.

After she adjourned the meeting, Faith took a few minutes to speak with each of the board members in turn before leaving her office in search of Bitsy. Emilee had offered to pick her daughter up from school, so that Faith could attend the board meeting. Juggling home and work was proving more of a challenge than Faith had anticipated. Bitsy had only a few more weeks left before summer vacation, but in the fall, Faith would make the necessary arrangements for the school bus to pick her up and drop her off at Lovie's. They would have to wake up extra early in the mornings in order to dress and be at the home in time for breakfast, but she was sure Bitsy wouldn't mind. That was the only solution that made sense with Mike's fluctuating schedule at the hospital.

Faith was not surprised to find her daughter on the dock with her nephew. Bitsy was chewing Jamie's ear off about something mean her best friend Chloe had said to her at school that day, while he worked to detangle a rat's nest in one of the fishing reels. In recent weeks, Faith had sensed her daughter pulling away from her friends at school. Some of the girls were becoming bullies, and Faith was relieved that Bitsy found their behavior juvenile. She only hoped her daughter had the courage to stand up to them. Bitsy had been through a lot in her young life, and those experiences had made her wise beyond her years. But wise didn't always mean strong.

"You're a good man to do this for the residents," Faith said, tousling her nephew's dark wavy hair. "How'd it go?"

Jamie looked up from his rat's nest. "Overall, it went well. Some of the residents are more proficient at casting than others, but they're an enthusiastic bunch and I enjoyed working with them."

Faith glanced in the bucket on the dock beside Jamie. "Looks like you got a few crabs."

"String crabbing's easy," Bitsy said. "Anybody can do it."

Faith and Jamie shared a smile. There was a time, not long ago, when Bitsy was afraid of blue crabs.

Jamie held the rod out to his cousin. "Hey, squirt, do me a favor and put this back in the shed." Bitsy took it from him and sauntered up the dock, rod in hand.

"Check this out, Faith." Jamie opened a cooler beside him, revealing a mess of fish—several croakers and three nice-size flounder. "No one has worked this creek in years. The area around your dock is a sweet spot for fish and crabs."

"Good news at last," Faith said. "It'll help save on groceries.

But catching them is one thing. You also need to teach the residents how to clean and cook them."

"That's the plan. We'll begin tomorrow with steaming crabs. In the meantime, I'll clean these fish tonight. Cook can fry them up for sandwiches for lunch tomorrow."

"Hey, Mama," Bitsy called to Faith from behind the shed. "There's a pathway back here leading into the woods. Can I see where it goes?"

"Not without me, you can't." Faith walked up the dock and joined her daughter at the edge of the pine forest fifty yards behind the shed. "I bet it leads to the caretaker's cottage. I've never visited it, but I've seen it on the survey."

"Let's check it out," Bitsy said, peeling back a layer of undergrowth.

Exploring the woods was the last thing Faith wanted to do, but she hated to squash her daughter's enthusiasm. "As long as we stay close together."

After fighting their way through twenty feet of undergrowth, the path opened up into a clearing in front of a small gray-framed cottage with black shutters.

"Look!" Bitsy ran ahead of her. "It's like a dollhouse. Can we go inside?" Her hand was on the knob, opening the door before Faith could object.

"Wait for me, Bits," Faith said, hurrying to catch up with her daughter.

Faith took Bitsy by the hand and they stepped slowly across the threshold. Other than cobwebs in the corners and windows streaked with grime, the interior appeared surprisingly clean considering it hadn't been occupied in decades. The floors were worn heart pine and an exposed brick wall housed the fireplace. The kitchen, small and outdated, was off to the right side, and a hallway led from the center of the main room to the master bedroom and bath at the back of the house.

"What's in here?" Bitsy opened a door off the hallway and

darted up a flight of stairs before Faith could stop her. "Check this out. There's a whole room up here."

Faith trudged up the stairs to a finished attic extending the width of the house.

Bitsy peered out one of two dormer windows. "Look! You can see the inlet through the trees. This can be my bedroom."

Faith went to stand beside her. "Your bedroom, huh. Who says we're moving here?"

"But it's perfect for us!" Bitsy said, her face set in a steely determination that belied her years.

"I agree the cottage is cute, sweetheart, but it's only a fraction the size of our house. Imagine how crowded it would be with the three of us living here." Faith tugged on Bitsy's arm. "Let's go help Jamie clean the fish. It'll be dinnertime soon."

Bitsy tore herself away from the window. "Can we at least show the cottage to Daddy, to see what he says?" Bitsy asked, looking back at Faith as they descended the attic stairs.

"See what he says about what, honey?"

"About us living here. Duh."

"I already told you," Faith said, no longer able to keep the irritation out of her voice. "There's not enough room for the three of us to live in this tiny cottage."

"Whatever." Bitsy did that eye roll thing that was starting to get on Faith's nerves. Her daughter marched over to the door, and jerked on the doorknob, but the door wouldn't budge. "It's stuck."

"We've had a lot of rain lately. It's probably just swollen. Here, let me try." Faith said, hip-bumping her daughter out of the way. It took several minutes of yanking and pulling to pry the door open. "Whew. For a minute there, I thought we were going to have to call for help."

As they dug their way back through the tunnel of undergrowth, Bitsy said, "If we can't live in the cottage, can we at least eat dinner with the residents tonight?"

Negotiation had become a way of life for them recently. When Bitsy didn't get what she wanted, she felt compelled to try for some lesser prize, which Faith deemed a ploy for control.

"I don't see why not. Daddy's working late again. At least, I think that's what he told me." Faith had all but given up trying to keep up with Mike's schedule. Several doctors had resigned from the ER staff in recent months, leaving them short-handed and Mike to pick up the slack.

By choice, Faith had been spending more and more time at Lovie's. Her heart didn't ache for her mother as much when she was surrounded by the residents and their constant bustle of activity. And she couldn't bear to be in her own home alone with her memories of that horrible day she'd killed Curtis.

Faith felt a stab of guilt when she and Bitsy arrived home around eight to find Mike sitting alone at the kitchen counter eating a bologna sandwich.

"I'm so sorry, honey," Faith said, massaging his shoulders and kissing his neck. "I must have gotten confused. I thought you were working late."

"I don't expect you to organize your life around mine. I can hardly keep up with my own schedule these days," he said in an uncharacteristic grumpy tone.

She'd made him angry, but he was too nice a guy to ever admit it. She would have to try harder to be a better wife.

Faith was pouring a glass of milk for Bitsy when her cell phone rang. She thought about ignoring the call, but Mike motioned for her to answer it. "Go ahead. It might be important."

Emilee's urgent voice came over the line. "There's been an accident. Tilda cut her hand on a piece of glass. There's blood everywhere. She's gonna need stitches. Should I take her to the emergency room?"

Faith felt Mike's eyes on her, and she lowered the phone away from her mouth. "One of the residents cut her hand and needs stitches."

Mike had agreed to be the doctor on call for the home. To date, fortunately, his services hadn't been needed.

"Tell her I'm on my way," Mike said, stuffing the last bite of his sandwich in his mouth.

Faith repeated his words to Emilee and ended the call. "I'm going with you," she said, reaching for her purse.

"What about Bitsy?" Mike asked as he headed toward the front door.

"She'll have to come with us," Faith said.

Bitsy was getting out of the shower when Faith knocked on her bathroom door. She hustled her daughter into her pajamas and out to the car. She climbed into the passenger side of his truck. "Do you have your bag?"

"In the back seat," Mike said, aiming a thumb over his shoulder.

Although he used a small backpack instead of the traditional doctor's case, Mike never left home without emergency supplies. Under protection of the Good Samaritan Law, he'd frequently aided accident victims on sides of highways.

When they arrived at the home, Faith sent Bitsy to the kitchen for a cookie and raced up the stairs behind Mike. Molly was in bed, her face as white as the pillowcase beneath her head. She pointed to the adjacent bathroom where Tilda sat on the closed toilet lid with Emilee on the tile floor in front of her, holding a bloody towel around her hand.

Mike elbowed Emilee out of the way and knelt down in front of Tilda. "Can you tell me what happened?"

Tilda opened her mouth to speak but no words came out.

Mike cast an uncertain glance at Faith and tried again. "Do you remember how you cut your hand?"

Tilda squeezed her eyes shut and shook her head.

Faith's concern for the older woman was rapidly growing. She'd arrived at the home by taxi five days ago. Robin and Faith had questioned her repeatedly, but Tilda refused to tell them why she was seeking help, only that she needed it.

Emilee said, "According to Molly, Tilda was filling a glass with water and it slipped from her hands. She was fumbling in the dark to pick up the shards of glass when she cut her hand."

"Let's have a look," Mike said to Tilda in a gentle tone. He unwrapped the towel and examined the cut. "It's not bad, but you need a couple of stitches."

Faith leaned against the doorframe for support. She blamed herself for Tilda's accident. If she'd been on property, she could have somehow prevented it from happening. These women were vulnerable, some of them perhaps even suicidal. Why had she never thought to ban glassware from the property? Tomorrow, with Robin's help, they would scour the estate for other potential hazards.

9

MOLLY

The sight of Tilda's blood all over the bathroom floor was the stick of dynamite that blasted open the vault that housed Molly's bank of memories. She was assaulted by flashbacks from time spent, as a teenager, in a locked, damp, windowless basement with only bread to eat and water to drink. Her fingers raw from clawing at the wall. Her head bruised from banging it on the concrete floor. She wore a burlap sack and no undergarments, and every month, with no feminine hygiene products to stop the heavy flow, the blood from her period ran down her legs and onto the floor. To this day, the smell of mildew made her gag.

Peeking from beneath her covers, she watched Mike and Emilee walk Tilda out of the room. They were taking her downstairs to the kitchen to stitch up her hand while Faith stayed behind to clean up the mess. When she'd finished mopping up the blood, Faith came to stand beside her bed.

"Molly, are you okay? Your teeth are chattering. Are you cold?"

"Not cold," Molly said through clenched teeth. "Scared. So much blood."

"Of course you are," Faith said, lowering herself to the edge of the mattress. "Tilda's your friend, and she got hurt. Would you like me to stay with you until she returns?"

Molly nodded. "Please."

"Why don't I read to you?" Faith lifted the Nora Roberts novel from Molly's nightstand and turned to the earmarked page. Her soft voice settled Molly's nerves and after a few minutes she closed her eyes and drifted off to sleep.

She didn't hear Faith leave or Tilda return to the room. Around five the next morning, she bolted upright, gasping for air. She pressed her hand against her pounding chest. She'd had a nightmare that someone was strangling her. Only it had seemed so real.

Quiet, so as not to wake up Tilda, she got out of bed, dressed in the jeans and cotton blouse she'd worn the day before, and packed her suitcase. Wheeling it behind her, she tiptoed down the stairs and out of the house. She was halfway to the road on the gravel driveway when a baby blue sports car approached. The car skidded to a halt on the gravel and the passenger-side window rolled down.

"Molly! Where on earth are you going so early this morning?" Dr. Robin asked, leaning across the center console and craning her neck to see Molly through the window.

"Back to Charleston. I don't belong here," Molly said and kept walking.

Robin got out of the car and chased after her. "Wait a minute!" She grabbed hold of Molly's arm. "You can't just leave without an explanation." The therapist studied her face. "Something happened. Does it have anything to do with Tilda's accident?"

"Yes and no. The sight of so much blood brought all these memories back." Molly placed her hands over her eyes to block out the memories that threatened to return. "It's like a rerun of an old movie but it's not a movie. It's real."

"Can you tell me about the memories?"

"No! I don't want to think about them. I want them to go away." Molly lifted the handle of her suitcase and started marching toward the road.

Robin caught up with her. "That's not usually how it works, Molly. Something triggered these memories. You can't just make them go away. You've experienced a breakthrough, which is the first step toward getting your new life." The therapist rested a hand on her shoulder, forcing her to slow her pace. "Come back to the house with me. I'll get us some coffee and we'll sit on the porch and talk."

The memories came at her fast—snippets of an evil man doing unthinkable things to her. She stared down the driveway toward the road, wanting desperately to escape but realizing she no longer could. She'd escaped the memories for more than two decades and she was tired of running.

Allowing Robin to guide her back to the car, Molly got into the passenger side with her suitcase on her lap. Robin drove the rest of the way and parked under the covered area. When she went through the kitchen for coffee, Molly walked around the outside of the house to the porch. She wasn't ready to go back inside. Her dream was too fresh. She could still feel the fingers on her throat, choking the life out of her.

She plopped down in a rocker and rested her head against the back of the chair, watching the first pink rays of dawn peek through the clouds. Birds chirped their merry songs and down at the creek, a school of fish rippled the water. She'd been at Lovie's for only two days, but she missed the outdoors something terrible and was desperate to go back to the streets of Charleston. Which she realized in a light-bulb moment was home for her.

Ten minutes later, she was sitting on the edge of her chair, gathering her courage to take off again, when Robin came out with a tray of coffee and freshly baked blueberry scones. Molly relaxed back in her chair. She'd never been able to refuse free food. When Robin offered her a scone, she pinched it in half, popped it into her mouth, and swallowed it down with coffee.

"Let's talk about what you're remembering," Robin said.

Molly opened her mouth to protest, and much to her surprise, the words came tumbling out. "I was about sixteen at the time. I'd been living with the same foster family for . . . well, for about four years, I reckon. I come home from school one day to find that my foster mama had left her husband and taken their real children with her. My foster father's name was Rex, but he made me call him Daddy. He was madder than a hornet at his wife and he took it out on me. He threw me down the basement stairs and locked the door. He left me down there for months. Years maybe. It's all a blur. I tried to get away, Dr. Robin. I swear to you, I did. I kicked him and beat him with my fists. But he was too strong. In the mornings when I heard him leave for work, I hollered my head off for someone to save me, but no one ever came." Molly grimaced at the memories. "Do we have to keep talking about it?"

"Not if you don't want to," Robin said, patting her hand. "Can you at least tell me how you got out of the basement?"

"When I stopped showing up for school, the social worker came to the house to check on me. *Daddy* told her that his wife had skipped town with the children, including me. When she figured out that wasn't true— it took her awhile, mind you—she called the police in to rescue me." Molly stared down at the coffee mug in her lap. "I stayed in the hospital for a week. I was a month away from turning eighteen and there was talk of putting me in a group home until my birthday. I sneaked out of the hospital in the middle of the night and never looked back."

"What happened after that?"

"I got a job working as a waitress at a truck stop right outside of town and set up camp in the woods nearby. I spent my first paycheck on a tent. A month later, when Ed, my boss, learned I was living in the woods, he offered me the vacant apartment above the truck stop. I lived there for ten years."

"Did you ever try to find your sister?"

Molly nodded. "A lot of good it did. I waited until after my eighteenth birthday to go to social services, when I knew they couldn't throw me back in foster care. They told me that my sister's foster family had legally adopted her, and they'd moved to Michigan. Just like that." Molly snapped her fingers. "My sister vanished without no forwarding address. I've googled her on the computers at the library, but I ain't had no luck."

"Were you ever afraid, living alone in either the woods or the apartment?" Robin asked.

"Nope. I'm a fast runner, and I knew my way around them woods. As for my apartment, I had five bolts installed on the doors. And Ed looked out for me. He knew there was something not right about me and he made sure no one got too close. Until Brian. Ed loved Brian."

"And Brian is?"

"Was," Molly corrected her. "My fiancé. And the nicest guy I ever met. We were planning to get married. He was saving for a Las Vegas wedding. He called me one morning about a week before Christmas that year—I believe it was 2006—to tell me he finally had enough money for the airline tickets. He was killed in an accident on the interstate that very afternoon."

"That's so tragic, Molly. I'm sorry for your loss," Dr. Robin said, dabbing at her eyes with her napkin.

"Thank you." Molly had never talked to anyone about Brian's death, and Robin's sympathy warmed her heart.

Robin took a sip of coffee, but her scone remained untouched on a napkin in her lap. "Can you tell me how you ended up in Charleston?"

"I went outta my head after Brian died. Literally. A month after he died, I snapped. I broke into a hysterical fit of crying one day at work. When I couldn't stop, Ed took me to the local emergency room, and they transferred me to the state mental hospital in Columbia where I stayed for two years.

After that, I was discharged to a rehabilitation program in Charleston. I got a job working for a local community center, coordinating after-school activities for little ones." Molly paused, taking a deep breath. "Basically, I was a babysitter."

"Hold on for a minute," Robin said. "Let's take a step back. While you were institutionalized, did you ever discuss your past with your therapists?"

"Nah. We focused on Brian's death mostly. I'd locked the memories of what happened to me in that basement away in my mind, and they didn't know to ask me about it."

"Okay." Robin rested her hand on the arm of Molly's chair. "So where were you living at the time you were working at the community center?"

"I had a cheap apartment in a not-so-great part of town."

"When was this, and how long did you live there?"

Molly cast her eyes heavenward as she considered the dates. "For about three years, from about 2008 to 2011."

"Am I right in saying that 2011 was about the time you became homeless?"

Molly nodded.

"What happened?"

She got up from her chair and moved to the edge of the porch. "I don't want to talk about it."

Robin came to stand beside her. "We can save the details for another day. But I need to know what we're dealing with so that I can devise a plan to help you. We'll come to terms with all of it in due time."

Molly's words were barely audible when she said, "One of my neighbors raped me."

Robin didn't speak. She simply rested a hand on Molly's shoulder as they stood together in silence for what felt like a very long time.

Eventually, Dr. Robin said, "We don't have to talk about the heavy stuff anymore today. But let's sit back down for a few minutes," and led Molly back to their chairs.

"If you don't mind me asking, Dr. Robin, how is it that you always seem to know what I'm feeling?"

Robin shifted in her chair toward Molly. "Because you and I have a lot in common. I, too, had a difficult childhood. But unlike you, I remember every vivid detail of the havoc my father wreaked on our family when he got drunk. The past has a nasty habit of repeating itself. Many women, when searching for a husband, look for personality traits similar to their fathers. And I was no different. I made the tragic mistake of marrying an alcoholic. I eventually ended our marriage but not before he'd left permanent scars on our young sons. I was really hard on myself for a long time after the divorce. I couldn't understand how a woman in my profession could've made such a mess of her life and endangered her children. But my good friend, Moses—you met him at the opening ceremony—is also a therapist, and he helped me understand that I am only human. As a result of my experiences, I've become more passionate about my work as a psychologist and empathetic toward my patients." Robin chuckled. "That's probably a much longer answer than you were looking for."

"Not at all. I'm glad you told me." Molly stared out over the dewy lawn, thinking about how similar their lives had been, yet at the same time so very different. "If only I had a career like you."

"Did you ever try to get another job, Molly?"

"Nope. I never did. Besides, who would hire me? I ain't good at nothing. I break everything I touch. I dropped a whole stack of dinner plates clearing the table just last night."

"Cut yourself a break, Molly. You're settling into a new life, learning to do all kinds of different things. It's normal for you to make mistakes. You've learned survival skills from your time on the streets that will serve you well for the rest of your life in whatever endeavors you decide to pursue. I can't imagine the danger you've encountered—the people that roam around the streets at all hours of the night, the animals, and the elements."

"It's not so bad," Molly said with a flick of her wrist. "The drunks and druggies don't bother me none. Neither do the critters, honestly. As for the weather, summers are worse than winters in Charleston. I don't mind the cold so much, but the heat is unbearable. I camp out in the public library when it gets real bad."

Robin's eyebrows shot up. "You don't mind being indoors at the public library?"

"Nah. And I've stayed in shelters a time or two. I don't mind so much when there's people around. Like here, at the home. What I'm afraid of the most is being alone."

"We'll address that fear as we begin to confront your past," Robin said. "You have a lot of hard work ahead of you, Molly. It won't always be easy. But remember, back then, when all those bad things happened to you, you were an underage minor at the mercy of the foster care system. You're in control of your life now. You're one of the strongest women I've ever met, and I have faith that you will persevere."

Tears stung the backs of Molly's eyelids, and for the first time, she truly believed she could start a new life.

As she crossed her legs, Robin turned her body toward Molly. "Tell me, what's the one thing you enjoy doing that you're the most good at?"

"Catching fish with a cane pole," she said without hesitation.

Robin slapped the arm of her chair. "Then keep at it. There's certainly plenty of fish to be caught around here. And you can learn to clean and cook them. Let this be your focus for a few days. See where it leads you."

"K," Molly said as she inhaled an unsteady breath. She wasn't sure about the cleaning and cooking part, but she didn't see any harm in trying. As long as they didn't kick her out for making mistakes.

"And no more running away," Robin said. "Can I trust you to stay put?"

"Yes'm. I'm not going anywhere. Tilda needs me." As the words left her lips, she realized her roommate had been in the back of her mind when she'd been plotting her escape. She didn't know what was ailing Tilda, but she aimed to find out.

Robin gave her a knowing look. "Tilda does need you. You have a lot to contribute to this group. Don't be afraid to share your feelings."

She stood, reaching for her suitcase. "I better go check on Tilda."

"We'll talk more later," Robin called after her.

The house was quiet as she crept up the stairs, and Tilda was still sound asleep with her bandaged hand against her chest. Molly left her suitcase inside the door and retraced her steps, down the stairs and out the back door. She ventured across the lawn to the dock. The marsh came to life as the sun rose higher in the sky. Fish jumped in the creek, and a pair of egrets stood in the shallow water, bobbing their heads for minnows.

Molly removed a rod with a spinning reel from the shed, took it to the end of the dock, and baited it with a minnow from the bait pen. She took a deep breath, remembering Robin's words —*Keep at it. See where it leads you.* Holding the line against the rod with her right hand, she opened the bail thingamajig with her left. She brought the tip of the rod upright, and using her elbow and wrist, she pushed the rod forward. The minnow landed with a splash in the water five feet in front of her. Molly stared down at the reel, thrilled to see there was no tangle. She closed the bail, and reeled in the line. She managed three more successful casts, and on the fourth try, she caught herself a spotted sea trout.

10

CAROLINE

*W*hen Caroline still hadn't heard from Troy by Tuesday morning of her week's anniversary at the home, she walked her cell phone out to the dock and hurled it into the water. "Take that, you bastard!" His attorney would have to hire a private investigator if he wanted to serve her with divorce papers. No one knew where she was, and Caroline had no intention of going anywhere anytime soon. For the first time in years, she was enjoying the company of other women. And she had a whole vacant field to plant if she chose to do so. If only she could embrace the therapy.

"You'll have to talk sooner or later if you want to stay in the program," Robin had warned. But the more Robin questioned her about her problems, the more Caroline retreated to her garden. The woman was relentless. "How do you feel about this and that?" Caroline knew, deep down, that she would have to address Robin's questions in order to move on with her life, but she felt so exposed, so vulnerable, opening up to a virtual stranger about her innermost feelings.

At her own expense, Caroline planted four more raised beds —one with wildflowers and the other three with a variety of herbs and vegetables. She created gravel paths between the beds and installed wire fencing around the entire plot to keep squirrels and deer out. She watered every morning and weeded every afternoon, and her plants thrived in the warm Southern climate.

While she avoided Dr. Robin at all costs, she bonded with the residents as they rotated through the garden. With the exception of Tilda who was difficult to connect with and of little use to Caroline with her injured hand. She spoke with the others, friend to friend, about their problems, and she was surprised at their eagerness to open up. Their complicated lives intrigued her, and she spent a lot of time thinking of ways for them to improve their situations. Focusing on their problems helped Caroline forget her own.

While she still visited the garden from time to time, Molly had put in a request to work full-time on the dock. Caroline missed her, even though she thought the fishing and crabbing experience with Jamie better suited Molly than gardening. Keenly aware of Jamie's presence on the property, Caroline had waved to him and he'd waved back. They had not yet spoken to each other. She sensed he was waiting for her to make the first move but she wasn't ready. She feared she would fall apart and that's not the kind of reunion she wanted to have with Jamie, the young man who had been like her second son.

That evening, Caroline entered the parlor after kitchen duty to find Molly slumped over the communal computer with her eyes glued to the screen. Sheila was playing solitaire with a deck of cards at the square table in the corner while Tilda, who sat on the sofa in front of the TV, seemed more interested in watching Rosalie cut Louise's hair through the doorway to the solarium than *The Good Doctor*.

Rosalie's in-house salon was thriving. Faith contributed the necessary supplies—a cape, a pair of professional shears, which Emilee kept for her for safety when not in use, and an assortment of hair coloring kits—and the residents volunteered to be her guinea pigs. To express her trust in her roommate's talent, Caroline had given Rosalie free rein to demonstrate her creativity on her shoulder-length hair. She'd cut it super short in a style Caroline found flattering to her face and easy to blow-dry. Molly's hair makeover was the most dramatic of all. Rosalie trimmed off several inches of split ends and added layers and blonde highlights to her dull brown locks. Molly had been thrilled with the results, and for the rest of that evening, she'd stood in front of the mirror admiring herself.

Caroline pulled up a chair close to Molly. "Looks like you're working on something important. Can I help in any way?"

"I'm trying to find my sister," Molly said, without looking up at Caroline. "I've googled her name and searched all them social media hangouts and people-finder websites. There's no sign of her anywhere. I have a terrible feeling she's dead."

"But wouldn't her obituary show up if she were dead?" Caroline asked.

"Oh." Molly looked up at Caroline, her blue eyes wide. "I hadn't thought of that."

"Let me try," Caroline said, taking the keyboard from Molly. "What information do you have for your sister?"

"Her maiden name, birth date, and place of birth. Penny Maguire, born May fifth, 1980, in Aiken, South Carolina."

Caroline's fingers flew across the keyboard as she typed in the information. For the next thirty minutes, they explored all the major search engines, missing relative websites, and social media sites.

Caroline finally gave up and exited out of the internet. "Okay. So, your sister doesn't have a police record, she's not dead, and she doesn't have a penchant for social media. She's living a quiet life somewhere. We just have to figure out where."

"Yeah, but how?" Molly asked.

Emilee appeared in the doorway from the hall with the five-minute warning. At nine o'clock, the residents were required to retire to their rooms.

"I'll give it some more thought," Caroline said, pushing back from the computer. "Maybe you should talk to Faith and Robin. They might have an idea of how to go about finding Penny."

Caroline said goodnight to Molly at the top of the stairs before going into the bathroom to brush her teeth. When she crossed the hall to her room, Rosalie was already in bed, curled into a tight ball on her side with a worried expression on her face.

Caroline slipped beneath the covers and turned out the light. "I like what you did with Louise's hair." She enjoyed how they whispered in the darkness, well into the night, like best friends despite the difference in their ages.

"I wanted to cut more. I tried to tell her she'd look more professional with shorter hair, but she wouldn't listen."

Silence fell over the room. When she heard sniffling a few minutes later, Caroline rolled on her side to face Rosalie. The light of the full moon peeking through the blinds illuminated Rosalie's face and the tears that glistened on her cheeks. "What's on your mind, sweetheart?"

"I don't know," she said in a tone of exasperation. "I'm thinking I should call my mama. I miss her like crazy. Although I don't know how I'd call her without my cell phone. She made me give it back when I left. I guess that's fair since she's paying the bill. But she doesn't even know where I am."

Caroline sat straight up in bed. "Are you kidding me? You should totally let her know where you are. You can call her from the house phone downstairs. I'm sure she's worried sick about you."

"Ha. I was such a rotten daughter. She's probably relieved to be rid of me."

"I seriously doubt that, Rosalie."

"What would you have done, if you'd gotten stuck with a brat like me?"

Caroline stretched out flat on her back with her hands over her head. "Anything I could to keep you safe. Your mother made a tough decision to kick you out. But you're better off because of it. You may have been a brat back then, but you're not now. At least not the Rosalie I know. And I feel like I've gotten to know you pretty well."

"My mom is no angel either. She has her share of boyfriends. I guess maybe I was trying to get her attention. Until I came here, I always felt kinda lost. I suck at school. I've never really had any positive direction in my life."

"But now you do with your hairstyling."

"I forgot to tell you," Rosalie said, her voice suddenly full of excitement. "Faith's helping me look into cosmetology programs. I'm going to become a legit stylist."

A wave of disappointment washed over Caroline. Her affections toward this girl had grown. She couldn't take another loss. "When will you be leaving Lovie's?"

"Not anytime soon. There are not any good programs around here. I'll probably have to move to Charleston. I have to figure out how to pay for school and where I'm gonna live."

"Baby steps," Caroline said.

"I'm curious, Caroline. Would you have thrown me out of the house if you were my mother?"

"Honestly, I don't know if I would have had the guts to throw you out. Assuming your mom's a good person, and she would have to be to have a daughter like you, I admire her for making a difficult decision for the right reasons. If you're not ready to talk to her yet, you should have Emilee reach out to her, if for no other reason than to tell her that you're safe."

"That's actually a good idea. Thank you for not judging me."

"Rosalie, sweetheart. I am the very last person who should be judging others."

11

FAITH

On Wednesday morning, the residents bid a tearful goodbye to Louise. She was Faith's first success story. Her hands had stopped trembling, and she'd been conducting Skype interviews in search of a job. She'd accepted a position with a marketing firm in Raleigh, North Carolina—a new career path that promised less stress and more opportunity for her to express her creativity.

Jenny arrived an hour later to take her place. Faith worried they were in over their heads where Jenny Cannon was concerned. She'd been married for only a year when her husband had a very public affair with her best friend. Faith didn't blame Jenny for being furious with both the husband and the best friend, but the twenty-six-year-old was beyond angry. She appeared to be in some kind of trance. She kept her eyes glued to the floor, uttering a continuous monosyllabic hum that reminded Faith of a monk in prayer.

Jenny's parents had driven their daughter down from their home in Sumter. Jenny sat out in the hallway while Faith met with Catherine and Carl Logan in her office. They begged Faith to help Jenny. Catherine, an attractive woman in her midfifties whose manners and jewelry hinted at wealth, spoke openly about her daughter.

"She's an emotional train wreck. We've tried, but we can't reach her. We know our sweet Jenny's in there somewhere. But she won't let anyone near her. She's consumed by fury. She's tried to kill herself twice. Please, you must help her. You're our last hope."

The idea of having a suicidal resident in her care terrified Faith. "We don't have the staff to hold suicide watches. Perhaps she'd be better off in a psychiatric institute."

The Logans exchanged a look. "That's a last resort for us," Carl said. "We don't expect you to watch her 24/7. We've tried to do that these past few months, and . . . well, it's next to impossible."

Catherine said, "We feel that being around other women with similar problems will be good for her. Please, just give her a few days to see how she responds."

Faith reluctantly agreed. "But if I find her behavior is too disruptive to the other residents, I'll have to ask her to leave."

"We understand," the Logans said in unison.

After the Logans left, Faith and Robin showed Jenny to her room. "You'll be rooming with Sheila Thomas," Faith said.

"She's outside working in the garden at the moment," Robin added. "I'll introduce you to her at lunch."

Faith stood with Robin in the doorway watching Jenny unpack her things. "I can clear my calendar for the afternoon," Robin said in a lowered voice. "I'll show Jenny around and introduce her to the other residents. Once I determine her areas of interest, I'll assign her responsibilities and explain what's expected of her. She needs our help. If we all pitch in, I believe we can reach her."

Faith was learning that her psychologist never backed down from a challenge. Much like Faith, Robin had experienced things in her past that made her all the more determined to help others.

"Should I cancel my trip?" Faith had planned to make the forty-minute drive to Charleston in the hopes of learning something about Tilda's family from her neighbors. Tilda had grown steadily more despondent and agitated since the accident with her hand. She'd taken a sudden, almost obsessive, interest in the chickens, and spent most of her time out in the hen house. Concerned about her patient's mental health, Robin wanted to reach out to the next of kin, but when Tilda had filled out the requisite paperwork upon her arrival at the home, she'd revealed nothing about a husband or children. She'd even left blank the space to name her family doctor.

"No, you should go," Robin said. "We need to locate Tilda's family if she has any."

"All right then," Faith said, backing out of Jenny's room. "I'll try not to be gone for too long. Call me if you need me. And keep a close eye on our newest resident."

After a brief exchange with Emilee, Faith retrieved her purse from her office and drove off toward Charleston. She tuned in to her favorite country music station and opened the sunroof, feeling the warmth of the spring sunshine on her face.

The pressure of her responsibilities at Lovie's and at home was mounting. Most mornings, she arrived at Lovie's before breakfast and stayed until well past dinner. Bitsy didn't have a problem with it. She loved spending her afternoons in the outdoors with her favorite cousin. But Faith felt guilty when their laundry wasn't done and her husband didn't get a home-cooked dinner. Fortunately, Mike didn't seem to notice. He'd been working equally long and inconsistent hours.

Faith located Tilda's home several blocks from the harbor in downtown Charleston and pulled into the short driveway behind a silver Audi sedan. Tilda's postage stamp lawn was freshly mowed, and her two-story single house with double-decker piazza appeared well tended. As she was getting out of her car, she spotted a middle-aged woman emerging from the house next door. She wore a taupe-colored suit with pencil skirt and her dark hair pulled back in a tight bun as if on her way to a high-powered job.

Faith flagged her down, stepping over a clump of liriope into the woman's driveway. "Excuse me, ma'am. May I have a word with you?"

The woman brought her wristwatch to her face. "I'm late for a meeting. What's this about?"

"Your neighbor." She gestured at Tilda's house. "I was wondering what you could tell me about Tilda Watson."

"Very little, I'm afraid. I've only lived here a couple of years." She opened the door to her Mercedes. "You might talk to the neighbor on the other side. Her name is Margaret something or other. She's an older woman like Tilda. I'm sure she can help you."

The woman started her car and drove off, leaving Faith standing in the middle of her driveway.

Faith crossed Tilda's yard and clanged the brass knocker on the two-story stucco house on the other side. A woman wearing a floral-print housecoat and pink curlers that sprang from her gray hair answered the door. She appeared older than Tilda, but her blue eyes were bright and focused.

"I'm sorry, but I'm not buying any of what you're selling." The woman moved to close the door, but Faith stopped her.

"I'm not selling anything, ma'am. I'm here to speak with Margaret. Are you Margaret?"

Hand on hip, she asked, "And who wants to know?"

Faith worked hard to hide her smile. She appreciated the old woman's spunk. "My name is Faith Neilson. I'm the director of a woman's shelter in Prospect. I'd like to have a word with you about your neighbor Tilda Watson."

Margaret's expression softened as she gripped the collar of her housecoat. "A women's shelter? My gracious. I haven't seen

Tilda in two weeks. I've been worried sick about her. Is she okay?"

Faith debated how much to tell Margaret about Tilda's condition. "She's fine for the most part. May I come in?"

Margaret hesitated. "I'd rather you not. My house is a mess."

Faith looked past Margaret at the clutter piled up in the living room. "Is there somewhere else we can talk?"

"Why don't you come around to the back porch for a glass of lemonade." She pointed Faith to the driveway. "Don't let the dog out when you open the back gate. Her name's Lucy. She won't bite."

Faith rounded the side of the house and let herself in the gate, stopping briefly to pet Lucy, a medium-size mixed breed with a sweet face and gentle manner. She sat down on the metal sofa on the screened porch and waited for Margaret, who joined her a few minutes later with two glasses of lemonade.

"Tilda and I have been neighbors for going on thirty years," Margaret said. "We're not bosom buddies or anything like that, but we keep tabs on each other. It's not like her to disappear without letting me know. I don't understand why in the world she'd go to a women's shelter when she has a perfectly good home right here."

"Our residents have a wide variety of problems. Tilda is unwilling to confide in us about her problems except to say that she has some." Faith paused to sip the tart lemonade. "We'd hoped she would open up over time, but that hasn't happened."

Margaret scrunched up her face. "I wasn't aware that Tilda had any problems."

"Does she have any family that you know of?"

"No." Margaret settled back against the sofa cushions. "Her husband died a couple years ago. They never had any children. By choice, I assume, although Tilda has never really said. Her husband served three terms as a United States senator and held several positions in the state government prior to that. They lived a glamorous lifestyle, flying to exotic places and hobnobbing with important folks. Tilda is one put-together woman. She's clever and efficient, always immaculately dressed. At least she used to be."

A senator's wife, Faith thought. *I knew there was something dignified about Tilda.*

"Does she have any siblings that you know of?" Faith asked.

"A sister and a brother, both deceased."

"Do you, by chance, know who any of her doctors are?"

"I have no idea. We've never discussed it." Margaret removed a slice of lemon from her glass and chewed on the rind. "Now that I think about it, Tilda has been somewhat of a recluse since Frank, her husband, passed away. Then again, his career always dictated their social life." She spit the lemon rind back into her glass. "I'm not even sure who her friends are. Or if she even has any. I've never seen any women our age coming or going from the house, you know like for bridge club or girl's night out or anything like that."

Faith wondered what kind of friends Margaret had and what they did for fun.

"Like I said, Tilda and I are good neighbors but not best friends. On the other hand, I feel like she would've confided in me if something was bothering her. I wish I could be of more help." Margaret stood, which Faith took as an indication their visit was over.

Faith removed a business card from her wallet. "Please call me if you think of anything that might be of help."

As Faith was descending the porch steps with Lucy on her heels, she noticed a tiny carriage house in Tilda's backyard. She stopped midway down the stairs and turned to face Margaret. "Has anyone ever lived in Tilda's carriage house?"

Margaret shook her head. "I've only known out-of-town guests to stay there for the weekend. But I haven't seen anyone coming or going from the carriage house since Frank died."

Faith thanked Margaret for her time, and walked back to her car. She knew little more about Tilda than she'd known before she came. On the drive back to Prospect, she thought about how best to help Tilda, but when she reached the home, she hadn't come up with any solutions.

She found a frazzled Robin sitting across the dining room table from Jenny who was slumped over an untouched tuna salad sandwich in front of her. Robin rose to greet Faith in the doorway.

"I've tried everything I can think of," Robin said. "But I can't seem to get through to her. She hasn't said more than five words to me all day. She just hums and glares. She's throwing off some seriously angry vibes."

Faith's heart went out to the young woman who was obviously in so much pain. "Did you show her around outside?"

Robin nodded, her eyes on Jenny. "She expressed a slight interest in the chickens. When I showed Jenny the garden, Caroline made an effort to converse with her. Although she didn't get very far, my gut tells me that Caroline might be just the person to break through her shell."

"Smart thinking."

"How did it go in Charleston? Did you learn anything that might help us with Tilda?"

Faith shared what she'd learned about Tilda from Margaret. "It's worth talking to Tilda about her life as a US senator's wife and her husband's death."

Robin sighed. "It's worth a try. I still think we should schedule a neurological exam, if for no other reason than to illuminate the possibility of Alzheimer's."

As the words left Robin's lips, Faith caught a glimpse of movement out of the corner of her eye, of a person hurrying toward the front door. She couldn't be sure, but she thought the retreating figure might've been Tilda.

Faith turned back to Robin. "I'll take over from here."

Robin glanced at her watch. "If you don't mind. I don't think we should leave Jenny alone just yet, but I'd like to make Luke's baseball game. It starts in fifteen minutes."

"Go! I don't want you to miss his game. Besides, Jamie's brought his boat over this afternoon. I'll ask him to take Jenny and me for a ride when he finishes with the Salt Life program."

"That's a wonderful idea. Let me know how it goes." Robin started down the hallway, calling over her shoulder, "I'll see you in the morning."

Faith approached Jenny. "I'm going down to the dock. Why don't you come with me?" Without waiting for a response, she took Jenny's sandwich plate to the kitchen and returned for her. Grabbing onto her arm, she helped her from her chair. Jenny seemed unsteady on her feet at first, which Faith contributed to not eating. She was sickly thin. Could she possibly be anorexic?

On the way out to the dock, Faith told Jenny about her nephew's efforts to teach the residents saltwater life. "Have you ever been fishing?"

Jenny shook her head.

"Look what I caught, Miss Faith." Molly held up an enormous blue crab with its claws extended.

Faith inspected the crab closely. "I must say, Molly. You've become quite adept at Salt Life."

"She has," Jamie said, bobbing his head up and down in agreement.

Faith introduced Jamie to their newest resident. "Would you consider taking us for a short boat ride? If you're finished with your training, of course. I'd love to see the estate from the water."

"Can I go with you?" Bitsy hollered from across the dock and hurried over to join them.

"Fine with me," Faith said. "But you'll have to ask the captain."

"Sure, squirt," Jamie said, yanking his cousin's brown ponytail. "Run grab your life jacket out of the shed."

"Jamie keeps extra life preservers on the boat in case of an emergency," Faith explained to Jenny. "But if you don't know how to swim, you'll need to wear one."

"I can swim." Jenny's words, though barely audible, were spoken from her lips, a sign that she was capable of talking.

"Do you think your students will be fine by themselves?" Faith asked Jamie. "We won't be gone long."

A mischievous grin spread across his handsome face. "Students? Ha. They don't need me anymore. I only come here for the attention. These lovely ladies are crazy for me."

Faith smacked his arm with the back of her hand. "You are full of yourself, Jamie Sweeney."

Bitsy returned, slipping her arms into the life jacket. "I'm ready."

The foursome boarded the twenty-foot center console boat Jamie's mother, Sam, had bought him when he graduated from college in December. Faith sat with Jenny at the bow while Bitsy climbed onto the padded leaning post behind the wheel with Jamie. They pushed away from the dock and headed down the creek toward the inlet. Jamie turned his stereo to country music and they rode for a while without speaking.

She observed Jenny out of the corner of her eye. Aside from her pasty complexion and bruises under her eyes, she was a pretty girl, blonde and petite with classic features.

"Our residents are a special group of women," Faith ventured finally. "Each has her cross to bear and is working hard to overcome her problems. But they're supportive of one another as they work toward achieving their goals. I'm glad you've come to us. We can help you if you let us."

Jenny stared a hole right through Faith. "I don't want your help. I just want to be left alone." In a tone that sounded more angry than desperate, she added, "And I'd rather die than go back to Sumter."

Faith thought about what Jenny's parents had said. *She's tried to kill herself twice.*

"Suicide isn't the answer, Jenny. Look around you." She spread her arms wide at the marshland and calm waters and pelicans flying in formation overhead. "There's life all around you. You'll make new friends, and one day you'll find love again."

"I have no use for them," Jenny mumbled. "Men and friends, neither can be trusted."

Faith's heart broke all over again for this girl. "I can understand why you feel that way. You've experienced the worst kind of betrayal. But I sense that you're a survivor. You need to learn to trust again. That won't be easy, but in time, you'll find happiness. You're very blessed. You have parents who love you very much."

"Right. My parents love me so much they dumped me off in this hellhole."

Faith forced back her irritation. Jenny's parents had indulged their daughter's pain, but Faith didn't think coddling the girl would benefit anyone, least of all Jenny. "Your parents didn't dump you off here, Jenny. They sought us out in desperation to find help for you. Lovie's home is not a hellhole. I survived an abusive marriage, and when my ex-husband got out of jail, he came after me and I killed him in self-defense. I started Lovie's Home to help women suffering from all types of hardships. We respect one another here. We work together as a family to farm the land and fish the waters. We will do whatever we can to help you, but we expect you to cooperate in return."

Jenny's lip quivered, and Faith suspected she'd struck a chord. She grabbed hold of Jenny's hand and didn't let go for the rest of the boat ride.

Mike was waiting up for Faith when she finally got home close to ten that night. She walked an exhausted Bitsy to her bedroom, kissing her cheek goodnight, before joining him in the family room.

"I can't take it anymore, Faith," he said with an elbow propped on the arm of the sofa and his forehead resting in his hand.

Her heart sank as she sat down beside him. "I'm sorry, Mike. I've been so preoccupied with the residents that I let my household duties slip. I promise I'll do better."

"What?" His head shot up, his eyes narrowing as he focused on her sorrowful expression. "You misunderstood, honey. I'm not upset with you at all. You absolutely should be preoccupied with your work. I admire your commitment, and I've never seen you happier." He drew her in for a hug. "I'm talking about the ER. I didn't think I'd ever say this, but I need a change. I'm too old for these hours. Mark Howard approached me again about joining his family practice. I think I'm ready to take him up on his offer."

A wave of relief washed over her. "Are you sure this is what you want? Your hours have been crazy lately. Do you think maybe you're just tired?"

He shook his head. "I've been thinking about it for some time. Nine-to-five with one weekend a month on call and every Wednesday afternoon off sounds good to me. Think about it, sweetheart. I'd be able to take Bitsy to school in the mornings, and have dinner with y'all at Lovie's every night."

She craned her neck to look at him. "You're actually volunteering to have dinner with a bunch of broken women?"

"Heck yes! If you'll let me. I don't want to overstep my boundaries, but I very much want to be a part of Lovie's Home, more than just the unofficial doc on call. I was thinking I could set up a clinic on Wednesday afternoons for residents with medical issues."

She rested her head on his shoulder. "You're a good man, Mike Neilson."

He kissed her forehead. "Married to a good woman, Faith Neilson."

"When would you turn in your notice?"

"Tomorrow, if you approve," he said. "The timing's bad for the hospital. They're already short-staffed. But they'll survive. I was thinking about taking a couple of months off, maybe even the whole summer. We can afford it financially, and I could spend some quality time with Bitsy."

"She'd love that. She enjoys being at Lovie's, but I was worried she'd get burned out if she spent the whole summer there. Besides, I've noticed the women are careful about what they say in front of her. They need to be able to talk openly among themselves." She snuggled in closer to him. "I hope you're not doing this just for me."

"I'm doing this for all of us. It's been a long time coming. But mostly, I'm doing it for myself. I'm looking forward to a more structured lifestyle."

She elbowed him in the ribs. "You mean, so you can go fishing more often?"

"Fishing is the least of it. Although I plan on doing a lot of that with Bitsy this summer. Seeing the same patients on a routine basis will help me feel more grounded to the community. And working with your residents will be fulfilling, like I'm providing medical attention to women who are really in need."

JENNY

*S*uicide, *hell*, Jenny thought. She didn't want to kill herself. She wanted to kill her husband and best friend. Her slip of the tongue had prompted Faith's impassioned speech. *Suicide's not the answer, Jenny. There's life all around you. You'll make new friends, and one day you'll find love again.*

No doubt Jenny's mother had warned Faith that her daughter wanted to off herself. Catherine had been hovering over Jenny like a helicopter pilot since she'd fallen off the monkey bars in the third grade and broken her arm. The pilot had been afraid to let Jenny go to the playground again for a year.

Jenny had been the last person in Sumter to learn of Derek's affair with Christy. When she heard the rumor at her bridge club's Christmas luncheon, the pilot had taken it upon herself to conduct a stakeout, like an amateur sleuth, of the bank building where Derek worked as branch manager. When he left the bank early that afternoon, the pilot had followed Derek to Christy's townhouse, and when he went inside through the front door, she'd sneaked around to the back and snapped pics of the lovebirds through the sliding glass door. The pilot had summoned Jenny home from her work at her father's lumber company and broken the news to her, showing her the pics on her cell phone as evidence. Jenny, overwhelmed by emotions, had allowed the pilot to take control of the situation. By the end of the day, the pilot had spoken with their attorney about a divorce and moved all of Jenny's clothes out of the apartment she shared with Derek, and into her childhood bedroom.

The so-called suicide attempts had been accidents. Three days after Jenny had moved in with her parents, without realizing the pilot light in the fireplace had gone out, she'd turned on the fake logs and filled the family room with gas. A week later, after encountering Derek and Christy together at Starbucks, she'd taken three of the pilot's Xanax to ward off the migraine brewing behind her eyeballs. Jenny admitted the Xanax had been a bad choice when Advil would've probably done the trick.

She'd told her parents repeatedly, "I wasn't trying to kill myself." But they refused to believe her.

The pilot thrived on drama. During Jenny's high school days, her mother had loved playing mediator when Jenny got into fights with her girlfriends. And why not? Her mother had little else to occupy her time, aside from bridge club, online shopping, and lunches out with her friends.

Jenny had spent Christmas and New Year's wallowing in self-pity, but by mid-January, the hurt had morphed into anger. And things had gone downhill from there. When her parents had suggested she seek help at Lovie's Home, she'd jumped at the chance to get the hell out of Sumter and away from whirling heli-copter blades.

She'd been eavesdropping outside the open door to Faith's office when the pilot said, "We know our sweet Jenny's in there somewhere."

Had Jenny ever been sweet? She didn't think so. Subservient was more like it. She felt like a puppet performing an act onstage for their friends. She'd always done exactly what her parents had expected of her, even when she'd wanted to go to art school in

New York and they'd convinced her to get a business degree from Carolina in order to run the lumber company her father had poured his heart and soul into building. If her parents truly loved her, they had a funny way of showing it. They didn't want what was best for her. They wanted what was best for them.

Jenny wondered if she was even lovable based on the way Derek had dissed her.

The humming had started by chance. In the early days, when Jenny's emotions were raw and all she'd done was cry and mope around the house, the pilot had tried to make it all better by cooking her favorite foods and counseling her like a female version of Dr. Phil.

"I'm not listening to you anymore," Jenny had shouted one day. "See, I'm tuning you out. Hmmmmmm." She'd hummed for ten straight minutes until she'd driven her flustered mother from the room.

After that, she'd used the humming as a tactic whenever she wanted to be left alone. Before she knew it, she was humming all the time.

While she could tune out the psychobabble, Jenny couldn't escape the pity in her mother's eyes. In everyone's eyes, even the residents' at Lovie's when they learned Jenny's husband had cheated on her with her best friend. She didn't want people feeling sorry for her. She wanted to move on with her life. But that would never happen if she were to stay in the small town of Sumter where she would constantly be reminded of Derek and Christy's affair.

Christy had virtually taken Jenny's place in Derek's life. Christy had moved into *her* apartment, was sleeping in *her* bed, and was currently controlling Derek's social life, which included most of the friends Jenny had known since kindergarten. Jenny was still trying to figure out why those friends had sided with them, when *she* was the one who'd been betrayed.

Most of the residents, put off by the constant humming, shied away from Jenny. But Rosalie had sat beside her during dinner, babbling on about life at the home no matter how high Jenny raised the volume on her drone.

As they cleared the table together afterward, Rosalie said, "I'm the self-appointed hairstylist around here. I'm not a professional. At least not yet. I plan to go to cosmetology school when I get outta here. In the meantime, I practice every chance I get. Can I interest you in a new hairstyle?"

Eyeing Rosalie's streak of blue hair, Jenny saw an opportunity to infuriate the pilot. "Can you give me a streak of color? Although I'd rather mine be pink."

"Heck yeah!" Rosalie said, setting a stack of plates on the counter with a clatter. "I'll run upstairs for my supplies and meet you in the solarium in ten."

Rosalie had spoken openly during dinner about her problems at home, and Jenny admired her for rebelling against her mother's rules. Jenny's life might have turned out differently if she'd refused to go to business school. If she'd refused to take over the company. If she'd refused to marry Derek. They hadn't exactly insisted she marry Derek. They'd persuaded her into marrying him. After all, Derek was her father's best friend's son.

"He's a fine boy. He'll make a good husband," her father had said repeatedly. "In a couple of years, once he gets some experience at the bank, I'll bring him on board at the company."

She'd served her father those words for more than one dinner since her breakup.

As Rosalie piled Jenny's long blonde hair on top of her head and fastened it with a clip, she studied the stylist. "Do you think you'll live at home while you go to cosmetology school? I mean, it seems like things were pretty bad living at your mom's house. I don't imagine you want to go back there, but where will you go?"

"I'm not sure yet. The better schools are in Charleston. Faith is helping me figure it all out." Rosalie combed through the bottom layer of her hair. "I doubt I'll ever go home, though. I love my mama and I want to have a relationship with her. But from afar. I haven't been very nice to her, and she deserves better than that." She handed Jenny a mirror. "How much should I cut?"

Jenny thought about how much the pilot loved her long blonde hair. "Cut it all off," she said.

Rosalie's jaw dropped. "You mean like Britney Spears?"

"Well . . . maybe not all of it. How about to here?" Jenny patted her shoulders. "With layers and long bangs."

"That would be cute!" She raised her arms, comb in one hand and scissors in the other. "Last chance to change your mind."

Jenny gave her the nod. "Go for it."

Thirty minutes later, five inches of her hair lay on the floor at her feet. Rosalie once again handed her the mirror. "What'd you think?"

"I love it," Jenny said, admiring the way her hair danced on top of her shoulders with a single streak of pink adding a touch of badass up top.

"My best work yet. Let me take your pic," Rosalie said, removing her phone from her back pocket.

Getting her hair cut had distracted Jenny from her problems, and for the first time in as long as she could remember, she felt normal. But when she thanked Rosalie for the haircut and Rosalie flashed her a friendly smile, a switch flipped inside Jenny and the familiar anger took control. Friends were not to be trusted.

She trudged up the stairs and entered her room. Sheila was sitting up in bed reading a novel with the image of a half-naked man looking at her seductively from the cover. She rolled her eyes. Men. Romance was overrated.

Why did she have to have a roommate, anyway? For five months, she'd been suffocated by her parents. She needed her space to find herself again. As she went to her dresser for pajamas, Jenny remembered Sheila sitting next to her at dinner, so timid and anxious, afraid of her own shadow.

"I should probably warn you, Sheila, that I sleepwalk. Happens all the time at home. Just saying." She lifted her shoulder in a nonchalant shrug. "A few weeks ago, my dad woke one night to find me standing over him with a pillow in my hands, holding it near his face like I was going to smother him or something. I guess I'm still processing the anger. But don't worry. I'm not a murderer or anything."

Jenny went across the hall to the bathroom, and when she returned, the light on Sheila's bedside table was out.

Thoughts of Derek and Christy making love in *her* bed in the apartment she'd shared with *her* husband plagued Jenny's sleep. She heard Sheila tossing and turning in the bed next to her. At least she wasn't the only one not sleeping.

Jenny blamed the devil for making her do it. Dressed in his red suit, pitchfork in hand, he sat atop her shoulder as she rolled off the mattress, grabbed her pillow, and tiptoed over to the side of her roommate's bed. Jenny lifted the pillow high over her head, positioned to strike. Sheila's eyes shot open and she gasped, shielding her face. Jenny pretended to awaken, feigning alarm at having been caught sleepwalking. She fake-stumbled back to her bed, crawled beneath the covers, and rolled over on her side with her back facing Sheila.

See how sweet I am now, Mother?

13

MOLLY

*M*olly had encountered some mean people during her time on the streets. And the new girl ranked at the top of the list with the meanest. She suspected Jenny was behind Sheila's pale face and trembling hands at breakfast on Thursday morning. What was Faith thinking? If ever there were two ill-suited roommates. At least Faith had the sense to assign Jenny to the garden. Caroline's warmth and kindness made for a comforting presence. She was good at helping other people, even if she had a difficult time coping with her own sadness.

Molly pulled Faith aside after breakfast. "Can I talk to you a minute? I need your help with something."

"Sure! Let's go to my office," Faith said, motioning her down the hall.

Molly had never been in Faith's office. A long rectangular table surrounded by chairs occupied one whole side of the room, which was twice the size of Dr. Robin's and similarly decorated but in shades of taupe instead of gray.

"Have a seat," Faith said, gesturing to a chair in front of her desk as she sat down behind it. "I'm very proud of you, Molly. Dr.

Robin tells me you're making great progress in coping with your past."

Molly's face heated. "I'm really trying. I've learned a lot about myself." Therapy was hard work, but the more she discussed all that had happened to her with Dr. Robin, the more she felt her burden lifted.

"That much is obvious." Faith crossed her arms on the desk and leaned slightly forward. "And Jamie brags about what a hard worker you are all the time. And speaking of Jamie, I have something I'd like to talk to you about as well. But why don't you go first?"

Molly wrinkled her nose. "Am I in some kinda trouble?"

"Not at all. But we'll get to that in a minute. After you tell me what's on *your* mind."

Molly took a deep breath and blurted, "I was hoping you can help me find my sister." She told Faith about being separated from Penny when they were put into foster care after their parents were killed in the fire. "Caroline helped me look on the Internet. We searched the computer high and low, but there's no sign of her anywhere." She realized how ridiculous she sounded, as though her sister were hiding out inside the computer. She coughed to clear her throat. "Anyway, Caroline said I should ask you, that you might have a better idea of how to find her."

"As a matter of fact, I do. My sister's husband, Jamie's stepfather, is a detective with the local police department." Faith opened her top desk drawer and removed a small notepad. "Tell me everything you know about you sister, and I'll have him search his databases."

Molly slouched in her chair. "That's the problem. I don't know much. Her maiden name was Penny Maguire, and she was born on May fifth, 1980, in Aiken."

Faith scrawled the information on her notepad.

Molly continued, explaining to Faith about her long-ago visit to social services. "The lady there told me Penny had been legally adopted by her foster family and they'd moved to Michigan."

Faith lifted the receiver from the desk phone. "Let's give Eli a call and see what he says."

Listening in on Faith's side of the conversation, Molly's heart fluttered in her chest when it became evident that Eli would help them.

Faith thanked her brother-in-law and hung up the phone. "He's on it. He said to give him a day or two to look into the matter."

"That's terrific, Miss Faith. I can't thank you enough."

Faith raised a hand in warning. "Don't think me yet. We have to be prepared for him not to find anything." She lowered her hand. "Although I think he will. Eli's very good at his job."

"Now it's your turn," Molly said, unable to stand the suspense any longer. "What'd you want to talk to me about?"

"Well," Faith began, intertwining her fingers on the desk. "Has Jamie explained to you about our family's seafood business?"

Molly slowly nodded her head, unsure where Faith was going with this. "He mentioned something about a fire."

"Right. Jamie and his mother, my sister Sam, are rebuilding the business. They plan to reopen on June first. Sam has two full-time positions available, one in food prep and the other in retail. She'd like to interview you if you're interested."

The room grew small and Molly felt the walls closing in on her. "I haven't had a real job in years. I don't know if I can do it."

"You're a very determined woman, Molly. You can do whatever you set your mind to. Personally, I think you're an ideal candidate for the food-prep job, which would include cleaning fish and cooking crabs. But you'd also learn to do so much more."

The idea of having a real honest-to-goodness job with commitments and responsibilities appealed to Molly as much as it terrified her. She cast an anxious glance at the door. "Can I have some time to think about it? I need to get to my chores."

"Sure. But remember, part of getting your new life, Molly, is finding a job. We won't kick you out until you're good and ready, but you can't stay here forever." They both got up and Faith walked Molly to the door. "You need to let me know by tomorrow morning so I can set up the interview. I will personally drive you to the market and wait for you while you speak with Sam."

"Would you really do that for me?" Molly asked, surprised Faith was willing to go to such lengths.

Faith placed a hand on Molly's shoulder. "Of course. I wouldn't recommend you for the job if I didn't think you were ready for it. The bonus is, you would not only be working for Sam but for Jamie as well."

The idea of working with Jamie every day tickled her fancy. "Does he know about this?"

Faith grinned. "Who do you think suggested it?"

Molly beamed, and ten minutes later, as she pushed the vacuum around the downstairs, she felt like she was walking on a cloud. Her dreams were finally coming true. Having a job meant earning a regular paycheck, which meant getting a place of her own. Her enthusiasm slowed when she got to that part in her thinking. The living alone thing scared the bejesus out of her. She would have to find a roommate.

When she'd finished her inside chores, she put on the bucket hat she'd found in the thrift shop and went out to the backyard to cut the grass. The weatherman was calling for a scorcher, and the air was already heavy with moisture. Mowing the lawn was mindless work, and before long her thoughts began to drift. A job at Jamie's seafood market meant moving permanently to Prospect. And why not? She had nowhere else to go. Unless . . . if her sister was still alive, maybe Molly would move in with her. Then again, Penny probably had a husband and children, which left Molly out in the cold where she'd been for the past seven years. She'd often dreamed of running into Penny on the streets of Charleston. Would they recognize each other? Would Penny acknowledge her, a homeless person, as her sister? Had Penny ever tried to find her? It would've been difficult with Molly not having a permanent address. Still, if she had the means, she could've hired a private investigator. That's what Molly would've done if she had money. What if Penny still lived in Michigan or some faraway place like that? Molly wasn't interested in living a place where it snowed all the time. And hadn't she found a new family with Tilda and Caroline and Rosalie? Only they would soon go back to their lives or move on to new ones, leaving Molly all alone again.

Molly was nearing the end of her mowing when a commotion in the chicken coop caught her attention. She looked over in time to see Tilda stumbling out of the henhouse with a basket of eggs. She wobbled as she tried to catch her balance, and then tripped on her own feet, landing facedown in the dirt with the basket of eggs beneath her.

Molly parked the mower and ran to her aid. "Good heavens, Tilda, are you okay?" She grabbed her roommate by the arm and helped her to her feet. Tilda's jeans and knit polo were covered in crushed eggshell and yellow yolk.

With tears in her eyes, Tilda shoved the basket at Molly and took off running toward the house.

Setting the basket down beside the wire fence, Molly went to the garden shed for a bucket and a shovel and cleaned up the ruined eggs as best she could.

Tilda's behavior was growing stranger by the day. Her clumsiness caused constant accidents. During the night, when she wasn't thrashing around in her bed, she was fumbling around the room, using the toilet, flipping the light off and on, and rooting through her dresser. Tilda refused to talk about her problems. When Molly asked what was bothering her, Tilda snapped at her to mind her own business.

Molly finished cutting the grass and returned the mower to

the shed. She expected to find Tilda in the room when she went upstairs to wash up for lunch. But the room was empty, and when she went down to the dining room, Tilda wasn't seated at the table with the other residents.

"Has anyone seen Tilda?" Molly asked. "She had an accident in the chicken coop just now. She was headed to the house, like she was coming inside to change her clothes, but she's not in the room.

"How long ago was this?" Faith asked, emerging from the kitchen with a large platter of sandwiches.

Molly thought about it. "I'd say about a half hour ago. She tripped coming out of the henhouse and fell on her basket of eggs. She wasn't hurt. At least she said she wasn't. But she sure seemed upset."

Faith set the platter down on the table. "Rosalie, get some plastic wrap out of the kitchen and wrap up these sandwiches." She addressed the others. "We need to divide and conquer. Let's search inside the house first. Molly, Caroline, and Jenny, you take the upstairs. The rest of us will look down here and in the basement. Check in every closet and under every bed. We'll meet in the hallway when we're through. In the meantime, Emilee, you wait at your desk. If any of you find Tilda, let Emilee know immediately."

The residents hurried out of the room to the various parts of the house. Molly went back to her room, searching under the beds and in the closet. Noticing Tilda's dirty laundry basket, she dumped the contents on the floor, but there was no sign of the egg-stained clothes.

She reported her findings to Faith. "I watched Tilda walk toward the house. I could've sworn she was coming inside to change."

The other residents returned to the hall, either in groups or one by one. Not a trace of Tilda had been found inside the house.

"All right, then. Listen up." Faith clapped her hands loudly to get their attention. "Time is of the essence. It's getting hotter by the minute outside. Let's divide into the same groups of two to search the front and back yards. Check the sheds and down by the dock, but do not, I repeat, *do not* venture into the woods. Does everyone understand?"

The group said yes in unison. When Faith excused them, Molly dashed out the front door and ran across the lawn to the dock, which she now considered her personal domain. She was certain she'd find Tilda with her legs dangling off the end, but again, her roommate was nowhere to be seen. She paced up and down the dock, chewing on a hangnail as she decided where to look next. She was walking along the border of the woods, just beyond the boathouse, when she heard someone crying. Peeking through the overgrown shrubs, she spotted Tilda sitting on the front steps of a small gray cottage.

She was torn between going to find Faith or consoling Tilda. Faith had specifically said not to go in the woods, but Tilda was in plain sight. She was about to venture into the woods when she spotted Faith rounding the corner of the porch from the front yard.

Molly flagged her down, and when Faith was at her side, she pointed at the entryway to the forest. "She's in there."

Faith inhaled a deep breath and dug her way through the undergrowth with Molly quietly on her heels.

"Tilda!" Faith called as she approached the woman. "Thank goodness you're all right. We've been looking for you all over."

When Faith sat down on the brick step beside Tilda, Molly plastered herself against the front of the cottage out of Faith's line of vision. She didn't want Faith to send her back to the house until she knew Tilda wasn't hurt.

Faith patted Tilda's knee. "It's dangerous for you to go running off like that in this heat."

Molly agreed. It was hot as Hades, even in the shade of the

forest, and she worried that Tilda, in her frazzled state, might pass out.

"I'm sorry," Tilda mumbled.

"Do you want to talk about what's bothering you?"

Tilda stared straight ahead, avoiding Faith's gaze. "I heard you tell Dr. Robin that I have Alzheimer's."

"So that *was* you in the hallway, yesterday?" Faith said, and Tilda nodded.

"I didn't say you have Alzheimer's. I suggested we schedule a neurological exam to rule out the possibility. I don't know what else to do," Faith said, her tone frustrated. "We've tried everything we know of to get through to you. Something is troubling you, otherwise you wouldn't have come to us in the first place. But we can't help you if we don't know what we're dealing with."

Tilda buried her face in her hands. "I'm losing my mind. Maybe it is dementia or Alzheimer's. I came here because I was afraid, living alone in my house. I'm afraid that I'll fall and no one will rescue me. Or that I'll go to sleep and not wake up and the smell of my rotting remains will alert my neighbor to my death. I thought it'd be better here, surrounded by people. But it's not. I've never felt more alone."

"You're surrounded by women, but we're merely warm bodies unless you choose to communicate with us."

Tilda looked at Faith with wide eyes and brows raised as though surprised by her accurate assessment. "I didn't think about it like that."

"In my experience—and my mother had the disease so I know plenty about it—Alzheimer's patients rarely suspect that anything is wrong with them. In fact, they often become defensive when their loved ones suggest their memory is failing or their behavior is off. I'm not a doctor, but I think there's a good chance you don't have Alzheimer's. But wouldn't you like to know for sure? If you do have it, we can help you make arrangements for your care. If you don't, you can find out what, if anything, is making you so anxious and have so many accidents. It could be a simple problem with your balance."

Tilda looked over Faith's shoulder at Molly. "Do you think I should have the test?"

Before Molly could answer, Faith turned to her and said, "I didn't know you were back there. Please go tell the others we found Tilda and for them to go ahead and start lunch without us. We'll be up in a minute."

14

CAROLINE

*T*hursday was one of the most difficult days Caroline had experienced since Cory's death. Beginning first thing with Sheila's sudden and abrupt departure.

"I've made arrangements to go stay with my sister in Baltimore for a while," poor timid Sheila had explained in a voice so soft Caroline had to strain to hear her.

Caroline had grown fond of the woman, as she had all of the residents, and she worried that Sheila wouldn't be able to function in the real world with all her fears.

As the heat and humidity built, so did her anxiety. After the concern and confusion over Tilda's disappearance, she'd spent an hour with Dr. Robin in her office warding off her incessant questions about Cory's death and the breakup of her marriage. And then, as if things couldn't get worse, the new resident, Jenny, had been assigned to the garden for the afternoon. They worked well together as they prepared the soil for a new flower bed, but the girl's humming soon began to irritate her. By midafternoon, Caroline's nerves were crackling like the lightning in the pop-up thunderstorms sparking all around them.

She was relieved when Jenny left to go down to the dock for

Jamie's Salt Life program. With her peace restored, she was able to focus her attention and soon fell into her zone, digging holes and planting the flats of Queen Red and Zinderella varieties of zinnias she'd sown indoors. Her mind was so preoccupied with thoughts of Cory and her impending divorce, she failed to notice the darkening sky, but when the skies opened up, she welcomed the pounding rain that cooled off her body and massaged her back. Caroline worked best in the rain. She felt at one with the earth, communing with nature. She continued to dig and plant, oblivious to the flashes of lightning. And the tears streaming down her cheeks.

She was tamping muddy soil around the last seedling when a pair of hands took hold of her shoulders, lifting her from her knees to her feet.

"What're you doing Ma—" Jamie stopped himself. "It's dangerous out here."

Caroline experienced a revelation at the exact moment a bolt of lightning split the dark sky behind Jamie's head.

"Hurry!" Jamie took her by the hand, and they ducked their heads against the driving rain as they darted across the yard to the toolshed.

They stood together inside the shed, crowded by lawnmowers and wheelbarrows and yard tools, dripping rainwater onto the dirt floor and gulping in air to steady their breaths. The silence was awkward. Four years had passed since they'd last spoken. Jamie had become a man, yet she saw traces of the boy she'd loved as much as her own son.

"I want to hear you say it," she said, turning to face him.

His dark brows narrowed into one. "Say what?"

"Your nickname for me. You started to say it when we were outside."

"Mama Caroline," he said in a husky voice, the name he'd called her since he was a boy of six.

The revelation she'd experienced moments ago made sense

out of the grief that had consumed her for so long. "I've just realized something very important. I've been mourning the loss of not one son but two." She placed her hand on his face, cupping his cheek. "I've missed you so much, Jamie."

"I'm sorry. I—"

"Shh!" She pressed her finger to his lips. "It's my fault. Not yours. I came to visit you once when you were in the hospital. I don't know if you even remember it. You were so broken. The doctors said you might never walk again. After losing Cory, it was too much for me to see you like that. So, I never went back. I've been running ever since."

"Running from what?"

"From myself mostly." *Another revelation*, she thought. Had she known these things about herself all along and refused to accept them?

She moved to the doorway, watching the rain pouring down in sheets. "I haven't been out to the farm since the day of the accident."

"Really? That surprises me. You used to love it out there." He came to stand beside her. "I've missed that place."

A faraway look settled on her face as visions from the past flooded her mind. "You boys used to pitch your tent right outside the back door of the cabin. You were eleven or twelve before you made it past midnight."

"I remember. We roasted marshmallows by the bagful on our little campfire," Jamie said, leaning against the doorway. "The memories of the time we spent at the farm got me through the worst of days after Cory died. The tire swing. Shooting skeet. Getting up at the crack of dawn to go hunting."

"Fishing off the dock," Caroline added. "And the birthday parties. You insisted on having yours together even though your birthday was in December and his in June."

He chuckled. "Cory and I drank our first beer together at the farm on the Fourth of July the summer before our sophomore

111

year in high school. We had more than one beer that night, truth be told."

Confessions from their youth. "No telling what else you two rascals got into. If only Cory were here to help tell tales."

Jamie shot her a look. "But he's with us all the time. At least for me he is." He placed his hand over his heart. "I carry him around with me wherever I go. When I'm out on the water or in the woods alone, I talk out loud to him like he's right next to me. I still dream about him from time to time. I wake up the next day with a smile on my face."

Caroline thought about how she worked herself to the bone during the day so as to avoid dreaming at night. "I try not to think about the past," she said, remembering the ghosts that haunted her during the wee hours of the morning. "It's too painful."

"Cory's life was cut way too short. And it nearly killed me when he died. But I wouldn't trade one single minute of my time with him. I embrace the memories. They're all I have left of him. I revisit the good times we had together to keep Cory alive in my mind, to prevent the memories from fading."

The rain slowed to a drizzle, yet neither of them made a move to leave the shed.

"How is Mr. Becker?" Jamie asked. "He used to shop at Sweeney's. Before the fire."

I know, Caroline thought. *I sent him there. To avoid seeing you.*

"He left me last week. Up and moved across the country without a single word of warning."

"I'm so sorry, Ma—"

"Don't be. Our marriage hasn't worked in a long time." She realized the truth in her words as they departed her lips. The marriage had worked for as long as it did only because of Cory's presence. Now, without him, their marriage didn't stand a chance.

She smiled at Jamie. "And call me Caroline. It'll be easier for both of us."

Jamie pushed off the doorjamb. "The rain's almost stopped. I should go check on things down at the dock."

Caroline didn't want her time with Jamie to end. Now that they'd been reunited, she had much to talk to him about. "Do you mind if I walk with you?"

"Not at all. I was wondering when you were going to come see our operation." He offered her his arm and they started off across the lawn.

"Say Jamie, would you be willing to drive out to the farm with me one day? Troy insisted I put it on the market. But I'm not sure I'm ready to part with it just yet. As you know, it's been in my family for generations."

"I'd be happy to go with you. How about Saturday?"

Caroline gulped. Saturday seemed so soon. Would it be rude to retract the invitation? She found herself saying, "Saturday is perfect. I'll get Cook to pack us a picnic lunch."

"Our favorites?"

Caroline smiled. "Of course. We'll make a day of it, since the residents don't have normal chores on Saturdays." *Whoa, Caroline. You're getting ahead of yourself.* "I'm sorry. You may have other plans."

"Not at all. I'll bring along some rods. We can do a little fishing."

They parted when they reached the dock. The other residents had returned from the house after having been driven inside by the storm. They were storing away their fishing equipment and cleaning up in preparation for group therapy that would start in half an hour.

Caroline admired how easily Jamie interacted with these women. He teased them and they flirted with him. The sweet and thoughtful boy had turned into a generous and loving man. He would make some girl a good husband. She realized with a jolt that she very much wanted to be a part of his future. She'd lost one son, but the other was right in front of her. Jamie always said he had enough love in his heart for two mamas. She wondered if that was still true. Cory was the bond that had tied them together. That bond had been severed, but was it possible for them to forge a new one?

Caroline dreamed that night about Cory. They were having a picnic lunch at the farm. Her son looked up and smiled at her. He'd grown into a young man. She knew it was supposed to be Cory—he had her son's bright blue eyes. But the face belonged to Jamie.

She lay in bed for a long time after she woke thinking about the dramatic turn her life had taken in the past twenty-four hours. How wrong she'd been about so many things. The half hour spent with Jamie in the gardening shed had been her happiest in four years. The grief had not gone away. It probably never would completely. But she was ready to reenter the world of the living, to move on with her life.

The fog had cleared, and she was able to look at the past four years with a different perspective. She'd needed time to lick her wounds. But Troy had done her a favor. By leaving her, he'd set her free to begin the healing process. She would face the future alone. She was no longer afraid but excited. Well . . . not excited exactly. But optimistic. She would embrace the memories, answer Dr. Robin's endless questions, and start to build new relationships.

15

JENNY

*J*enny experienced a pang of guilt when Sheila packed her suitcase and hightailed it out of Lovie's on Thursday morning. She'd wanted to get rid of Sheila so she could have the room to herself. She didn't mean to scare her off completely.

Jenny's first full day at Lovie's did not go well. No one had bothered to mention that manual labor was expected of her. Seriously, gardening? What did she know, or care, about gardening? At least Caroline didn't run her mouth incessantly like the other residents. She knew they were only trying to befriend her, but Jenny didn't need them. No man. No friends.

The storm saved her from having to bait a hook with a live minnow and catch a fish. Her father, in the absence of a son, had taught Jenny to fish and hunt at a very young age. She'd hated every minute of it, but the subservient Jenny had planted a sweet smile on her face and gone along with him.

And what was with the old lady getting lost? It didn't take a doctor to know the woman had Alzheimer's. They needed to lock her up in a memory care unit like Jenny's parents had done with her granny. She had to work hard not to laugh at the eggshells crusted to the dried yolks on Tilda's shirt. Wasn't there some kind of saying about egg on the face? Whatever that meant.

She survived her first session with the shrink by shooting Dr. Robin death stares and raising the volume on her humming.

"I'll let you off the hook for today," the shrink said. "But you'll eventually need to share your feelings."

Eventually, hell. Jenny didn't plan on sticking around long enough for that to happen. She spent a good portion of the day planning her escape. She took note of the security cameras positioned around the property. Because Emilee was at her desk most of the day surveying the activity on her computer monitor, her best bet would be to sneak out during the night, which shouldn't be a problem since she no longer had a room-mate. She'd have to somehow get around the guard. But he was at least a hundred years old and Jenny was a fast runner. She would hoof it to that deadbeat town she'd passed in the car with her parents on the way to Lovie's. Prospect, she thought was the name of it. Surely, they had banks with ATM machines. The pilot had neglected to take away her debit and credit cards. She'd withdraw the maximum amount of cash allowed. Then, with her credit card, she'd purchase a bus ticket to Charleston and a plane ticket to a major metropolitan city like Dallas or Denver. From there, she'd use cash to buy another bus ticket under an assumed name to a small town in a surrounding state where her parents would never think to look for her. She would start a new life where no one would ever bother her again.

Faith wasn't as easy to evade as the shrink lady. When she asked Jenny to offer the blessing at dinner, Jenny said, "I don't really know one," even though she knew plenty.

"Make one up," Faith said.

If I do a bad job, she won't ask me to do it again. She'd learned this during her sorority days when she was appointed to committees she didn't want to be on. Jenny bowed her head and the words tumbled from her lips, "Good food. Good meat. Good God, let's eat."

To her credit, Faith looked up and smiled down the table at Jenny. "That was very nice. I knew that one as a child."

What else could Jenny do but smile back? The woman was proving a formidable opponent, much less a pushover than the pilot.

Faith's eyes traveled the table. "I'm sorry to have lost Sheila. She was a dear person and I hope she finds her way. Her departure has opened up an opportunity for me. For the next few nights, I'll be staying in the room with Jenny. Life seems a little unsettled around here, and I'd feel more comfortable being on property until things calm down."

Jenny thought she might vomit. She would never be able to escape with Faith as her roommate. "I hope you don't mind loud snoring," Jenny said to Faith as nonchalantly as she could manage.

"Won't bother me a bit," Faith said.

"Wouldn't you want your own room?" Jenny counted the residents at the table. "There are only five of us here now, which leaves two empty rooms."

"I prefer for the residents to have roommates. It's part of the bonding experience. Now, let's eat," Faith said, reaching for the platter of fried chicken in front of her. "This looks delicious."

In addition to the chicken, they shared bowls of salads, baskets of homemade breads, and a plate of deviled eggs around the table. When Rosalie handed the platter of chicken to Jenny, she thought about the hens out back and passed it on to Molly on the other side of her.

"Ain't you going to have any chicken?" Molly said, eyeing the meager portions of salads on her plate.

Jenny glared at Molly. "Obviously not, since I didn't put any on my plate."

"Then I'll have your share," Molly said, forking two thighs off

117

the platter. "I learned from living on the streets never to pass up food when somebody offers it to you."

"I wouldn't know," Jenny snapped. "I've never been homeless."

Tilda shot Molly a look of sympathy that made Jenny feel ashamed for hurting her feelings. But she didn't apologize.

"What do you do for a living?" Rosalie asked, bumping her elbow in a chummy show of friendship that irritated Jenny. Just because she'd let Rosalie cut her hair didn't mean they were friends.

"I manage the business office in my father's lumber company," Jenny said, stabbing her lettuce with her fork.

"And where are you from?" Caroline asked.

"Why does it matter?" When she lifted her gaze, bringing the fork to her mouth, four sets of expectant eyes were watching her. She set the fork down. "What? Do I have food on my face?" she asked, wiping her mouth with her napkin.

Caroline smiled softly at her. "You don't have anything on your face. We just want to get to know you better. If you'll let us, we'd like to be your friend."

"I'm not interested in making friends." As she picked her fork back up, Jenny began to hum and she hummed all the way through the rest of dinner.

When the others congregated in the parlor after dinner, Jenny went upstairs to her room. She stood at the window for a long time, contemplating her situation as she watched dusk fade to night. Faith had ruined her escape plans. She wouldn't make it to town before Faith discovered her missing. Jenny considered texting her mother. But if the pilot knew Jenny was unhappy, she'd make her go back to Sumter. And Jenny couldn't live another day in the same town with Derek and Christy. She certainly didn't belong at Lovie's with all these old women and their problems. But where did she belong?

She started humming, this time to pacify herself. She wasn't getting better. She was getting worse. And she had no clue what to do about it. She was just so damn angry. Angry at Derek and Christy. And angry at her parents. But angry at herself mostly for not being able to control her own life.

Think, Jenny. She left the window and paced circles in the middle of the room between the two beds, humming to herself all the while. *There's gotta be a way outta here.*

She could hit on Jamie. Ask him to show her his town. He was damn hot, even if he was three years younger than she. But she'd sworn off men and he had a girlfriend. Unlike Derek, Jamie didn't seem the type who would cheat.

She could try another suicide attempt. An earnest one, just for show. But her mother had threatened to put her in a psych ward. *Talk about prison.*

She was left with only one option that made sense. She would bide her time until she saw an opportunity to sneak off the property. Until then, she'd make everyone around her miserable so they would leave her the hell alone. The idea brought a smile to her face. *I'm not a sweet girl, Mother. I'm mean and unlovable. Hadn't Derek already proven that?*

16

FAITH

aith was both disappointed and disturbed when timid Sheila Thomas announced she was leaving the home despite Dr. Robin's assertion that she wasn't yet ready to face the real world. She suspected the real reason for Sheila's abrupt departure had to do with her new roommate, that Jenny had somehow antagonized poor Sheila. Faith couldn't help but feel responsible, and she made a vow to give more consideration to rooming assignments in the future. But she deemed Sheila's case a failure, and it gnawed at her that she let her down.

Jenny's aggressive behavior had set all of the residents on edge. Faith and Robin agreed that, based on the warning from Jenny's parents, they could not yet rule out the danger of suicide.

Faith had made the split-second decision during dinner to spend a few nights on the property, at least until Jenny settled down or another resident arrived to take Sheila's place as her roommate. She called Mike after dinner to explain her reasoning. "She's just so angry. I don't want Jenny to be alone, in case she . . ."

"Tries to hurt herself," Mike said, finishing her sentence. "I understand, and I think you're making the right decision."

Faith slept with one eye and ear open, but her first night as

Jenny's roommate passed uneventfully. The humming stopped the minute Jenny drifted off, and throughout the night, she didn't utter another sound despite her warning that she snored.

She was tired and a little grumpy when she took Tilda to her doctor's appointment on Friday morning.

Mike had reached out to a colleague, a geriatrician, asking her to fit Tilda into her schedule at her earliest convenience. Much to Faith's relief, Dr. Audrey Welch had a cancellation and was able to see Tilda right away.

Unburdening herself to Faith about her health concerns had made for a visibly more relaxed Tilda at dinner the previous evening, but she was a bundle of nerves again as she sat wringing her hands in the waiting room. "What if the doctor says I have it?"

Faith rested her hand on top of Tilda's to steady them and looked her square in the eye. "Then we will cope with it together. You are not alone in this. For now, I want you to think positively and hope for the best."

Faith remained in the waiting room during the examination. After ninety minutes, a nurse in pink scrubs called Faith back to the doctor's office where Tilda was already seated across the desk from Dr. Welch, a serious no-nonsense woman in her midforties.

"Based on my examination, at this time, I see no reason to refer Tilda to a specialist for additional testing. Anxiety is my diagnosis, not Alzheimer's. I believe that Tilda's anxiety is causing her to be forgetful and accident prone. I'm putting her on an antidepressant specifically designed to control anxiety. Tilda has the prescription. Will you see that she gets it filled?"

"Of course," Faith said. "As soon as we leave here."

"I want you to carefully read the information provided by the pharmacist regarding side effects. It can take a couple of weeks to adjust to the medication," Dr. Welsh said to Tilda and then to Faith, "In addition to the antidepressants, I recommend that

Tilda seek counseling to determine the cause of her anxiety. Is this something you can help her with?"

"Yes," Faith said. "She's already working with our staff therapist. Now that we know better what we're dealing with, I'm hopeful that Tilda will begin to make progress."

The doctor stood and came out from behind her desk. "I have another patient waiting. If you don't mind showing yourselves out whenever you're ready."

Tilda shook the doctor's hand, and Faith said, "Thank you so much, Doctor, for fitting us in on such short notice."

Faith waited for the doctor to leave the room before turning to Tilda. "I say this is cause for celebration. How about I treat you to lunch at the Pelican Roost?"

Tilda's smile—the first Faith remembered having seen from her since arriving at the home—transformed her face from a haggard woman to an elegant lady. A senator's wife. "Can we get the prescription filled first? I'd like to get started on it right away."

"You bet, we can," Faith said, and ushered Tilda out of the office to the car.

They stopped in at the local pharmacy on Main Street where the clerk promised to have the prescription ready for them within the hour. "In that case, we'll pick it up after lunch," Faith said.

They left Faith's SUV parked in front of the pharmacy and walked two blocks to the Pelican's Roost restaurant located atop the Inlet View Marina. They were seated at a table overlooking the waterfront. Through the window, they could see boats of all sizes coming and going and pedestrians moseying about on the boardwalk, stopping for hot dogs or ice cream at the food stands.

Faith broached the subject of Tilda's anxiety over fried mahi sandwiches. "Have you always suffered from anxiety, or is this a recent development?" she asked in an offhanded manner so as not to alarm Tilda.

Tilda looked down in thought before answering. "This is something new. It started after my husband died. His political career dictated almost every aspect of my life from the time we were first married, nearly fifty years ago. Don't get me wrong. I loved the jet-set lifestyle. We met fascinating people, dined in the finest restaurants, and vacationed at lavish resorts. And we always had housekeepers and bellmen and personal secretaries around to take care of our every need." She paused to take a sip of her sweet tea. "Frank's funeral was an elaborate affair attended by dignitaries and their wives from all over the country. But the day after, as I sat at my desk in my empty house, staring at my blank calendar, I realized I'd been living a borrowed life, that none of those people were true friends. I have no family, no career, and no hobbies to speak of. That's when it dawned on me that I could die and no one would ever even miss me. That's when the loneliness set in. I thought I was losing my mind. But now in hindsight it makes sense. It was anxiety all along."

"But, Tilda, you have so much to offer others." Although Faith couldn't name specifically what Tilda had to offer, she remembered that Tilda's neighbor had described her as clever and efficient. And Tilda struck Faith as clever and efficient enough to find a sense of purpose.

"Like what?" Tilda asked, her lips pressed thin.

"That's for you to figure out. Maybe volunteer work. The possibilities are limitless. With all the socializing you've done, you'd be great at planning events for nonprofit organizations. Or you could always get a part-time job, something you enjoy doing, simply for the sake of adding structure in your life."

Tilda narrowed her eyes as she considered this. "That's a thought."

Faith ate her last bite of sandwich and wiped her mouth. "Have you ever considered moving to a retirement community? Not only would you make a whole new set of friends, you'd have activities and opportunities for outings at your fingertips."

Tilda pushed her plate away and folded her hands on the table. "I haven't, but maybe I should. Are you throwing me out of the home?"

"Not at all! You still have a lot of hard work to do with Dr. Robin in learning how to cope with your anxiety. You're welcome to stay as long as you like. Within reason, of course. We'll kick you out eventually," Faith teased.

"Good!" Tilda said, her blue eyes bright. "Because I'm not ready to leave my friends."

Faith signaled for the waitress to bring the check, and they sat for a moment, gazing out the window at the beautiful day, lost in thought. Using the silence to debate with herself whether to tell Tilda about her trip to Charleston, she finally said, "I have something to confess, Tilda. I went to Charleston on Wednesday, hoping to learn more about your family."

Tilda opened her mouth, as though to protest, but closed it again with a sigh.

"You didn't give me much choice, Tilda. We've been trying so desperately to help you, but you wouldn't let us."

Tilda dropped her chin to her chest. "I know, and I'm sorry. Thank you for your concern."

"I had a nice chat with your neighbor Margaret. She told me what she knows about you, which didn't seem like much considering how long you've been neighbors. She seems like a nice person. I bet she'd make a good friend."

Tilda stared out the window, avoiding Faith's gaze. "Margaret's a bit of an odd bird, but I guess one friend is better than none."

"Odd birds make for good entertainment. Who knows? You might enjoy her company."

Tilda's lips parted in a slight smile. "Maybe."

"Anyway, while I was there, I noticed you have a carriage house in your backyard. Maybe you should think about renting it out. You might find comfort in having someone living so close."

"I'll give it some thought," Tilda said with a nonchalant shrug that left Faith wondering if the idea even appealed to her.

The waitress brought the check, and as Faith was signing the credit card receipt, Tilda said, "Thank you for lunch. My sandwich was delicious."

"I'm glad you liked it. As of now, the Roost is the only place in town to get a decent lunch. But that's going to change soon." Faith slipped the credit card receipt in her wallet and slid out of the booth. "Come on. I'll show you what's going on across the street." She led Tilda through the maze of tables to the bank of windows along Creekside Drive on the other side of the room. "You may remember that our family seafood business burned to the ground last May, and that Jamie and his mother, my sister Sam, are in the process of rebuilding." She pointed to the L-shaped brick building across the street on the corner of Creekside and Main. "The storefront on Creekside will house the new seafood market, and Jamie's half sister, Annie, is opening a sandwich shop in the part of the building facing Main Street. The two businesses will share a patio in the common space outback. I'm bringing Molly for an interview with Sam later this afternoon."

"She mentioned that," Tilda said, turning away from the window. "Molly's a good person. She deserves a break."

"All our residents are good people." When skepticism crossed Tilda's face, Faith added, "Deep down, buried beneath their troubles, they are."

But Faith was given reason to doubt her own words fifteen minutes later when they arrived at the home to find Jenny and Molly screaming at each other in the yard. Caroline and Rosalie stood between them trying to break up the squabble.

Faith killed the engine and jumped out of the car. "Shh! Lower your voices. You're acting like children."

Molly and Jenny stared at Faith, their faces beaming red with anger, and then starting shouting again.

"Stop it this minute!" Faith pointed at the front door. "Inside! Now!"

With Faith leading the parade of five, they marched single-file through the front door, stopping midway down the hallway.

Emilee looked up from her computer. "Is something wrong?"

Faith considered whether to send the others back to their chores and discuss the matter with Jenny and Molly in the privacy of her office, but then decided it best to work through the problem as a group.

"That's what I'm about to find out," Faith said. "I want to hear both sides of the story, starting with you, Molly."

"Jenny accused me of stealing her watch. I ain't never even seen her watch, Miss Faith, I promise."

"That's not true," Jenny blurted. "I saw you eyeballing it last night at dinner. A Rolex would earn someone like you a fair price at a pawn shop."

"That's enough, Jenny," Faith said with a warning tone. "Do you have any proof that Molly took your watch?"

"I put it in the top drawer of my dresser when I went to bed last night. And now it's gone. Molly vacuumed and dusted my room this morning. She's the only other person who's been in there." Jenny glared at Faith. "Unless you took it."

"Accusing me is as ridiculous as accusing Molly. There must be a logical explanation. I want everyone to stay down here while Jenny and I go search the room." Faith motioned Jenny to the stairs. "After you."

Faith followed Jenny as she stomped up the stairs. When they reached the top, Faith said, "Whenever I lose something, I find it helps to retrace my steps."

Jenny balled her fists at her sides. "I'm telling you, it's not lost. She stole it. She's a homeless bum. I don't know why you let people like her in here."

Faith forced down her anger. "The same reason I let people

like you in here. Now humor me. When's the last time you remember wearing your watch?"

Jenny hung her head and stared at the ground. When she looked up again, guilt was written all over her face. "Last night when I took a shower."

With Faith on her heels, Jenny entered the hall bathroom and grabbed her plastic toiletries basket from her designated shelf. One by one, she lined up her shampoo, conditioner, and liquid soap bottles on the sink counter. Together, they peered inside the basket at the missing watch. "Oops. I guess I made a mistake."

"I guess you did." Faith bit back the reproach that was on the tip of her tongue. "But we all make mistakes. And that's okay as long as we learn from them. Instead of accusing Molly, you should've come to Dr. Robin, Emilee, or me and let us handle it. You're not the only one here who has problems. We have to respect one another in order to have a successful program."

"I understand," Jenny said, but Faith wasn't sure she did.

"I believe an apology to Molly is in order."

"If you say so." Jenny returned her bottles to her basket and sulked out of the bathroom.

17

MOLLY

*M*olly knew a sincere apology when she heard one. And Jenny's mumbled sorry was definitely not sincere.

"Okay, show's over," Faith said, breaking up the group huddled in the hallway. "Let's get back to work."

Caroline and Rosalie returned to their chores, but Tilda remained at Molly's side for support.

"Would you like to reschedule your interview for another time?" Faith asked Molly.

Molly's desire to have a new life had multiplied significantly in the past hour. "No'm, I'm fine." She looked down at her dirty clothes. She'd been working in the garden with Caroline when Jenny attacked her. "But I need to change first."

"I'll go with you to the room." Tilda looped her arm through Molly's and dragged her down the hall.

"How'd your doctor's appointment go?" Molly asked as they climbed the stairs together.

Tilda flashed her a bright smile. "Great news! I don't have Alzheimer's!"

"That is very great news." Molly skipped a step when they

reached the top of the stairs and headed down the hall. "I'm happy for you but sad for me if this means you'll be going home."

"I'm not going anywhere just yet. The doctor says I have anxiety. I have to learn how to cope with that first." Tilda held the door open for Molly to enter the room. "Jenny was wrong to accuse you like that. I'm sorry for her troubles, but I don't care much for that girl."

"I'm used to it. People always assume I'm a thief because I'm homeless. But I ain't never took a single thing that wasn't mine to begin with, not even an apple from the vegetable cart on my hungriest of days." Molly opened the closet and removed her nicest pair of khaki slacks and a white cotton blouse. "I'll just have to work harder to make everybody forget I was ever homeless. Which means I need to get this job."

"You'll get the job," Tilda said. "Faith's sister is going to love you, like everyone else loves you."

"Everyone except Jenny," Molly said and went into the bathroom to change her clothes.

She washed her face, combed her hair, and brushed her teeth, pausing for a minute to scrutinize her appearance in the mirror. When she exited the bathroom, Tilda was sitting on her bed thumbing the screen on her cell phone.

"If I don't smile, do you think there's a chance Faith's sister might not notice my missing tooth?" Molly asked, pointing at the hole where her canine tooth once resided.

Tilda looked up from her phone. "But your smile is your best attribute. How will you win Faith's sister over if you don't smile? Besides, your missing tooth adds character."

"Not the right kinda character," Molly said, plopping down on her bed facing Tilda. "It screams homeless."

"Why don't you get it fixed if it bothers you that much? I'm not a dentist, but there must be some way to fix it. People lose teeth all the time."

Molly frowned. "I'm homeless, remember? I don't have the money for expensive dental work."

"You won't be homeless for long." Tilda set her phone down on the bed beside her. "Why don't you let me pay to have your tooth fixed?"

Molly waved away the suggestion. "I couldn't ask you to do that."

"Why not? What's the point of me having money if I can't use it to help a friend?"

"I'm honored you think of me as your friend."

"Trust me, the honor is mine." Tilda picked up her phone again. "While you were in the bathroom, I was sitting here looking through my contacts, realizing that I have hundreds of acquaintances but no true friends. Not one single person I know well enough to invite to lunch."

"You have friends here."

Tilda smiled. "I'm beginning to see that."

Molly glanced at the clock on the nightstand. "I better go," she said on her way to the door. "Wish me luck."

"You don't need luck with your smile. And I'm serious about paying to have your tooth fixed," Tilda called after her.

Faith was waiting for her at the front door. "You look very nice, Molly. I can't wait for you to meet Sam."

"I hope she likes me," Molly said.

"I'm sure she will."

They went outside to the car and started down the driveway. "About what happened today with Jenny. I'm sorry if she hurt your feelings."

"She didn't." Molly had already gotten over the incident. She'd learned a long time ago that worrying about people like Jenny was a waste of time. "I try not to let people like that get to me."

"Oh?" Faith cast a quick glance at Molly before taking a left out of the driveway. "What type of person do you think she is?"

Molly suspected that Faith was baiting her, but she didn't

care. "A pampered one. Don't get me wrong, Miss Faith. I'm real sorry about what happened with her husband and best friend. But she's beautiful and rich with parents who worship her. I'd be willing to bet that everything has come easy in her life until now. She's hurting, and she has reason to be, but she wants everyone around her to suffer with her." At a red light, she looked over to see Faith staring at her with an expression on her face Molly couldn't read. "I'm sorry. I've said too much."

"Not at all. You're very perceptive." Faith pulled into the packed parking lot and located a spot between two white vans with Morris Plumbing painted on the side. "As you can see from all the trucks, there's still a lot of work that needs to be done before they can open."

Faith unbuckled her seat belt, and as she was reaching for the door handle, Molly grabbed onto her arm. "Can I ask you a question before we go inside?"

"Fire away," Faith said, settling back into her seat.

"Tilda offered to pay to have my missing tooth fixed. She seemed serious. Do you think I should let her?"

Faith took a moment to ponder the question. "That's very generous of her. I imagine it would mean a lot to Tilda to be able to do that for you. My dentist is a good friend of mine. She might be willing to give you a discount. Would you like me to set up the appointment?"

"Yes!" Molly clasped her hands together. "Would you please?"

"I'll make the call when I return to the office. Now, let's go get you a job."

The interior of the new building was designed to look old with brick walls and concrete floors. In a beehive of activity, a woman that could only be Jamie's mother stood in the middle of the chaos directing the workmen with respectful authority. Sam was as pretty as her son was handsome, her blonde looks as day and night to his dark hair and eyes. She greeted Molly with a warm embrace.

"My son speaks highly of you," Sam said.

"And I think the world of him," Molly answered. "I'm excited at the possibility of working with both of you."

"From what I've heard from Jamie, you'll make a fine addition to our staff. Would you like the tour?"

"Please!" Molly said.

Molly and Faith followed Sam around the front of the store as she pointed to where the refrigerator display cases and merchandise shelves would go. Faith knew enough to ask intelligent questions, but Molly mostly listened, absorbing as much as possible.

When they went into the back room, Sam said, "I'd like for you to start out on the kitchen crew. I've hired a new chef. He's an old-school cook with an innovative flair. You'll clean your share of fish, but you'll also assist him in cooking the prepared foods."

Molly's heart sank. "I'll be honest with you, Miss Sam. I don't have much experience in the kitchen."

"Don't worry," Sam said. "He'll teach you everything you need to know. Eventually, I want you to learn to work the front as well. I like for my employees to know every aspect of the business. It gets crazy around here sometimes, and we all have to pitch in whenever and wherever we're needed."

Molly bounced on her toes. "Does this mean I've got the job?"

Sam shot her sister a look of mischief. "Was there ever any question?"

"When can I start?" Molly asked, eager to get on with her new life.

"Hmm." Sam tapped her chin, thinking. "How about a week from next Monday, which will be two weeks before we open? There will be plenty to do ahead of time to get ready."

Molly heard a squeal and turned to see a beautiful young

woman with hair the color of spun gold throw herself into Faith's arms. After a minute of intense hugging, Faith pushed away from the girl. "I haven't seen you in months. Let me get a good look at you. You look radiant. Have you found yourself a young man yet?"

"Ha," Sam said. "She doesn't have time for men. She's a workaholic."

"I'm saving myself for someone special," the girl said, and noticing Molly, she extended her hand. "You must be Molly. Jamie's told me all about you. I'm his sister, Annie. Half sister really, but that's just a technicality. The Sweeneys adopted me. They'll adopt you too if you let them. Everybody's like family to them."

Molly's heart somersaulted across her chest. There was nothing she wanted more than to be a part of the Sweeney family.

Annie took hold of Faith's hand. "Do you want to see the shop? The tables and chairs were delivered today."

"Lead the way," Faith said.

Molly filed in behind the others as they exited the back door onto a covered patio.

"The outdoor tables are coming next week," Annie said as they crossed the patio and entered the building through a different door.

An open threshold connected one end of the room to the seafood market. The tables were light-colored wood. A long one —Annie called it a community table—stood in the middle of a dozen smaller ones. The wall opposite the bank of windows overlooking Main Street was painted a soft green color to match the fabric on the chairs.

"I love it," Faith said. "It's so bright and airy."

"Like an indoor garden," Molly said.

Annie pointed at her. "That's exactly the look I want for my lunch spot. My shipment of potted plants and ferns is coming next week."

Molly crossed her arms over her chest, hugging herself. She felt at home here in this building with the Sweeney family.

"Are you excited?" Faith asked when they were back in the car heading for the home.

"You have no idea," Molly said in a shaky voice. "All my dreams are coming true, thanks to you."

"We still need to figure out a place for you to live. But I don't want you to worry about that just yet. You'll stay at Lovie's until you have money in your bank account and we've found the right living situation for you."

Molly nodded, afraid to ask what type of situation she had in mind. For the first time, the realization she would eventually have to leave her new friends at Lovie's hit home.

18

CAROLINE

*C*aroline prepared the picnic lunch herself. As promised, she made all Jamie's childhood favorites—egg salad sandwiches with dill relish on soft white bread with crusts removed, sweet green grapes, barbecue potato chips, and cans of root beer. *Jamie truly was, and still is, like my second son,* she thought to herself as she placed the items in a cooler she'd borrowed from Cook. The boys had been inseparable from the time they were in kindergarten. The demands of the seafood market had preoccupied much of Jamie's mother's time, and Sam had been grateful to Caroline for taking care of him, especially when school was out during the summer months. And, since Cory was an only child, having a friend along made for more pleasurable outings and long weekends at the farm for both children and adults.

She stuffed her garden clippers and gloves in a small backpack along with her sunscreen and a floppy hat and was waiting on the front porch when he arrived as planned at precisely eleven o'clock. Hopping out of the truck, he took the cooler from her and placed it on the back seat.

"Geez, Jamie. I need a stepladder to get in this truck," she said as she hoisted herself into the passenger side.

He laughed. "You know how South Carolina men like their trucks jacked."

"Boy, do I ever." She couldn't help but remember how Cory, from the moment he got his driver's license, had begged Troy and her for a pickup. He didn't care much about the color as long as the tires were big and the body lifted. They'd been planning to give him one for graduation. Troy had met with the dealer just the week before the accident happened.

"Do you mind swinging by my house on the way to the farm?" Caroline asked when they got to the end of the driveway. "I want to pick some flowers from my garden to place at the site of the accident."

"Not at all. That's a nice idea," Jamie said and turned left in the direction of town.

When they passed by the new seafood market, Caroline said, "The building is really coming together. When's the reopening?"

"June first," Jamie said, staring past her at the building.

"Coming up soon. I imagine Sam's getting excited."

"You have no idea," Jamie said with a shake of his head. "We're changing the name of the market to Sam Sweeney's. Mom argued that it wouldn't be right, since I'll likely be taking over when she retires. But I finally convinced her. With the fire and all, it seemed like a good time to make a change. And I think it's fitting. Sam is the heart and soul of Sweeney's, at least now that Gran is gone."

"Sam Sweeney's has a catchy ring to it. I was so sorry to hear about Lovie. She was an inspiration to us all. I know you miss her."

"Very much," Jamie said as he turned down Oak Lane.

Caroline stiffened as he pulled into her driveway. She hadn't been back to the house in almost two weeks, and the grass in the front yard was knee-high. She imagined the mail piling up beneath the slot in the front door, mold growing on leftover items in the refrigerator, and voicemail messages waiting for her on the house line. Perhaps she should get a replacement cell phone for the one she'd chunked in the creek. *Not yet*, she decided. *Being out of touch is liberating.*

Still, she couldn't let the bills pile up. Troy had left her with the responsibility of taking care of the house. She would carve out some time the following afternoon to tend to the chores and pay bills.

"This won't take but a minute." With Jamie on her heels, she walked down the driveway, unlatched the wooden gate, and entered the backyard. She'd set her irrigation system to water every night at midnight and her garden was in full bloom and more than a little overgrown.

"Whoa," Jamie said when he saw it. "There's like a whole ocean of flowers back here."

Caroline laughed. "Troy calls it my obsession. I think of it as my sanity. I can't help myself. I start planting and can't stop. The same thing's happening at Lovie's." She went into her gardening shed and returned with a mason jar. "Why don't you fill this with water from the spigot on the side of the house while I snip a few stems."

Caroline clipped a small mixed bundle of brightly colored perennials, placing them in the mason jar when Jamie handed it to her. "I don't expect them to last long in this heat."

Jamie shrugged. "It's the thought that counts."

They returned to the truck and drove ten miles outside of town. They chatted about Jamie's four years of college at the University of South Carolina but grew quiet as they neared Winding Creek Farm, named after the creek that meandered through the marsh in front of Caroline's family's property. The Realtor's sign announcing the farm for sale marked the entrance to the farm and served as a reminder of her imminent divorce.

Jamie clicked on his blinker and turned off the highway onto the dirt road that twisted and turned through the pine forest for half a mile before reaching the cabin. Caroline wasn't aware she'd been holding her breath until they reached the bend in the road where the accident had happened. As she exhaled slowly, she was transported back in time four years. Unbeknownst to any of them, a tree had fallen across the road during a windstorm that New Year's Eve. When Jamie and Cory had gone out trail riding in the ATV after lunch on New Year's Day, they'd rounded the bend too fast, careened off the downed tree, and rolled the vehicle several times down the road.

Caroline slid out of the truck, barely aware of her feet hitting the ground, and set the mason jar of flowers in a patch of grass near the dirt tracks in the road. In her mind, she heard the sirens of the rescue vehicles and smelled the wood smoke from the fire Troy had built in the pit in preparation for the oyster roast planned for later that day. Her hands flew to her eyes at the memory of the paramedics removing Cory's mangled body from the wreckage.

She sensed Jamie's presence near her, but she didn't dare look at him. She wept silently into her hands for the son she'd loved with all her heart. Would she ever be able to drive down the road and not fall to pieces? Probably not. But instead of avoiding the spot, she would commemorate it with a permanent marker.

"I'll keep it simple. A wooden cross underplanted with some type of shrub, something the deer won't eat that doesn't require sunlight."

She wasn't aware she'd spoken out loud until Jamie said, "A roadside memorial is a nice idea. Cory would approve."

"I'd like to think he would. At least more than the granite headstone marking his grave in the church cemetery. I was too distraught at the time to make rational decisions. If I had to do it over again, I would have him cremated and scatter his ashes here, over the place he loved the most."

Caroline suddenly felt the urge to see the rest of the farm. "Are you ready to move on?"

"If you are," he said, and they got back in the truck and drove the rest of the short distance to the waterfront cabin.

Someone, presumably Troy, had taken excellent care of the grounds in her absence. Her husband had always worked long hours, but after Cory's death, Caroline assumed he was burying himself in his accounting ledgers when, judging from the looks of things, he'd been hiding out at the farm.

She dug her keys out of her backpack. "Four years is a long time. I'm a little afraid of what I'll find inside." She wasn't sure whether that meant rat droppings, a new leather sofa to replace the green chenille one that had occupied the same spot in front of the fireplace for as long as she remembered, or ghosts.

"Do you want me to come with you?" Jamie asked.

"Please. I don't think I can face it alone."

Despite her apprehension, only happy memories greeted her when she opened the front door, from her earliest remembrance of childhood until four years ago. She'd been wrong to stay away. The farm was her home, more than her house on Oak Lane had ever been.

"Nothing's changed since I was a little girl," Caroline said as she wandered around the main sitting room. "I think the place could use some sprucing up."

"I hope that means you're not going to sell it."

"I think it does, Jamie," she said as she stood in front of the wall of framed photographs representing the good times spent at Winding Creek Farm over the decades. "I may even sell my house on Oak Lane and move out here. Would that be crazy?"

"Not at all." He joined her in front of the photographs. "You're only ten minutes from Prospect. As fast as Prospect is growing, it's only a matter of time before this farm is considered the outskirts of town."

"That's very true." She turned her head toward him. "Thank you for coming with me today. All this time I've been avoiding this place when right here is where I needed to be."

ASHLEY FARLEY

"I know what you mean. I feel the positive vibes. My sister, Annie, would say this place has good karma."

They left the cabin and walked down to the dock.

"I'd forgotten how peaceful it is here," Caroline said as an osprey made a swooping dive for a fish in the water in front of them. "Everything is suddenly much clearer for me. I'm ready to begin the healing process. I'll never get over losing Cory, but I'm tired of being miserable. I want to set goals and work toward achieving them."

"I hope that means gardening, since it's obviously your passion." Jamie turned his back to the water, looking in the direction of the cabin. "How many acres do you have here?"

"A hundred and twenty including the forest and the fields." Caroline smiled as she watched the wheels spinning in his mind. "What intriguing idea is formulating in that clever brain of yours?"

"I'm thinking you should start a plant nursery out here. You have plenty of room. You can build greenhouses and a small building to use as your office and gift shop. You can plant pumpkins and have a pumpkin patch for kids at Halloween. The possibilities are endless. Plenty of goals for you to work toward."

"Ha. No kidding." As she considered his suggestion, she experienced a flutter of excitement in her belly. It would be a massive undertaking, but what else did she have planned for the rest of her life?

"That's a seriously brilliant idea, Jamie. One that scares the heck outta me, and I'll have to give it a lot of thought. But you're right. Gardening is my passion. It was a hobby before Cory died, but since then, as you saw in my backyard, it's taken on a life of its own. The process of seeding and watering and nurturing is therapeutic for me."

Jamie offered up a high five. "Sounds to me like you've found yourself a new career. I hope you'll let me be a part of it."

19

JENNY

*J*enny had accomplished her objective. By accusing Molly of stealing her watch, she'd turned all the other residents against her. She'd gotten her wish. They were leaving her the hell alone. And she'd never felt so lonely.

When Friday rolled around, she could not stop obsessing about what was happening in the world outside the home. She even wondered about her parents' plans for the weekend. Had her mother organized a dinner party to celebrate their empty nest? She tried preoccupying her mind by watching TV after dinner, but Faith had clearly never heard of Netflix, and she couldn't find any decent shows, which only made her feel more depressed. Listening to the others chatting and laughing while they worked a jigsaw puzzle grated on her nerves. Seriously? A jigsaw puzzle. Lovie's wasn't a home for wounded hearts. It was a home for little old ladies.

At ten minutes till nine, she turned off the TV and went upstairs to her room. She crawled into her bed fully clothed with her phone. *My life sucks*, she thought as she visited her social media sites, scrolling through pics of her friends living it up on

Friday night. So many of her girlfriends from college had moved to exciting places like New York and were working cool jobs and hanging out at hip places on the weekends. Some of them had serious boyfriends. A few were engaged or already married. But most of them were still searching for that special someone. Jenny, married and already on her way to being divorced at twenty-six, had set herself apart from the crowd. Woo-hoo. Wasn't she proud?

Stuffing her phone under her pillow, she rolled over on her side and stared out the window at the bright night, the full moon and starry sky, a romantic setting for lovers.

She shut her eyes, swiping at the tears running down her cheeks. She forced her mind to go blank, and before long, she drifted off to sleep. She never heard Faith enter the room, and when she woke at eight the following morning, she was already gone. According to the other residents, Saturdays at the home were meant for rest and relaxation, a time to reflect on the progress they'd made in therapy during the week. Was there such a thing as negative progress? Because that's what she was experiencing.

Retrieving her phone from under the pillow, she was alarmed to see a missed call and voice message from her mother. Faith had asked her parents not to call Jenny except in an emergency. She tapped on the message and listened to her mother's weepy voice. "Oh, Jenny, honey, I'm so very sorry. I'm sure you've heard the news by now. I know how connected you are to your social media. You can't let this development hinder your recovery."

Jenny stopped the recording. *What development?* She tapped on her Instagram icon and the top image in her feed was of Derek with his arm around Christy who was showing off a diamond engagement ring considerably larger than the one he'd given Jenny.

She'd been angry for months, but the rage that overcame her was altogether different, an emotion she'd never before experienced. With her phone gripped in her hand, and still wearing yesterday's clothes, she stomped out of her room, down the stairs, and out the front door, crossing the lawn to the toolshed. She placed her phone on the dirt ground, faceup with the pic of Derek and Christy showing on the screen, and whacked it repeatedly with a pointed long-handled shovel from the wall rack of tools.

"Ah, that felt good!" she said out loud to the empty shed when the phone's screen was shattered and it no longer powered on.

Stuffing the ruined phone in her back pocket, she returned to the house for breakfast. She could barely see the eggs and bacon on her plate for the fury that blinded her vision. She attacked her household chores with vigor, and for the first time since arriving at Lovie's, she wished for something to occupy the long afternoon hours, like weeding the garden or mowing the lawn—any task demanding sufficient physical exertion to release the angry energy that was making her crazy. Then it dawned on her that she could make up her own *chores*. When the other residents—sans Caroline who had driven off somewhere with Jamie—headed down to the dock for a swim, Jenny retrieved the same pointed shovel from the shed and dug a hole three feet deep in the ground near Caroline's garden. Removing the damaged phone from her back pocket, she placed it in the hole and covered it up.

Check. Phone buried. She moved on to the next chore on her list.

Opening the garden gate, she dropped to her knees and assaulted the weeds with her bare hands. But she quickly grew bored with weeding. She eyed the flowers in the adjacent bed with their colorful array of blooms, taunting her with their happy faces. Flowers represented love, and she was done with love. Grabbing clippers from the shed, she snipped every single flower from the bed, leaving the stems on the ground wherever they fell.

Check! Flowers destroyed.

She was returning the clippers to the shed when she caught sight of three hens perched on a nest of eggs. She entered the henhouse, and ignoring the hens' angry cackles, she removed four eggs, two for each hand, from their nests. Exiting the henhouse, she crossed the yard to the small gravel parking lot. She chose a white pickup truck with Lovie's logo painted in green on the side as her victim. Setting the eggs on the ground, she hurled them one at time at the truck, receiving great satisfaction with each splatter.

Check! Truck egged.

In search of more chores, she walked along the side of the house and peeked around the corner of the front porch. The other residents were coming up from the dock with their hair dripping and towels wrapped around their wet bathing suits. Their voices, loud and merry, drifted toward her as they discussed what Cook might possibly be serving for lunch.

Jenny waited for them to enter the house before dashing across the yard to the dock. With frequent glances toward the house, she let the crabs out of the traps, dumped the live minnows out of the bait baskets, and tugged the fishing line out of the reels.

Check. Salt Life program sabotaged.

Exhausted from her chores, she returned to the house, entering through the back door and darting up the stairs before anyone could see her. She stretched out on her bed with her hands behind her head, feeling a sense of accomplishment. She'd proven herself as a mean girl. But the minute she closed her eyes, guilt and remorse set in.

She waited all afternoon for the dreaded knock on the door, which finally came around four o'clock.

"Come in," she called out from her bed.

The door opened and Rosalie stood in the threshold without entering the room. "Faith wants to see you in her office," she said, and left before Jenny had a chance to ask her why. As if she didn't already know.

Realizing she must look a mess in day-old, dirt-smeared clothes, she took a quick shower and put on a clean pair of cutoff shorts and an old T-shirt. Faith was none too pleased to be kept waiting, and she told Jenny about it as soon as she entered her office.

"When I ask to see you, Jenny, I mean right away, not thirty minutes later," Faith said from behind her desk.

"Sorry," Jenny said, plopping down in the chair in front of her.

"For the safety of our residents, I had the security company install surveillance cameras at key positions on the property. I spent the last hour reviewing the footage from this morning."

Jenny gulped. She'd forgotten about the surveillance cameras. But wasn't that the goal? To get caught so they'd kick her out?

"When I started this shelter, I never dreamed I'd be dealing with a disciplinary issue. Addiction, abuse, homelessness. But never one of our own residents deliberately vandalizing our property. I must say, I'm disappointed in you." Faith steepled her fingers on the desk in front of her. "Your mother left an urgent message on my office line this morning. I assume you know what that's about?"

"About my darling husband proposing to my BFF," Jenny said in a sarcastic voice. "I'm aware of it. They blasted it all over social media."

"I understand you're going through a difficult time, but I will not tolerate destructive behavior." Faith inhaled a deep breath and slowly let it out. "Frankly, Jenny. I'm about at my wits' end with you."

Jenny was surprised when she experienced a pang of disappointment. "Does this mean you're giving me a get-out-of-jail-free card?"

"Jail?" Faith said with a raised eyebrow. "No one is holding you here against your will. You are free to leave anytime you wish." She held her hand out, motioning her toward the door.

Jenny leaped to her feet and strode across the room to the door. She froze with her hand gripping the knob. Where would she go? Certainly not back to Sumter. Moving alone to a small town in the middle of Texas or Colorado suddenly seemed intimidating. She realized with a jolt that she felt safe at Lovie's home. The pilot wasn't hovering over her, and she could interact, or not, as much as she wanted with the others. She hadn't given the program a fair chance. Perhaps if she tried, she might find a way to get rid of the anger instead of venting it.

She dropped her hand from the doorknob and turned back around. "I know it's unfair of me to ask this, but would you be willing to give me another chance?"

Standing, Faith left her desk and walked toward her. "Against my better judgment. And only under strict conditions."

"Such as?"

Faith ticked the items off her fingers. "Wash the truck. Clean up the garden as best you can and apologize to Caroline for desecrating her flowers. Fix all the reels, rebait the crab traps, and replenish the supply of minnows."

"Done," Jenny said.

"And that's only for starters. You must also participate in your therapy sessions and treat the other residents and staff with respect. This is your last chance, Jenny. If you cause one more ounce of trouble, I will send you home to your parents. I have a sneaking suspicion that Sumter is not where you want to end up. If you let us, we can help you figure out your future. But that only works if we trust one another. And we're a long way from that."

20

FAITH

aith stood nearby while Jenny washed the truck and raked up the ruined flowers, transporting them by wheelbarrow to the compost pile. Watching her was like super-vising a teenager. She seemed remorseful about her wrongdo-ings, yet she didn't put much effort into making things right. Faith pointed out splatters of egg Jenny missed on the truck's fender, and down at the dock later, when Jenny failed to get the hang of casting a net, Faith was the one who replenished the supply of minnows.

She feared she'd made the wrong decision in allowing Jenny to stay. She was beginning to think Jenny's problems were a result of deep-seated character flaws more than her husband's betrayal. Her parents had obviously spoiled her rotten. And Faith had no clue how to go about repairing the damage. If it was even possible.

At four o'clock, she left Jenny on the dock detangling the fishing reels and returned to the house for her scheduled meeting with Rosalie and her mother, Teresa. Robin had agreed to take time out of her weekend to accommodate Teresa's busy work

147

schedule as a physical therapist, and the threesome were already gathered in Robin's office when Faith arrived.

"I'm sorry if I kept you waiting," Faith said, and introduced herself to Teresa, an older and slightly more conservative version of her daughter, as she slid into the empty chair beside Robin.

"Not at all. We were just about to start." Robin locked eyes with Teresa across the coffee table. "Your daughter requested this meeting. Faith and I are here simply to lend moral support." Her gaze shifted to Rosalie. "The show's all yours."

Rosalie angled her body toward her mother. "Let me start by saying, I've given up the drugs and alcohol. And my head is much clearer because of it. I've grown up a lot since I first came here. I realize what a shit I was to you, Mama. And I'm so, so, so sorry for that."

Tears glistened in Teresa's eyes when she said, "You have no idea how much I was hoping to hear those words." She cracked a smile. "But that doesn't mean I'm ready for you to move back home."

Rosalie laughed out loud. "Don't worry. Unless I'm destitute, I will never move back home. That was not a good situation for either of us. I love you. And I want us to have a healthy mother-daughter relationship."

"There's nothing I want more," Teresa said, taking Rosalie's hands in hers.

Rosalie continued, "Miss Faith and Dr. Robin and my friends, the other residents here, have helped me discover a new direction for my life." Her eyes met Faith's. "Miss Faith is helping me research cosmetology schools. The one that interests me the most is in Charleston."

"How much does something like that cost?" Teresa asked, and didn't wait for Rosalie to answer. "I've put some money aside in case you decided to go to college one day. I'm happy to pay for your tuition to cosmetology school, but you'll have to get a job to cover your living expenses."

Rosalie's face lit up. "Really, Mama? That'd be great! The school offers daytime and evening courses. I'd prefer daytime if I can swing it. There are so many restaurants in Charleston. I'm sure one of them would hire me."

Faith thought Tilda's carriage house would make for an ideal living situation for Rosalie, but she was hesitant to make the suggestion. She'd rather have Tilda come to that conclusion on her own. But she saw no harm in dropping a few subtle hints.

Rosalie placed her head on her mother's shoulder. "Thank you, Mama. I don't deserve it, after the way I behaved, but I promise I won't let you down."

Teresa stroked her daughter's thigh. "You call this a new direction, but you've been cutting hair since you were a child. Your poor Barbies were bald by the time you finished with them. I've always known this is what you were meant to do. But you had to grow up and figure it out for yourself."

"She has talent. I can vouch for that myself." Faith smoothed her hand over her hair. "She's cut most everyone's hair here except Robin's."

Robin protectively placed her hands on her head. "You can practice on my hair *after* you finish school," she said, and they all laughed.

"When will you start school?" Teresa asked.

"The next session doesn't begin until August," Rosalie said. "I'm hoping Faith will let me stay here until I figure out a place to live."

"I wouldn't want you to overstay your welcome," Teresa said, casting a doubtful glance at Faith.

"I'm not worried about that at all. Rosalie is eager to get on with her life, and I'm confident the right living arrangement will present itself." Faith patted Rosalie's knee. "I'm sure the two of you would like some time alone. Rosalie, why don't you show your mama the grounds? And be sure to stop by the kitchen for some of Cook's homemade lemonade."

Faith and Robin shared a smile as mother and daughter left the room arm in arm.

"Another success story," Robin said, retrieving her purse from behind her desk.

"Rosalie is a sweet girl," Faith said. "She deserves a happy ending."

Robin turned off the overhead lights and they walked out into the hall together. When Faith noticed Tilda standing at the paned glass door looking out across the front yard, she said, "Excuse me, Robin. I need to grab a word with Tilda. Thank you so much for coming in on a Saturday. Enjoy the rest of your weekend."

Faith joined Tilda at the door. "It's a lovely day, isn't it?"

"It most certainly is," Tilda said with a dreamlike quality in her voice. "And this is such a lovely place. I never tire of looking at the marsh."

Faith glanced around to make sure they were alone. "I don't want to put any pressure on you, but Molly mentioned that you offered to pay for the dental work to fix her missing tooth. My dentist might be willing to give us a discount, but I wanted to talk to you before I reach out to her. Even with the discount, I imagine it will be costly. I wouldn't blame you if you've changed your mind."

Tilda appeared horror-struck. "Not at all! That's all I've been thinking about since I made Molly the offer yesterday. Doing something nice for her has given me this unexpected happiness. My husband and I were never very philanthropic, aside from taking care of his constituents of course. I have the means, and I'd like to do more of it. I just need to identify the right types of nonprofits."

"That's wonderful, Tilda. Whatever organizations you choose will be blessed to have your support." She nudged Tilda with her elbow. "Be careful, though. If you do a good job, you might find yourself on their board of directors."

"I wouldn't mind that so much. I have nothing but time on my hands. I could make new friends, and help organize benefits. As a senator's wife, I had plenty of experience in party planning."

Tilda and Faith waved at Rosalie and her mother through the window as they strolled across the porch with ice cold glasses of lemonade in hand.

"I'm glad to see things are going well for Rosalie," Tilda said.

"She's not there yet. She still has a few things to sort out like her living arrangements in Charleston. Have you given any more thought to your situation?"

Tilda shook her head. "Only that I'm not ready to move into a retirement facility. I love my home. If only I didn't have to live there alone."

"I really think you should consider renting out your carriage house. Having a tenant nearby might offer you reassurance without cramping your style."

Tilda furrowed her brow as she considered it. "You mentioned that the other day. I like the idea. But who would I get?"

Rosalie's name was on Faith's lips, but she decided to let Tilda come to that conclusion on her own. "I'm sure if you put your mind to it you could come up with someone. In fact, you may already know somebody. Give it some thought." She touched Tilda's arm lightly in parting. "I'll see you at dinner. Mike's grilling burgers for us."

Tilda grinned. "I'll look forward to that. I can't remember the last time I had a juicy hamburger."

Mike had taken Bitsy to Folly Beach for the day, but he promised to be back no later than six o'clock to cook for them. Faith went to her office to catch up on some work while she waited. She listened to the voice messages on her office line, one of them from a board member relaying the disappointing news that her request for grant funding from the state had been denied. With elbows propped on the desk and face inches from her computer, she was studying her accounts, searching for more ways to cut back their budget, when her cell phone rang with a call from Eli.

"I've found Molly's sister! At least I think I have. According to social services, the Drake family adopted her when she was twelve. She went to college at the University of Michigan and medical school at Johns Hopkins where she met her husband, Roger Moss."

"So, she's a doctor," Faith said, settling back in her chair. "That's great news. Where does she live?"

"That's the best part. Penny and Roger Moss live just up the road in Charleston. She's a cardiovascular surgeon. I'll text you her contact information when we hang up."

"I don't know how to thank you, Eli. This will mean so much to Molly."

"Happy to help," he said and ended the call.

While she waited for Eli's text to come in, she googled Penny Drake Moss in Charleston, South Carolina. A professional image of a woman who bore a striking resemblance to Molly popped up with a link to her medical practice.

Faith's phone pinged and she stared at the contact information for ten minutes before summoning the nerve to place the call. After four rings, a woman answered with an irritated tone.

"May I speak with Penny Moss, please."

"This is Dr. Moss. Who's calling, please?"

"My name is Faith Neilson, and I'm the director of a women's shelter down in Prospect. I'm calling about your sister."

"My sister?" Moss asked in a startled voice. "Which sister? I have four."

That confused Faith for a minute, and then she remembered that Penny had been adopted by her foster family. "I'm calling about Molly."

A moment of silence passed before Penny said in a soft tone, "I haven't thought about Molly in years."

Little hairs on the back of Faith's neck stood to attention. "Oh really? Because she thinks about you all the time."

Penny ignored her comment, but instead of asking about Molly's well-being, she said, "You mentioned a women's shelter. I assume Molly is in some kind of trouble. I'm not in the habit of giving handouts to strangers. And Molly is just that to me—a stranger. I haven't seen her since we were separated as children. I barely remember that time in my life."

Faith felt sick to her stomach. *What kind of heartless woman is this?* "She is not in any kind of trouble. And she's not looking for a handout. Life has not been easy for Molly. She wants nothing more than to be reunited with her only sister."

She waited for Penny to say something. When she remained silent, Faith continued, "I understand this has come as something of a shock to you. Why don't you give it some thought? Can I give you my number in case you decide you'd like to see your sister?"

"I guess there's no harm in that," Penny said with a sigh. "But whatever you do, don't give her any false hopes."

2 1

CAROLINE

C aroline was dismayed at the sight of the ruined flower
bed. It wasn't so much the flowers. They would bloom
again in no time. It was the thought of that poor young woman
being angry enough to destroy such beauty. She understood a
little about what Jenny was going through. While the fog had
lifted and she could see clearly that divorce had been the only
solution for their troubled marriage, she was still furious with
Troy for the sneaky way he'd interviewed for jobs and made
plans to move to the West Coast behind her back. But she
couldn't imagine how Jenny must feel, having been blindsided by
her husband's affair with her best friend. Although this affair
would have been hard enough at any time for her, that they'd
been married only one year compounded the situation. Who
wouldn't be devastated? Caroline prayed someone would get
through to Jenny before she destroyed more than flowers. She'd
made no new friends with the residents and more than one
enemy. As Caroline left the garden and walked to her car, she
promised herself she'd be more attentive to Jenny going forward.

She hadn't driven her car since arriving at the home, two days
shy of two weeks ago, and she was relieved when the engine

started right up. Her thoughts drifted to Cory as she drove the short distance to her house on Oak Lane. It was Mother's Day. Caroline had ignored Mother's Day for the past four years, and she had every intention of ignoring it this year. Which is why she'd bailed on the prayer service and brunch Faith had organized to celebrate.

She parked the car in the driveway and went straight to her garden to visit with her flowers. Her beds needed tending, but she wouldn't have time for them today, not if she wanted to make it back to Lovie's for the nature boat cruise Jamie had promised the residents for the afternoon.

She entered the house through the kitchen door, grabbed a yard-size trash bag out of the broom closet, and attacked the contents of her refrigerator, throwing out everything except the condiments. With the kitchen wall phone on speaker, while she emptied the clean dishes from the dishwasher, she listened to forty-three voice messages. Most were spam. Several were from Troy, each growing more frantic when he was unable to reach her on her cell. One was from Gilbert Griffin, the divorce attorney Troy had hired. And none were from friends or acquaintances inviting her to lunch or girls' night out.

She considered calling Troy, to let him know she was alive. But then she decided to let him stew a little longer. When he walked out on her, he gave up his right to know her whereabouts.

Caroline went to the front door, raked the mountain of mail into a pile, and took it to her small desk in the family room. For the next two hours, she sorted the mail and paid every bill due for the foreseeable future. She noted through her online banking app that Troy had deposited money in their joint account as he did at the beginning of every month. She imagined that would soon stop. All the more reason to avoid calls from the divorce attorney awhile longer.

She stuffed the stamped stack of bills into her purse on the kitchen counter and turned her attention to tidying up the rest of the house. On her last night there, she'd been so frantic to get away from her demons, she'd left clothes strewn from her dresser drawers and the contents of her medicine cabinet scattered on the sink counter. As she moved from room to room, picking up and straightening, it dawned on her that the furnishings—the carpets and fabrics and wall coverings—were not at all to her liking. When they'd bought the house ten years ago, she'd decorated it to accommodate her husband's tastes. The only son of a wealthy investment banker, Troy had grown up in a formal home with priceless antiques, silk draperies, and an art collection worth millions. As with so many other aspects of their lives, she'd put his wants and needs ahead of her own. She was a no-frills kinda girl, at her best in the outdoors.

She stood in the open doorway of Cory's bedroom, listening for sounds of laughter, hoping to see his face looking up at her from his homework, but the room was empty, the drone of the air conditioner piercing the silence.

Caroline slumped to the floor and squeezed her eyes shut. As she rested her head against the doorjamb, she imagined pelicans flying overhead, waves lapping against the marsh grasses, and the pungent odor of low tide. In her mind's eye, the cabin was calling her home.

She got to her feet, looked up the number she needed on the computer, and returned to the phone in the kitchen. She wasn't surprised when her call was forwarded to an answering service. It was Mother's Day, after all.

"I need to leave a message for Jasmine Hughes to call me back as soon as possible," she said to the woman on the other end. "My name is Caroline Becker. She's the listing agent for my property, Winding Creek Farm."

"I'll pass the message on," the polite female voice said. "I'm sure she'll call you back shortly."

Caroline brewed a cup of chai tea, grabbed a notepad from the junk drawer, and sat down at the kitchen table. Now that she'd made her decision, she couldn't wait to make the move. At the top of the notepad, she wrote *Replace cell phone*, followed by a long list of people to call for repairs and updates that needed to be made to both houses. Would she need a security system, living out in the woods alone? For safety's sake and peace of mind, she would have one installed, but she hoped she never had to use it.

Jasmine finally returned her call forty-five minutes later. "What can I do for you?" she asked in an irritated tone.

"I want to take Winding Creek Farm off the market right away," Caroline said.

Jasmine hesitated. "Do you mind if I ask why?"

Caroline gripped the receiver. "My situation has changed considerably since the last time we spoke. I won't bore you with the details of our marriage. Or I should say our pending divorce. My husband . . . um, Troy has moved to the West Coast. Eventually, I'd like to list my home on Oak Lane for sale. But I need to consult with a divorce attorney first."

"Understood. I will take Winding Creek Farm off the market today. I hope you'll consider me as your listing agent when you're ready to sell Oak Lane."

"I absolutely will," Caroline said and hung up the phone.

Her next call was to Geraldine Rose, a woman whose daughter had dated Cory briefly in their early years of high school. Geraldine, known to her friends as Gerri, had shown exceptional kindness toward her when Cory died by stationing herself at Caroline's front door, making order out of the chaos of food and flower deliveries during the days following his death. She was also a divorce lawyer with a reputation for being the best in town.

Gerri was surprised to hear from her, but she didn't sound irritated at being disturbed on Mother's Day. They spoke for a few minutes about Kelli, who was in her last year at Chapel Hill, gearing up to take the LSAT in preparation for law school.

"Like mother like daughter," Caroline said. "Which is why I'm calling you, Gerri. I'm in need of a divorce lawyer, and I understand you're the best."

"Oh, honey. I'm so sorry. You've already been through so much, and now this. I'd be happy to help you. Let me get my calendar."

Caroline said, "I know this is asking a lot, with it being Mother's Day and all, but is there any chance we could meet this afternoon? I'm eager to get things rolling."

"I totally understand," Gerri said, and the sound of pages turning came over the line. "In looking at my calendar, that would probably be best for me as well. Especially since my daughter is spending the afternoon studying. Shall I come to you?"

"That would be perfect."

Gerri arrived twenty minutes later with her briefcase. She was an outgoing, attractive woman with similar interests, someone Caroline would like to know better. She wondered why'd they'd never been friends and realized it was because she had never made the effort. Gerri had reached out to her before Cory died, back when Kelli and Cory were an item, inviting Caroline to join her book club. But Caroline had been too busy being Cory's mom and Troy's wife to make friends of her own.

Over a pot of coffee, she brought Gerri up to speed on the events of the past two weeks. Gerri explained the divorce process in detail, and Caroline signed the papers giving her new attorney approval to set things in motion.

When Caroline walked her to the door, Gerri said, "Will you promise me you'll get yourself a replacement phone and let Troy know you're safe?"

Caroline nodded. "I promise." Gerri started down the front sidewalk and Caroline called after her. "Would you like to have lunch sometime? I mean, as friends."

Gerri turned around, walking backward. "I'd like that very much."

Caroline waited for Gerri's car to pull away from the curb before going inside. On her return to the back of the house, she paused in the doorways of her living and family rooms, wondering what furniture she would take with her to the farm. Moving to the kitchen window, staring out at her luscious garden, she realized that her flowers meant more to her than anything in the house, aside from the contents of Cory's room, which she would pack away in boxes in the storage room at the farm.

She hated for the flowers to go to waste with no one living in the house to enjoy them. She would take them to her new family at Lovie's home. She locked up the house, tossed her purse into the car, and retrieved two large buckets from the garage. She added three inches of water to each bucket and packed them full with assorted blooms from her yard. She would enlist the residents help in arranging them into bouquets. The sweet fragrance and colorful blooms would brighten their days. Goodness knows they needed brightening.

22

MOLLY

*M*olly had never ridden in a boat before. She was as excited about Jamie's exploration cruise as a kid on a Ferris wheel for the first time. He took them deep into the marsh, pointing out the various wildlife along the way. She learned about tidal changes and the names of a variety of different birds. She hated for the trip to come to an end, and was surprised to find Bitsy waiting for her when they returned to the dock.

"Mama wants to see Molly in the solarium," Bitsy said, taking the bowline from Jamie and looping it around a cleat.

"Me?" Molly asked, placing a hand on her chest. "Am I in some kinda trouble?"

Bitsy giggled. "Did you do something wrong?"

"Not that I know of." Jamie offered his hand, and Molly grabbed onto it as she stepped out of the boat and onto the dock.

"We have a visitor," Bitsy explained. "I don't know who she is."

"Then I'd better go find out," Molly said, leaving Bitsy on the dock with the others.

Faith and the guest rose out of the chairs to greet Molly when she entered the solarium. The woman, who was about Molly's age, seemed vaguely familiar, and she had the eerie feeling she'd known her from somewhere before. On closer inspection, Molly felt as though she was looking at an altered version of herself in a mirror. Her hair was dark, instead of blonde, and pulled back in a severe hair knot, but her eyes were the same pale blue as Molly's.

"Penny?" she mouthed the name, afraid to give voice to it for fear it might not be true.

"Hello, Molly. It's been a long time."

Molly flung herself into her sister's arms. "I can't believe it," she cried. "After all this time, we're finally together again."

Penny pushed her away, smoothing her hand down the front of her linen blouse as if Molly had wrinkled it. "I wasn't going to come. And now that I'm here, I'm not sure why I did."

Molly shot a glance of uncertainty at Faith who looked as though she wanted to disappear into the jungle printed on the fabric of her chair. Faith nodded encouragement. "Eli found her."

Suddenly overwhelmed, she sank to the sofa, pulling her sister down beside her. "We had such good times together as children. Remember I used to call you my shiny penny?"

Something that resembled a smile crossed her sister's tight lips. "And I called you Molly Pop. But that was a long time ago. I go by Penelope now."

"But you used to hate it when Mom and Dad called you Penelope." Molly fidgeted with her hands unsure of how to react to the strange vibe Penny was giving her.

Penny crossed her legs and held her shoulders back. "I don't have many memories from that time in my life."

"But I don't understand." Molly shook her head in bewilderment. "How could you forget how happy we were on the farm? And how much our parents loved us?"

"That was a different lifetime. After our parents died, I was adopted by my foster parents. I have four sisters. They're my family now. Just as I'm sure you have a family of your own."

When she noticed her sister studying her missing tooth,

Molly pressed her upper lip tight over her top teeth. "But I don't. Have family of my own. You're the only one." She'd dreamed of being reunited with her sister ever since the day after the fire when social services sent them to different foster homes. "Did you ever try to find me?"

Penny's cheeks grew pink. "I never saw the need. I always assumed that, like me, you'd been adopted by a nice family. Didn't you ever marry?" she asked, as though getting married was something everyone did.

Molly stared down at her lap. "I was engaged once. To a trucker. He was killed in an accident on the highway." She paused for a minute to steady her voice. "Do you? Have a husband and children?" She braced herself for the answer. She didn't want to hear about her sister's happy marriage and loving home full of children. She didn't consider herself the jealous type, but it hardly seemed fair how life had treated her sister so well and her so poorly.

Penny brushed a speck of imaginary lint off her black slacks. "My husband and I have been married for ten years, and we have three little children, all boys ages eight, six, and four. I'm a cardiovascular surgeon, or did I already mention that?"

"No, I don't believe you did." Molly thought she could've been a doctor too, if she'd had nice adopted parents who made certain she got a good education. Instead, she'd had an abusive father who locked her in the basement and tortured her. She squirmed on the sofa. Suddenly, she wished her sister would leave.

Penny reached into her designer pocketbook and removed an envelope. "I assume, since you're living in a shelter, that you're in some kind of trouble. My conscience got the best of me after speaking with Faith yesterday. I feel obligated to give you this." She thrust the envelope at Molly, whose eyes bugged out at the sight of so many hundred-dollar bills inside. "There's three thousand dollars there. I hope that's enough to get you out of whatever kind of trouble you're in. But that money comes with one condition."

"What's that?" Molly asked, still staring at the money.

"That you never contact me again. My family doesn't know about you, and I'd like to keep it that way."

"Do you mind if I ask where you live?" Molly said in a weak voice.

Penny folded her hands, with their red lacquered fingernails, in her lap. "I live in Charleston. But, as I just said, I have to insist that we don't see each other again."

Molly jumped to her feet. "I don't want your money," she said, dropping the envelope in Penny's lap. "And, for your information, I'm not in trouble. I asked Faith to help me start a new life, because for the past seven years, I've been living on the streets of Charleston."

Confusion crossed her sister's face, and then her lips curled up in disgust.

She experienced a surge of anger. "That's right, Pen-ny," she said, pronouncing her sister's name slowly and deliberately. "I'm homeless. I'm sure our paths have crossed before, and we didn't even realize it. I know your type. You're one of those snooty women who looked at me with that same look of disgust when you passed me on the street. You never dreamed that one of those pathetic women in threadbare clothes, wheeling a suitcase bearing all her possessions, could possibly be your blood kin."

"Humph." Penny stuffed the envelope into her handbag and stood to face Molly. "This is the thanks I get for trying to do something nice for you."

The anger in her voice sounded foreign to Molly when she said, "Something nice for me? You offered me three thousand dollars for my *trouble* without even asking me what kind of trouble I was in. You didn't want to do something nice for me. You wanted to get rid of me once and for all. You don't have to pay me off. I'm more than happy to stay out of your life for free. Pen-e-lop-e."

Faith rose from her chair and came to stand beside Molly in a show of allegiance. "I think this visit is over. I trust you can see yourself to the door."

They watched Penny cross through the parlor, and when she paused at the entrance to the hallway, looking right and left unsure which way to go, Faith hollered, "To your left!"

"I'm so sorry, Molly. I should've told you that Eli had located her. I tried to arrange a surprise visit, thinking you'd have a happy reunion, but when I spoke with Penny yesterday, she seemed so . . . disinterested. I was shocked when she showed up here today."

"That's not the same Penny I remember," Molly said, near tears.

"No, I'm sure it's not." Faith sat down on the sofa and patted the cushion beside her. "Let's sit for a minute and process what just happened."

Molly plopped down on the sofa and snatched a tissue from the box on the lamp table beside her. "I'm not sure what to think of what just happened. It hurts so much." She sobbed into the tissue. "She never even tried to find me."

Faith placed an arm around Molly's shoulders and pulled her close while she cried. She couldn't remember when she'd last shed tears. She'd learned a long time ago that crying was for the weak and usually made her feel worse about a situation. But as she bawled her eyes out, she felt a weight being lifted from her shoulders. Ever since she was ten years old, she'd been burdened by guilt for having allowed social services to take her sister away from her. But she'd been a child with absolutely no control over the situation. Over the years, she'd worried herself sick that Penny was trapped in a destitute life like her own, that her foster parents had mistreated her, and later, that she might be living on the streets somewhere. But things had turned out pretty darn good for Penelope. Much better than they had for Molly. She owed her sister nothing. She was beholden to no one.

A smile spread across her lips as she thought, *I'm free to live my life for me.* She lifted her head off Faith's shoulder and blew her nose. "I'm better now. In a weird way, I'm relieved. I no longer have to worry about my baby sister. Except for her soul when she goes to meet her maker."

Faith burst into laughter. "You're a funny one, Molly Maguire. I'm lucky you came into my life."

Molly shook her head. "I'm the lucky one. I can't thank you enough for all you've done for me."

"It's been my pleasure." They sat in silence for a minute, each lost in her own thoughts. "I wonder if the court system allows families to adopt adults. That would be merely a formality, anyway. I consider you part of my family, Molly. Sam and Jamie both adore you. Your home is here now, in Prospect, with us."

23

FAITH

aith returned home after supper on Sunday for the first time since Thursday morning. Jenny appeared to have mellowed a bit, and Faith prayed the threat of suicide was over, but at bedtime, when she turned out the lamp on her night table, her concern for the girl—for all the residents—came rushing back.

"What is wrong with me, Mike?" she whispered in the darkness. "I feel so torn. When I'm here, I'm worried about the residents. But when I'm at Lovie's, all I can think about is how much I miss you and Bitsy."

"What're you talking about, Faith? We've had some quality time together this weekend. Bitsy and I spent all day with you at Lovie's today, and last night, we were there for the cookout." Mike rolled over on his side, propping himself up on his elbow. "Happy Mother's Day, by the way."

"That's not the first time you've wished me Happy Mother's Day. But thank you." She craned her neck to kiss his lips. "You're a good sport. I'm sure there are other ways you'd rather spend your Mother's Day than with a group of broken women at a women's shelter."

"As I told you the other day—and I meant it—there is nowhere I'd rather be, Faith. You're doing great things at Lovie's. You're changing lives for a lot of women, and I'm a hundred-percent committed to helping you." He toyed with a lock of her hair. "You must see how good this is for Bitsy. Not only are you providing a great role model for her, but she's thriving there. She's been through a lot in her young age. Thanks to you, she finally appears to be healing."

"I just wish I could be two places at once," Faith said. "I've neglected my household chores here. I'm behind on the laundry, and there's nothing to eat in the refrigerator. I haven't been a very good wife these past couple of weeks, and I fear it's only going to get worse."

"You're the best kind of wife, sweetheart. It's me who's at fault. You are now in a full-time job, which I wholeheartedly support, and it's my responsibility to help pick up the slack around here. I've been so busy at the hospital, but after this week, I'll be able to do that and more."

Faith sat up straight in bed. "That's right! I almost forgot. Your last day is Friday. We should have a retirement party for you. Family only. We'll invite Sam and Jackie, their husbands and sons."

"Ha! You can't even get the laundry done. When will you have time to plan a party?" He pulled her back down beside him. "I'm not retiring, anyway. I'm changing career paths. I'll have plenty of time on my hands after Friday. Why don't I plan a family cookout for your birthday in June? Your mother's illness prevented us from having a proper party for you and your sisters last summer."

The sisters' special tradition was one Faith held especially close to her heart. The three Sweeney sisters, all born the first week of June—the first, second, and fourth—typically celebrated with one party on June third, usually out at Jackie's farm. "That sounds perfect. We've all been so busy. I'm sure Jackie will appreciate being let off the hook." She snuggled up close to him, and with the warmth of his body comforting her, she fell into a deep sleep.

Faith left for Lovie's before sunrise on Monday morning, entrusting Mike with getting Bitsy to school on time. She stopped by the kitchen for coffee on her way to her office. With three residents on the verge of leaving the home, she felt responsible for helping them make the next step. If Tilda hadn't figured out by Wednesday that having Rosalie move into her guest cottage was the ideal solution for both of them, Faith would be blunt in asking her to consider it. But Molly's situation was more complicated. She would need to work for several months before she could afford to pay rent on an apartment. Faith had a responsibility to her board of directors to make sure their funds were appropriated responsibly; otherwise, she'd let Molly continue to live at the home indefinitely. She could always offer Molly the guest room in her own home for a while, but she didn't think that was fair to either Mike or Bitsy. And there was the matter of transportation. Regardless of where she was living, without a driver's license, how would Molly get to and from work when she started at the market in a week?

Faith spent an hour at her computer, studying the accounts, before placing the dreaded call to Moses, her most trusted member of Lovie's board of directors. He answered on the second ring.

"This better be good," he grumbled. "I haven't had my coffee yet."

"It's not," Faith said. "Wanna call me back?"

"Not at all," he said, his voice suddenly alert. "I always make time for my favorite ex-patient turned director of a women's shelter."

"I'm afraid I'm not doing such a great job of directing. Our financial situation is dire. As you know, the state denied our request for grant funding. We can probably make it through the summer, but I don't know how much longer we can remain open past that." She planted her elbow on the desk, face in hand. "I feel like such a failure, Moses."

"Come now, Faith. Where's your fighting spirit?"

She sensed movement out in the hallway and looked up to see Rosalie standing in her open doorway. "Breakfast," Rosalie mouthed.

Faith lifted a finger, signaling she would only be a minute. As she watched the young woman walk away, she thought about how far Rosalie had come in a few short weeks. She'd stopped abusing drugs and alcohol, made peace with her mother, and was on her way to a career as a hairstylist. And Faith had been partially responsible for making that happen.

Feeling a renewed sense of self-assurance, she said, "I'm not giving up. But I need a miracle right now. Can you find one for me?"

"I'm on it," he said, and ended the call.

The conversation was lively when Faith joined the others in the dining room for breakfast, a sure sign that hearts were on the mend. Caroline seemed almost joyful, and Jenny had emerged from her funk. Molly and Tilda could not stop talking about how much they enjoyed Jamie's nature cruise. Only Rosalie was quieter than usual, and Faith wondered how much of her conversation with Moses she'd overheard.

Cook had prepared a feast—eggs, pancakes, and a variety of homemade Danishes, including brown sugar and pecan scones and blueberry muffins. The food was delicious, and Faith helped herself to some of all of it, but immediately following breakfast, she had yet another conversation with Cook about the importance of being frugal.

Returning to her office, she placed a call to her dentist who agreed to consult with Molly about her missing tooth and offered a discount on whatever solution they agreed upon. Faith set the appointment for the following day at noon.

She'd only just hung up with the dentist when Mike called. "I have a young woman who needs your help."

"How young?"

"Eighteen. She and her mother were brought in by ambulance during the night. They'd both been beaten badly by the girl's stepfather. The mother's condition is critical. We've admitted her, and she's not going anywhere anytime soon. The daughter, on the other hand, refuses treatment."

Faith furrowed her brow. "Why?"

"I'm not sure. Scared, probably. As best I can tell, her wounds appear superficial—black eye, busted lip, scratches on her arms. But obviously, we can't send her home to the stepfather."

"I'm on my way," Faith said, pushing back from her desk and reaching for her purse.

"Let me bring her to you," Mike said. "I've spent some time talking to her, and I think I've finally gotten her to trust me. Her name's Bridget, by the way. Bridget Cooper."

Faith lowered herself back to her seat. "What about the step-father? Has he been arrested?"

Mike's silence sent an all-too-familiar chill up her spine. "Not yet," he said in a tone that conveyed her fear. "He managed to get away from the police. That's all I know."

Faith sighed. "When should I expect you?"

"We'll be there within the hour," Mike said. "Oh, and one more thing. She came in with only the clothes on her back. And she's on the heavy side. Do you think you have something that might fit her in your thrift closet? If not, I can make a run to Walmart after work."

"I appreciate the offer," Faith said, "But I'm sure we can find some clothes that will work."

She had no sooner hung up with Mike than her cell phone rang again with a call from Moses. "I know you're a miracle worker," she said. "But that was fast even for you."

"I'm calling on a different matter," he said, his voice serious.

"A colleague has a client who needs your help. She's the victim of a recent armed robbery of a jewelry store where she was employed as the manager. She's suffering from PTSD. She's been in Florida at a treatment facility for several weeks, and she's made great progress. But she's a widow—her children live in other parts of the country—and she's not yet ready to be alone. Any chance you have room for a new resident?"

Adding two new residents to the program in one day would put a strain on the relationships that had finally begun to develop between the five currently in-house, but Faith would never turn away a woman in need as long as she had empty beds. "Three, possibly four, of my five are ready to leave the nest. But Mike is on his way here with a young girl who was beaten by her stepfather. The short answer is yes, we'd love to have her."

"That's good news," Moses said. "I'll have my colleague get in touch with you soon about the arrangements. He's planning to bring her in himself later this afternoon."

Tossing her phone onto the desk, Faith fell back in her chair as she considered her options for room assignments. Bridget was only eighteen years old. Her mother was in the hospital in critical condition. And she was virtually homeless, since she obviously couldn't live with an abusive stepfather. She would assign Bridget to Jenny's room in the hopes that Jenny would take Bridget under her wing. It wouldn't hurt for Jenny to be around someone with problems more severe than her own. And Jenny, with her constant humming, would not be a good fit for someone suffering with PTSD.

She buzzed Robin over the intercom. "Prepare yourself. Our lives are about to get crazy," she said, and explained about the incoming residents. After an in-depth discussion about security, Robin and Faith agreed their measures in place would be enough until the police advised them otherwise.

When Mike texted that he was arriving, Faith went outside to greet them. She felt the stabbing pain of her heart ripping in two at the sight of the battered girl when she slid out of Mike's truck. The years disappeared and Faith was an abused wife again, her nose broken by her husband's fist. She'd been terrified with no safe place to hide from Curtis. Women like Bridget and her mother were Faith's primary motivation for starting Lovie's Home. She would take whatever measures necessary to protect them.

Faith went to her, taking Bridget's clammy hands in hers. "Welcome. I'm Mike's wife, Faith, and I'm the director here at Lovie's Home. I understand a lot about what you're going through, and I want you to know you're safe here." As the words left her lips, she had a very bad feeling in her gut that perhaps she was wrong.

24

JENNY

$\mathcal{J}$ust when Jenny was beginning to make friends with the others, Faith had to throw her a curveball by getting two new residents. And what whack jobs they were. One poor teenager whose stepfather beat her face to a pulp, and another woman about the pilot's age who jumped out of her skin every time someone made a sudden move. While she felt sorry for them, Jenny didn't understand why she had to share her room with one of them. And she confronted Faith about it before group therapy that afternoon.

"There's plenty of empty rooms," Jenny argued. "Why can't we all have our own?"

"Our policy is to place residents together whenever possible," Faith said. "For the purpose of bonding, you understand."

"Then why not put the two new residents together?" Jenny asked, refusing to give up.

The muscles in Faith's face tightened and a vein pulsed at her temple. "Because, in my opinion, Bridget will feel more comfortable with you since the two of you are closer in age. This is your chance to make a difference in another person's life, Jenny. She's been through a terrible ordeal. The least you can do is summon some sympathy for her. I'm counting on you to make her feel at home."

"Whatever." Jenny rolled her eyes, but she made a point of sitting next to Bridget in group therapy anyway.

Paula Bowen, the woman with PTSD, monopolized the majority of the sixty-minute session with her story. "I was held up at gunpoint in the jewelry store I managed. It happened in Atlanta where I've been living for the past twenty years. I'm originally from this area, and I moved back after the robbery, hoping that being in a peaceful small town would help me get better. But it hasn't."

"What kind of jewelry did they sell?" Rosalie asked, sitting on the edge of her chair, impatient for more details.

Jenny glared at her. "What difference does that make?"

Rosalie shrugged. "I'm just curious."

"It was a small boutique with contemporary custom pieces made by a talented young designer," Paula said. "Anyway, the robbery happened on a cold night, this past January. We had no business staying open until nine, and I'd told the owner that a hundred times. The store was in an upscale area, but not exactly the safest part of town."

Rosalie needs to do something with this woman's hair, Jenny thought. Her gray hair curtained her face with only her wild green eyes, like marbles rolling around in their sockets, peeking through.

Paula continued, "I was locking up the back door when two men forced their way in. They were brothers who looked enough alike to be twins. Gingers, orange hair and freckles with yellow specks of evil glinting in their hazel eyes. They bound my hands and feet with zip ties and covered my mouth with duct tape. One of them pointed a gun at my head while the other kicked me with his steel-toed boots. They were aiming to kill me, and I played dead to get them to quit. They bruised my kidneys, ruptured my spleen, and broke every rib in my rib cage. They fractured my humerus bone so badly it tore through the skin. I lay in a pool of my own blood, in unbearable agony, until the janitor found me at six o'clock the next morning.

"I was in the hospital for over a month. I worked with the police for weeks to identify the robbers. When we finally got them, I had to face my vicious attackers in court. The judge sentenced them to thirty years in maximum security prison. You'd think that'd make me feel better, but it doesn't. It's been 110 days, but every time I close my eyes, I see those Marcus brothers as vividly as if the robbery happened yesterday."

Jenny glanced around at the other residents who were spell-bound by Paula's story. Molly, an expression of horror on her face, and Rosalie, clinging tight to Caroline's arm. Even Jenny was intrigued, until Dr. Robin began bombarding the poor woman with her shrink questions.

Suddenly bored, Jenny crossed her arms and legs and studied Bridget out of the corner of her eye. What could she possibly have done to her stepfather to make him mad enough to bash her face? She was curious to hear Bridget's story, but when Dr. Robin finally got around to asking her if she wanted to share, the girl shook her head.

———

It was past ten o'clock that evening and Jenny was still reading *Lord of the Flies*. Bridget had not stirred in over an hour, and Jenny assumed she'd fallen asleep. But when she reached over to turn out the light, Bridget sat bolt upright in bed.

"Please leave it on! I won't be able to sleep if you turn the light out."

"And I won't be able to sleep with it on." In response to the look of despair that crossed the girl's face, Jenny said, "Okay. We can try it, if it'll make you feel better."

"Thank you," Bridget mumbled, sliding back down in bed. "I

175

don't mean to be difficult. It's just that . . . well, last night was really bad. And Faith called the hospital awhile ago. My mama's not any better. I'm afraid she's going to die."

Jenny didn't know what to say. This seemed like a good time to pray, but she'd given up on God when Derek cheated on her. It dawned on her then, after months of being angry at him, that it wasn't God's fault. How naive she'd been about so many things. "I'll pray that she doesn't, not that I have much leverage with the Lord at the moment."

"You have more than me," Bridget said in a voice so soft Jenny worried she hadn't heard her correctly. What could this eighteen-year-old possibly have done wrong to make God mad?

"It's none of my business, and I don't blame you if you don't want to talk about it. But what made your stepfather angry enough to do this to you?"

Bridget rolled on her side to face Jenny. "He got mad because Mama didn't cook his hamburger enough. The week before, Vern —he's my stepfather—busted Mama's nose when she forgot to take the supercan out to the street on trash day. There was the time Mama smiled at the mailman, and Vern accused her of having an affair. He really got angry about a year ago when she accidentally spilled bleach on his favorite shirt. He almost put her in the hospital that time."

"But those are all things your mom did," Jenny said. "Why'd he beat you?"

"Last night, he attacked me because I got in his way when he was beating Mama. But he comes after me all the time, like when my grades aren't good enough and when I stay out too late. And by late, I mean nine o'clock on the weekend. He's run off every boy who's ever been interested in me. Not that there have been that many. He's an equal opportunity wife and child abuser."

Silence fell over the room, and after a few minutes, Jenny heard sniffling.

"I'm so scared," Bridget said finally. "What if he finds out where I am and comes after me?"

"That's why you're in a shelter. There's security everywhere here. The place is locked up tight. I know, because I was thinking about escaping."

"Did you ever try it?"

"Nope. Faith told me I could leave anytime I wanted on my own free will. Unfortunately, I have nowhere else to go."

"That makes two of us."

"Don't worry, Bridget, the police will catch the bastard. He can't bother you from jail."

"They've gotta find him before they can arrest him. Knowing Vern, he's hiding out somewhere."

The thought of Bridget's evil stepfather on the loose made Jenny's skin crawl. "But that's good. If he's gone into hiding, he can't bother you, right?"

"Wrong. You don't know Vern. If he finds out where I am, he'll get to me one way or another."

Great, Jenny thought. *And being your roommate puts me directly in the line of fire.*

Bridget flipped over on her back, staring up at the ceiling. Jenny couldn't help but notice the large mound under the blanket that was Bridget's midsection. She wondered if her stepfather gave the girl a hard time about being overweight. She had a pretty face despite her black eye and fat lip, if only she lost a few pounds.

"If my mama doesn't die, she'll go back to him," Bridget said. "She always does."

Jenny's mouth fell open. "But why? I don't get that at all."

"Because we're poor. Because Mama doesn't have an education, and she's never held down a job. I only turned eighteen in March. I'm supposed to graduate from high school in a month. I'm hoping to get a job and save some money so I can move out of that house."

Jenny got out of bed to comfort her roommate. Sitting on the edge of Bridget's mattress, she stroked her arm while her roommate cried. "Faith is a good person, and she really cares a lot. She'll help you figure this out," Jenny said, shocked when she realized she actually believed it was true.

"Not when she finds out about the—" Bridget finished her sentence with a sob.

"About the what, Bridget?"

"I don't want to talk about it. I didn't sleep at all last night. I'm exhausted, but I can't stop thinking about Mama. I'm so worried about her."

Jenny glanced at the *Lord of the Flies* on her nightstand. "Why don't I read to you? It might help you take your mind off your trouble?"

Bridget looked at her in surprise. "Would you? No one has read to me since my daddy died."

Jenny gasped. "How old were you when that happened?"

"Five. He was a fireman. He went to work one day and never came home."

While Jenny found her parents controlling, she'd always taken their presence in her life for granted. She didn't know what she'd do if she ever lost one of them. "I'm so sorry," Jenny said in a sincere tone. "That must have been horrible for you."

Bridget lowered the lid on the eye that wasn't already swollen shut. "I barely remember him, but I know he was a good man. My life would've turned out so much differently if he'd lived."

Jenny returned to her bed and picked up her book. Propping herself up against her pillows, she opened *Lord of the Flies* to the first chapter. At first, she felt awkward reading out loud, and even though she'd nearly finished the novel, she soon relaxed as she settled into the story all over again. She kept reading, even after she heard the sound of Bridget's soft snoring. It was nearly three in the morning when she read the last word and closed the book. Keeping her promise to Bridget to leave the light on, she rolled over onto her side, facing the window with her back to the lamp. She drifted off to sleep with her thoughts on Golding's characters—Ralph, Jack, and Piggy. Caroline was the most like Ralph, the golden child, the obvious leader. Jenny was Jack, obsessed with killing a hog, only Jenny's hog was Derek. And Bridget was Piggy, not because of her weight but because beneath her awkwardness Jenny sensed determination and strength.

———

At breakfast the following morning, Jenny asked Faith to assign her to the same chores as Bridget. "Someone should show her the ropes. I figured that someone should probably be me, since I'm her roommate."

"That's very thoughtful of you, Jenny." Faith studied her as she sipped coffee. "What's different about you?"

Jenny lifted a shoulder. "I don't know? My new hairstyle, maybe."

"It looks nice. I like the pink streak. But that's not it." After studying her some more, Faith's eyes widened. "You've stopped humming."

Jenny's head shot up in surprise. When had that happened? At least since dinner the night before, because Jenny specifically remembered Rosalie making a good-hearted joke about the humming. "Maybe worrying about Bridget has caused me to stop obsessing about my own problems."

"And that's a good thing, don't you think?" Faith asked with a twinkle in her eye.

"I guess so." Truth be told, she was relieved to be thinking about someone else for a change.

So, when Faith pulled Bridget aside after breakfast, Jenny, as her self-appointed guardian, went with her, standing nearby in case the girl needed her.

"Mike called from the hospital a few minutes ago," Faith told

Bridget. "He checked on your mama personally this morning, and she's doing better. She asked about you, and he assured her that you were in a safe place, being well cared for."

When she tried to smile, Bridget grimaced at the pain in her lip. "What about my stepfather? Has there been any word about Vern?"

Faith shook her head. "My brother-in-law is a detective on the local police force. I asked him to look into the case for us. According to Eli, the police have reason to believe your stepfather has left the area."

"I'd feel better if he was in jail," Bridget said, gnawing on a hangnail.

Faith said, "Me too, honestly. But we have ample security here, and there's a policeman stationed outside of your mama's room at the hospital."

Bridget's shoulders slumped as the tension drained from her body. "That makes me feel a little better, anyway. Thanks for telling me."

Faith placed a supportive hand on Bridget's shoulder. "We're doing everything we can to keep you safe."

Concerned for the safety of her new friend, and herself, Jenny heightened her awareness of her surroundings throughout the day. She felt only marginally better knowing Emilee was monitoring the surveillance cameras installed around the property. And she had little faith in Elmer, the ancient security guard, who could barely walk up a flight of steps without getting winded much less chase down an intruder. Nonetheless, while collecting eggs from the henhouse, when Jenny thought she spotted someone lurking behind the trees at the edge of the forest, she reported it to Elmer, who investigated the situation but found no evidence of anything out of the ordinary.

To further add to Jenny's angst, when she went to the kitchen to help prepare lunch, Cook was beside herself over a missing loaf of bread.

"That loaf of bread was right there a minute ago." Cook smacked the counter with her plastic spatula. "I went downstairs to get a jar of Duke's mayonnaise out of the basement pantry. When I came back it was gone."

"Are you sure, Cook?" Jenny asked in a concerned tone. "Maybe you took the bread with you to the basement and accidentally left it down there."

"I've already checked, thank you very much." She smacked the counter again. "I'm telling you, it was right there. I know it, like I know my name is Alberta Summers. Miss Faith's gonna have my head. She's been after me to cut back. And here I go losing whole loaves of bread."

"Chill, Cook. It's just a loaf of bread. We should be more worried about who took the bread."

25

CAROLINE

*C*aroline waited for Jamie to finished with the other residents on the dock Monday afternoon before approaching him. "I wanted to thank you for going with me to the farm on Saturday. Because of you, I've decided to sell my house in town and move out to Winding Creek permanently."

He looked up from cleaning the dead minnows out of the bait basket "That's a big move. Are you sure you're ready for it?"

"I believe I am. A lot has happened to me recently that's changed my life. With Troy leaving me and me coming here." She gestured at the group of residents moseying toward the house together. "Making all these new friends. But mostly because of you, Jamie. You've helped me reconnect with the past in a way that brings me joy instead of pain. And you made me realize that gardening is more than a hobby. It's a way of life. I'm going to take your advice and open up a nursery."

Jamie dumped the bait basket into the water and stood to face her. "Good for you, Caroline! I'm certain you'll be a success."

"You sound more convinced than I feel. I'm scared to death. I'd feel better if I had a partner."

"But then you'd have to share the profits," Jamie said with a playful smile.

Caroline hesitated, considering the pros and cons of partnership. "True, but sharing the profits also means sharing the risks and headaches."

"If you really want a partner, I'm sure you can find one. Surely you have a friend who likes gardening as much as you."

"Maybe." Caroline was unwilling to admit to him that her very short list of friends included the other residents and perhaps her divorce attorney but that was a stretch.

She noticed his boat tied to the dock and dark clouds building in from the west. "Looks like we may get a storm. You should probably get your boat home before it hits."

"It's not supposed to storm until later tonight, but I need to get going, anyway." Jamie got in his boat, and she helped him untie it from the dock. As he was pulling away, over the sound of the outboard motor, he called, "I'll talk to Mom. We're always looking for suppliers. I'm sure we can work something out for Sweeney's to buy your produce."

Caroline felt a rush of adrenaline at the prospect of a relationship with a business as successful as Sweeney's. Could this really be happening for her? Cupping her hands around her mouth, she yelled, "That'd be great," and gave him a thumbs-up.

As she walked back to the house, her mind was so preoccupied with thoughts of growing vegetables, she failed to notice Rosalie sitting alone on the porch until she was right on her.

"What's wrong?" Caroline asked, taking a seat in the rocker next to her. "You look like you lost your best friend."

"I'm worried about Faith," Rosalie said. "Well, not Faith personally but about the future of Lovie's. I overheard her talking on the phone yesterday. I don't think she has the funds to keep the home open much past this summer."

"That's disappointing to hear. She's worked so hard."

Rosalie nodded. "And think of the people she's already helped in the weeks since she opened her doors."

"There's gotta be something we can do," Caroline said, although she had no clue how to help Faith. Any meager donation she could afford wouldn't go very far. The least she could do was offer to continue working the garden after she left the home and moved to the farm.

When Robin called them inside for group, Rosalie and Caroline joined the others already gathered in the parlor. Dr. Robin pressed Bridget to talk about the abuse she'd experienced at home, but every time Bridget opened her mouth to speak, her lower lip quivered and she clammed up again.

"Just leave her alone," Jenny said, taking the words out of Caroline's mouth. "Can't you see she's not ready to talk about it?"

Robin shifted in her seat, turning her attention to Jenny. "You're obviously feeling protective of Bridget. Do you want to talk about that?"

Jenny shot Robin an angry look. "What's there to talk about? She needs protecting. She's been through so much. And she's only eighteen."

"That's very true, Jenny," Robin said. "But Bridget doesn't need protecting from me. I'm here to help. As are you. Your compassion is a side of you I've never seen. How does it feel?"

"I hate talking about shrink stuff." Jenny jumped to her feet and went to the window, placing her back to the group as she stared out at the stormy sky. "But I have to admit it feels good. Worrying about Bridget has made me stop obsessing about my own problems."

Robin left the circle and went to stand beside Jenny. "You've stopped humming, which is a positive sign," she said, loud enough for everyone to hear. "What makes you think you've had a breakthrough?"

Jenny shrugged. "I just know I'm tired of thinking about

Derek and Christy. I want to move on with my life. But I don't know how to do that or where to go."

Robin placed an arm around Jenny. "Baby steps. We'll address those issues as we move to the next stage of your recovery."

Robin turned around to face the group, leaving Jenny alone at the window. "Now, who else wants to share?"

Molly's hand shot up, and she spent ten minutes telling them about her visit to the dentist and the course of action the dentist planned to take to bridge the hole in her mouth. "I'm starting my new job on Monday, but I'm worried about where I'll be living and how I'll be paying for it. I can't stay here forever."

"I'm worried about that too," Rosalie chimed in. "I've applied to cosmetology school in Charleston, but I need to find a part-time job and a place to live. And I don't have a clue how to go about doing that."

Caroline thought about the money problems Faith was having at Lovie's. She wasn't operating a boarding house. She couldn't allow the residents to stay at the home when they were strong enough to leave.

"I don't want any of you to worry," Robin said. "We want all of you to succeed when you leave here. We won't turn you out into the world until you're ready. That includes finding suitable accommodations for those of you who have nowhere to live as well as making certain those of you who already have a home are prepared to be on your own."

"I'm worried about that part," Caroline said, leaning forward, engaged in the conversation. "I'm going to put my house on the market, and I'm excited about moving out to my farm. But I was married for twenty-six years and I'm terrified of being alone."

Tilda raised a tentative hand. "Living alone is the cause of the anxiety that drove me here. But what do we do about it?"

"Everyone's situation is different. We'll sort through these issues individually." Robin stood, signaling the end of the session. "Before you go into dinner, I just want to say how proud I am of all of you. For the first time today, I felt like you're working together as a team. You're the first group of residents to go through our program, which makes you special. You've formed close bonds that I hope you'll continue to nurture when you leave here. You need one another, whether or not you realize it yet."

Robin's upbeat words instilled hope in the residents, and Caroline sensed the mood shift within the group as they migrated into the dining room. Even the newcomers seemed more at ease as they found their seats. Faith and Emilee occupied their usual places at opposite ends of the table. Caroline sat between Bitsy and Rosalie, opposite Bridget. Sitting next to Bridget, Molly offered one of her quirky blessings, and after everyone had helped themselves to a serving of Cook's delicious crab stuffed flounder, Faith announced that her husband was retiring from the emergency room at the end of the week and going into private practice.

"But he's taking the summer off to spend with us before starting his new job." Faith rested her hand on Bitsy's arm. "Isn't that right, sweetheart?"

Bitsy, who seemed oddly out of sorts from her usually jovial self, brushed her mother's hand away and stared down at her plate. "I guess."

Concern crossed Faith's face in response to her daughter's surly response. She tucked a stray strand of hair behind Bitsy's ear. "One more week of working nights and he'll be all ours."

Poor Faith. Caroline thought. *She has so much on her plate.*

Faith and Bitsy left immediately following dinner in order to make it home before the bad weather set in. When Cook also left early to beat the storm, the residents plus Emilee pitched in to clean up the kitchen. After the dishes were put away and the leftovers stored in the refrigerator, they retired to the sitting room for bingo.

Emilee volunteered to be the caller, and while she hadn't played bingo in years, Caroline admitted to having fun. The wind picked up—they could hear it howling through the eaves of the porch—but when eight thirty rolled around and it had not yet begun to rain, Caroline wondered if the storm might bypass them. Which meant she would be up early the next day watering the gardens.

Nine o'clock arrived, and Emilee was threatening to call lights out, when her cell phone rang. She took her call to the solarium, and when she returned ten minutes later, the color had drained from her face and her hand trembled as she pressed her fingers to her lips.

"My mother's had a stroke," she said in a weak voice. "It's serious, and I need to be with her. I couldn't reach Faith, but I'll keep trying. I'll let Elmer know I'm leaving on my way out. I want you all to stay in this house. Do you understand? No one is to leave for any reason."

"We understand," they said at once. Why would they leave when most of them had nowhere to go?

26

FAITH

uring the drive home, Faith tried unsuccessfully to get
Bitsy to open up about what was bothering her. And
she questioned her again when she kissed her goodnight at
bedtime, but Bitsy refused to talk. Grabbing a lightweight
sweater from her bedroom, Faith brewed a cup of hot tea and
took it out to the rocking chairs on her screened porch. She
missed Mike. They relished stormy evenings like these, watching
lightning flashes on the horizon and listening to the wind
rustling the palmetto fronds. Soon, he would have a normal nine-
to-five schedule like most husbands. Only her schedule may
never be normal again.

She wondered for the umpteenth time that day whether she'd
gotten in over her head with the shelter. Earlier in the afternoon,
Moses had texted the idea of hosting a benefit to raise funds for
Lovie's Home—a black-tie dinner in conjunction with a silent
auction. While such an event would give them the opportunity to
show off their facilities, she thought the money spent on elaborate food, alcohol, and decorations would be a waste.

And it wasn't all about the money. Now that so many of her
residents were preparing to move on with their lives, she felt

responsible for setting them up with jobs and housing in the outside world. And that was proving difficult. She'd discovered an efficiency apartment that would be ideal for Molly, close enough to Sweeney's that she could walk. But Molly would need to pay first and last month's rent in advance. Faith was on the verge of using her own money. Even if she never got it back, it was for a good cause. As for Rosalie, she planned to speak with Tilda first thing the following morning about allowing the girl to live in her carriage house until she could find a part-time job and affordable housing.

But the situation with Bridget and her mother had really gotten Faith down. Seeing that poor child's battered face and having her stepfather on the loose brought back the horrible memories she'd thought she'd laid to rest. And she couldn't ignore the uneasy feeling that danger was on the horizon. The past was haunting her. And Bitsy had been so uncharacteristically quiet and moody. Faith couldn't help but worry the same thing might be happening to her.

Suck it up, Faith. You survived Curtis. You can survive anything. You're exhausted and need some rest.

"You're right," she said out loud to herself. "Go to bed. Things will look brighter in the morning."

After returning her mug to the kitchen and locking up the house, Faith was on her way to bed when she found Bitsy lurking in the hallway outside her room.

"What're you doing still up?" Faith said, placing an arm around her daughter's waist.

"I can't sleep. Something happened today at school that I need to tell you about."

Faith brushed a lock of hair off Bitsy's damp forehead. "Why don't we get in my bed and you can tell me about it?"

"Can I sleep with you?" Bitsy asked, looking up at her with fearful eyes.

"I guess," Faith said in a teasing tone. "Just this once."

189

Hands on shoulders, Faith steered Bitsy into the master bedroom. She threw back the covers, and helped her daughter into bed, climbing in behind her with her clothes on.

"Now tell me what's been bothering you, sweetheart. I don't like it when you're feeling blue."

"Chloe got me in trouble today with Mrs. Granger. Chloe's mean, Mama. I don't like her anymore."

Faith's stomach twisted. "I don't understand. How'd you get in trouble?"

"Well . . . you see, Chloe, who sits behind me in class, was pulling my hair and flicking little balls of paper at me. When I asked her to stop, the teacher got mad at me for disrupting the class." Bitsy drew her knees up to her chest. "I may have been a little loud when I told her to stop. Mrs. Granger said I screamed. I don't remember. I was just so angry."

"Did she send you to the principal's office or make you stand in the corner?"

Bitsy laughed, despite herself. "Stand in the corner?"

"That's what my teachers always did when we got in trouble. We had to stand with our noses in the corner for thirty minutes. That was our version of time out."

"That's funny." Bitsy's face grew serious again. "But no. Mrs. Granger just asked me to be quiet."

A wave of relief washed over Faith. "Then you didn't really get in trouble."

"I felt like I was in trouble." Tears welled in her eyes. "I don't want Mrs. Granger to be mad at me."

Faith took her daughter in her arms. "Oh, sweetheart, she's not mad at you. Mrs. Granger has probably already forgotten about it." It dawned on Faith that her daughter might be upset about another matter entirely and was using the incident at school as a tangible reason to vent. Maybe she'd been spending too much time with the residents. Maybe, like Faith, seeing Bridget's battered face had brought back traumatic memories she wasn't able to process.

"Is there anything else bothering you that you want to talk about?"

"Kinda," Bitsy murmured. "I don't want to be Chloe's friend anymore. But she's turned all of my other friends against me."

"I'm so sorry, honey," Faith said, kissing the top of her daughter's head. "I know how that feels."

"You do?" Bitsy asked, propping herself on her elbow to look at Faith.

"All too well," Faith said, and told her daughter about Cecily, the girl who'd tormented her in the fourth grade. "But I ended up making new friends, who were nicer to me than Cecily had ever been."

"You mean like Tilda and Molly and Rosalie are my new friends?"

"Not exactly, sweetheart. I'm glad you think of the residents as your friends. But you need friends your own age too." Another concern Faith had never considered entered her mind. "You realize the residents won't be living at Lovie's forever. Will you be sad when they leave?"

Bitsy thought about this before answering. "I'll miss them, but I'll be happy for them, because they'll be going home or starting new lives like Molly."

Faith was pleased that her daughter seemed to have a realistic perspective on the residents. "You're a very smart girl," Faith said, touching her daughter's nose. "I want you to promise me you'll try to make new friends your own age."

"There is this one girl in my class," Bitsy said. "Her name is Tracy. She seems kinda lonely. I thought maybe I'd be her friend."

"I bet she'd like that."

Rain began pounding the roof and a loud clap of thunder shook the house, bringing Bitsy closer to Faith. "I'm scared."

"There's nothing to be scared about, sweetheart. The storm will pass. You're safe here with me."

Her daughter's breath was warm against her neck when she said, "Where do you think Molly went on stormy nights when she was living on the streets?"

"I'm sure she found shelter somewhere," Faith said, thinking that *shelter* was probably in the doorway of a dilapidated building. "Fortunately, she's not homeless anymore."

Faith heard her cell phone ringing in another room. "I'd better get that." She rolled off the bed. "Don't go anywhere. I'll be right back."

By the time she located her phone in her purse on the kitchen counter, it had stopped ringing. She realized she had two missed calls from Emilee, one from earlier when she'd been on the porch. She tapped on the number and returned the call.

"Faith!" Emilee yelled over the sound of wind and rain in the background. "Thank goodness. I've been trying to reach you."

"Where are you?" Faith asked, stuffing her finger in her ear to better hear. "I can barely hear you. I take it the storm's bad."

"That's an understatement. I'm in my car on the way to the hospital. My mother had a massive stroke. I'm not sure she's going to make it."

Faith's breath hitched. "I'm so sorry, Emilee. What can I do for you?"

"Pray. That's all anyone can do. I asked Elmer to look out for the residents. I wouldn't go out in this mess unless you have to."

Fear gripped Faith's chest as that nagging feeling of imminent danger returned. "Go! Be with your mother. Text me when you have an update on her condition."

"Will do."

As she was ending the call, she heard a loud crash on the outside of the house near the front door. Seconds later, Bitsy was at her side. "What was that, Mama?"

"I'm not sure, sweetheart. It sounded like a tree falling." With

Bitsy glued to her arm, she walked down the hall and peered out of the sidelights to the right of the front door. "Yep. A tree fell across the driveway."

She tapped on Eli's cell number and pressed the phone to her ear. "Are you on duty tonight, by any chance?" she asked when he answered on the second ring.

His voice was alert. "I can be. What's up?"

She explained about Emilee having to leave the residents alone and the tree blocking her driveway. "I have a feeling that something is terribly wrong. I'm sorry to bother you, but Mike's at the hospital, and I'm sure they're probably swamped because of the storm."

"Why don't I come pick you up. We can drop Bitsy off with Sam on our way to check on the residents."

Faith exhaled a sigh of relief. "You're a lifesaver, Eli. We'll put on our rain gear and be waiting at the front door. Blow your horn when you get here. Hopefully, we can climb over the tree."

"You'll need a flashlight. And be careful."

MOLLY

*M*olly felt like an adolescent who'd been left at home alone for the first time. She waited until she heard the front door bang shut, announcing Emilee's departure, before addressing the others. "Why don't we live a little and stay up past curfew?"

"I'm game!" Jenny said and the others vocalized their agreement.

"This calls for ice cream," Molly said, already on her feet on the way to the kitchen.

Jenny fell in behind her. "I'll help you."

The freezer was stocked with half gallons of ice cream in a variety of flavors. "If the power goes out from the storm, the ice cream will melt," Jenny said.

She flashed Jenny a wicked grin. "And we wouldn't want it to go to waste."

Molly loaded Jenny's arms up with three half gallons of ice cream—one salted caramel, one butter pecan, and one strawberry cheesecake. She grabbed seven spoons from the silverware drawer and followed Jenny back to the sitting room. In their absence, despite the heat and humidity outdoors, the others had turned on the gas logs and slid the furniture back to make room for the group to sit in a circle on the floor in front of the fireplace.

Molly handed everyone a spoon while Jenny removed the lids on the cartons. Passing the cartons around the circle, they savored heaping spoonfuls of ice cream as the storm raged outside the floor-to-ceiling windows.

"I hope everything's okay with Emilee's mother," Bridget said with a faraway look as though thinking of her own mother.

The group let out a collective mm-hmm.

"You know," Tilda said, licking her spoon and pointing it at the ceiling. "I've been thinking a lot about our discussion with Dr. Robin earlier. And what she said about us being a special group and staying friends after we leave here. I live in downtown Charleston not far from the harbor, and I have a carriage house I would like to offer to anyone who needs a place to live." Her gaze landed on Rosalie. "This might be a perfect solution for your needs."

Rosalie eyed her wearily. "I'm not sure I can afford the rent on a carriage house."

"But that's the point. I wouldn't charge you rent. I would only ask that you check on me from time to time, maybe have coffee with me some mornings and dinner every now and then. I'm not looking for a constant companion. Having someone occupying the carriage house might ease the anxiety of living alone."

"Really, Tilda?" Rosalie got to her knees with her hands clasped together. "That would be so perfect. I'll water your plants. Run errands for you. Whatever you need."

Tilda smiled. "The only thing I'll need is your sunny disposition to brighten my days." She wagged a finger at Rosalie. "But no wild parties."

Rosalie placed her hand over her heart. "I promise. My partying days are over."

"If there are any other takers," Tilda said, "the carriage house has two bedrooms, and I have plenty of spare guest rooms in the main house."

"The same goes for me," Caroline said. "I have two spare bedrooms in my cabin if anyone wants to help me work my farm in exchange for rent. I can't afford to pay anyone until I start making a profit. And I'm not sure how long that will be."

"How far out of town is your farm?" Molly asked, thinking she could help on the farm when she wasn't working at Sweeney's.

"About ten minutes," Caroline answered.

"That won't work for me," Molly said, lowering her head. She would need a car and a current driver's license, and she had neither.

"I might be interested," Jenny mumbled. "I'm not sure what I'll be doing when I leave here. Only that I won't be returning to Sumter."

Hope filled Caroline's face. "Think about it. We can talk more about it tomorrow if you'd like."

Molly noticed that Bridget had begun to fidget and Paula to twitch. It was inconsiderate of them to talk about moving on with their lives when these two had only just begun the process of healing.

She elbowed Bridget beside her. "Are you okay?"

"I'm fine. I just really want to check on my mama. Does anyone have a cell phone I can use? I left mine upstairs in my room." Bridget's eyes traveled the circle, pausing for each resident to respond. Molly had never owned a cell phone. Jenny and Caroline had destroyed theirs. Rosalie's mama had confiscated hers when she left home. Tilda's battery was dead. Paula was the only one with a phone, but she did not offer to loan it to Bridget.

"Please! It won't take but a second." Bridget fished a scrap of paper from the pocket of her dress. "I have the number to the nurses' station right here."

Paula reluctantly handed her phone over to Bridget who took

one look at the screen and handed it back. "No cell service. Because of the storm, I guess."

"Why don't you use the phone on Emilee's desk?" Jenny suggested.

"Press nine to dial out," Paula added.

"How do you know that?" Jenny asked.

Paula shrugged. "Because I've done an extensive investigation of the grounds."

With head to the side and lips pursed, Rosalie asked, "Why would you do that?"

"Because of the robbery," Paula said. "Being prepared for an intruder lessens my anxiety."

"Oh right," Molly said with a nod. "A survival tactic."

Bridget hauled herself up off the floor and crossed the room. She turned to the right, but instead of continuing down the hallway to the phone, she froze in place. Her hand flew to her mouth, she let out a blood-curdling scream, and dropped to her knees. A streak of lightning lit up the rooms for a split second before everything went pitch-black.

"What in the world, Bridget? Are you okay?" When Paula aimed her phone's flashlight across the room, Bridget was crawling on the floor toward them.

"My stepfather's inside the house!" Bridget hissed. "In the hallway. He's got a knife."

"Are you sure you didn't imagine it?" Jenny's question was answered by a loud crashing noise and the sounds of glass shattering and a man's whispered cusses.

"Follow me!" Paula waved them on as she hurried, crouched down, from the parlor to the solarium. Molly had never noticed that the two floor-to-ceiling windows directly behind the sofa in the solarium were actually French doors. With Paula in the lead and Caroline bringing up the rear, the residents climbed in single-file over the sofa and escaped the solarium.

Paula ran away from the porch, into the storm. "Where should we go?" she shouted to the group when they were a safe distance from the house.

"To the cottage!" Molly hollered back.

"I don't know where it is." Paula handed Molly the phone. "Show me the way."

A streak of lightning cracked the sky and Molly took off running toward the woods. She'd only been to the cottage once, on the day Tilda went missing, but in spite of the blinding rain, she found the entrance to the tunnel of undergrowth right away. She trudged through the mud in the clearing in front of the cottage and shoved the door open. One by one, they fell into the small living room. Caroline slammed the door behind them, collapsing against it as she struggled to catch her breath. Their hair and clothes were drenched, the excess water dripping on the worn oak floorboards of the cottage.

"He'll never find us in here," Rosalie said.

"I wouldn't be so sure." Paula shone her light about the room, pausing in the far corner. "Looks like he's already been here. And left behind his provisions."

"Is that a loaf of bread?" Jenny asked, squinting in the darkness. "Earlier today, Cook was complaining about a loaf that had gone missing from her kitchen."

Caroline left the door and went to inspect the items. She held them up one at a time—a roll of duct tape, an empty 24-ounce can of Olde English 800 malt liquor, and a battery-operated lantern. She flipped the switch and dim light filled the room. "Thank goodness it works."

"That's the kind of beer Vern drinks," Bridget said, her good eye on the empty can.

"We can't stay here. He'll come after us." Paula ran for the door, reaching for the knob. The knob turned, but when she tried to open it, the door wouldn't budge. She yanked and tugged at it frantically, with no result. "It's stuck."

Molly felt her own panic rising. "There's gotta be another way out of here."

"Everybody stay calm, and let's search the house." Caroline led the way with her lantern as they traveled from room to room. The windows were either painted or swollen shut. And the only other exterior door in the kitchen was locked with a deadbolt, but there was no key to be found.

Back in the living room, Tilda said, "Look on the bright side. If we can't get out, he can't get in."

"You don't know that!" Paula's tone was nearing hysteria. "He's gonna bust his way in and beat us just like the Marcus brothers did to me. Look what that maniac did to her face," she said, pointing at Bridget.

Five sets of eyes followed Paula's finger to where Bridget stood off to the side, her purple eye a stark contrast to her pale face. She let out a yelp and doubled over.

Jenny rushed to the girl's side. "What's wrong, Bridget?"

"My water just broke," Bridget said, clutching her belly.

Jenny's jaw hit the floor. "Wait, what? Did you say your water broke, as in you're pregnant?"

Molly had thought from the beginning that there was something fishy about the girl, like maybe she was hiding something.

"Yes!" Bridget cried, and fell to the floor, rocking back and forth on her knees in pain as the first contractions hit her.

Jenny waited for the pain to subside. "So, you knew you were pregnant?"

"Of course I knew I was pregnant," Bridget said, sucking in air. "But no one else knows. Being fat has its benefits."

Caroline knelt down beside Bridget on the floor. "Bridget, honey. You need to answer some questions so we know how to help you. Have you seen a doctor?"

Bridget shook her head.

"Do you have any idea when the baby is due?"

She grimaced. "Not for sure. I think it's too early."

Jenny leaned over, hands propped on knees. "Do you know who the baby daddy is?"

"Vern is the daddy. He did this to me! I don't even want to see the baby. I'm getting rid of it as soon as I get it outta my body."

Molly knew all too well what it was like to have a creepy stepfather—in her case it had been her foster dad—take advantage of her. Only Molly had been fortunate enough not to get pregnant.

Bridget closed her good eye shut. "Oh! Oh! I need to push."

The residents looked at one another in horror over the top of Bridget's head. "Has anyone ever delivered a baby?" Caroline asked.

Molly slowly raised her hand. "I ain't actually delivered one myself, but I've seen it done several times."

Caroline appeared doubtful, but she held her shoulders back and sucked in a deep breath. "All right, then. We'll have to do the best we can. Molly and I will stay here with Bridget. Paula, keep trying to get through to 9-1-1 on your cell phone. Try from different spots around the house, including the attic. The rest of you go search this house for anything we can use to wrap the baby in."

"We can use my shirt." Rosalie attempted to peel her wet shirt off her body. "Or maybe not."

Tilda, Rosalie, and Jenny took off on their scavenger hunt, scurrying about the house looking in closets and cabinets, while Paula waltzed around the downstairs with her phone before climbing the stairs to the attic.

Molly sank to the floor beside Bridget, doing her best not to think about the jammed door or the evil lurking beyond it. Memories from what seemed like another lifetime flooded her. Memories of being locked in a basement waiting for a lunatic to come for her. At least she wasn't alone this time. Although she almost wished she were. Seven women breathing hard and sweating in wet clothes with no ventilation was causing the heat and humidity to creep up in the cramped quarters.

The evening had been so pleasant with bingo and eating ice cream by the fire. Then thirty minutes later, they found themselves locked in a cottage delivering a baby for a young woman, no more than a child herself, who they didn't even know was pregnant, and being stalked by her deranged stepfather who happened to be the baby daddy.

Bridget cried out in agony. "I feel the baby's head. Please! God! Let me push!"

Molly cast an uncertain gaze at Caroline. "You can do this," Caroline said. "I have faith in you, Molly. We all do."

Molly pulled Bridget's dress up and felt her belly. It was hard as a rock, and she could feel the baby moving inside of her. Bridget didn't look nine months pregnant. But what did Molly know? She'd never been pregnant. *If* the baby was coming prematurely, Molly questioned whether they could save it.

"Paula's been up in that attic an awful long time," Molly said, casting her eyes to the ceiling.

As if on cue, they heard banging overhead followed by the sound of a hard object rolling across the attic floorboards.

Jenny appeared at Caroline's side with an old flannel pillowcase she'd found at the back of a closet. "We've looked everywhere. This is all we could find."

"Thank you," Caroline said, taking the pillowcase from her. "Will you please check on Paula? See what that noise was and if she's had any luck getting through to 9-1-1."

As Jenny was heading up to the attic, Paula came barreling down the steps with a newel post from the railing at the top of the stairs, holding it tight against her shoulder like a baseball bat. "I saw him through the upstairs window. He's right outside the cottage. He's coming for us. And I aim to be ready." Paula positioned herself by the door with the newel post suspended in midair.

Seconds later, every pair of eyes in the cottage watched the doorknob turn. When he couldn't open it, Vern pounded on the door. "Let me in. I don't want no trouble. I just want what's rightfully mine. Send Bridget on outta there and we'll be on our way."

The residents stared at one another, but nobody uttered a word or moved a muscle except Paula who altered her stance, spreading her feet farther apart and lifting her weapon higher, preparing to strike.

When a contraction ripped through Bridget's body, she could no longer remain silent. "Damn you to hell, Vern Parry," she screamed. "You're gonna get what's coming to you for what you did to my mama and me."

"You can't hide from me, little girl. We're family, you and me."

He threw his weight against the door repeatedly, and when that didn't work, he started kicking. On the sixth kick, the door splintered, and with another thrust of his body, the door banged open. In a rush of cool air, the monster of a man was inside the cottage with them. Paula went after him, swinging. She knocked the butcher knife out of his hand, and then aimed for his head. He turned, but when he tried to flee the cottage, she landed a solid hit on his right shoulder, knocking him to his knees. She attacked him, beating his back and cracking him over the head with the newel post.

"Stop!" Jenny shouted. "You're going to kill him."

"That's the idea," Paula said, taking another whack.

Jenny and Rosalie charged Paula, wrestling the post from her hands. The threesome stared down at Vern's unmoving body, and from inside the cottage, Molly could see blood pouring from a gash in the side of his head.

"Is he dead?" Tilda asked, frozen in fear just inside the door.

Jenny leaned down and felt his pulse. "He's still alive."

Caroline, who'd been coaching Bridget through contractions during the commotion, ordered Jenny and Rosalie to go back up to the house to call for help. "And hurry. With any luck the main phone line is still in service."

28

FAITH

*B*itsy was none too happy at being made to stay with her Aunt Sam.

"Please, Mama," she begged. "Let me go with you. I promise I won't get in the way. The residents need me."

Faith placed her hands on the side of Bitsy's face, cupping her cheeks. "What the residents need is for you to be safe. Which is why you're staying here with Sam. I'll call her as soon as we know anything."

As she hugged her daughter, she mouthed a thank you to Sam over the top of her head before hurrying back to her brother-in-law's patrol car. Eli had met Sam when he was helping Faith through her ordeals with her abusive first husband—the beatings and threats on her life. He was gentle and compassionate, always willing to help a friend—or in the case of the Sweeneys, a family member—in need.

The streets were flooded as they drove through town, and they made more than one detour to bypass fallen trees. Stoplights were out and sirens from rescue vehicles blared as they sped past them. All off-duty police officers had been called into work, but only one unit had been available to dispatch to Lovie's Home. So far, Eli had heard nothing back from them.

"I'm not worried yet," Eli said. "On a night like tonight, communication is tough."

"Which explains why I can't get through to Elmer. I'm sure everything is all right . . ." Her voice trailed off. She didn't believe everything was all right. With each passing minute, the feeling that something was terribly wrong was growing more urgent.

By the time they arrived at the home, the rain had slowed to a drizzle but streaks of lightning were still visible off in the distance. The patrol car was parked under the porte cochère with two uniformed officers seated inside. Policemen Pittman and Porter—both with rugged good looks, neither of them older than thirty—got out of the car to greet them. They began speaking at once, explaining that they'd been trying to get through to Eli on the radio and that they'd conducted a thorough search of the house but not a soul was in sight.

"How can that be?" Faith asked.

When they started talking in unison again, Eli held up his hand to silence them. "One at a time. Porter, you go first."

Porter removed his hat and scratched his head. "It's the darnedest thing, Detective. It's like a ghost house in there. The gas logs are on in the fireplace and cartons of melted ice cream with seven spoons were left on the floor, as though the seven people eating that ice cream just up and left in a hurry."

"Have you seen my security guard?" Faith asked. "An older man with balding gray hair and pink chubby cheeks. His name is Elmer. Drives a white pickup with blue lights on top and Security written on the side."

"We haven't seen anyone that matches that description," Pittman said.

Faith scanned the property, as far as she could see in the dark. "Did you check the toolshed?"

"Yes'm," Pittman said with a firm nod. "It's empty."

Her eyes lingered on the shed. "Something's not right. What the—" she said, taking off for the shed at a jog.

"Faith! Wait!" Eli called out as he and the other two officers ran after her. "Let us handle this."

Faith slowed her pace, letting the policemen catch up with her. "I see the rear bumper of the security truck sticking out from behind the shed. Something's wrong, Eli. Elmer always parks the truck beside the kitchen door."

"Stay right here," Eli insisted, removing his revolver from his hip holster. "Let us check it out first."

Ignoring him, Faith followed on their heels as the three officers approached the truck with caution.

"There's someone in there," Pittman said, peeking through the window. "On the floorboard over here."

When he opened the passenger door, Faith saw Elmer on the floor of the car, his feet and hands bound with gray duct tape.

"Is he alive? I can't look." Faith placed her hand over her eyes. "Please, God, tell me he's alive."

"He's alive," Eli said.

It took all three of the policemen to help Elmer off the floorboard and out of the truck. He was visibly shaken, but otherwise unhurt.

Elmer started talking as soon as Eli ripped the duct tape from his lips. "He attacked me from behind. I never saw him coming. Got a glimpse of him, though, when he was taping my hands. Large man, angry red face with pitch-black eyes."

"What time was this?" Eli asked.

Elmer consulted his watch. "Must've been around nine o'clock. Right after Emilee called to say she was leaving and that the residents were in the sitting room cleaning up from their bingo game."

"Can you call for more help?" Faith asked Eli. "We need to search the grounds."

She'd started toward the house when she noticed two figures

running toward her. As they grew nearer, she recognized Jenny and Rosalie and called their names as she hurried to meet them near the dinner bell.

"Call an ambulance," Jenny said, as she struggled to catch her breath. "Bridget's having a baby."

Faith shook her head, unsure she'd heard correctly. "Did you just say—"

"Yes!" Rosalie said. "We need two ambulances, one for Bridget's stepfather. He came after us with a butcher knife but Paula took him out. He's unconscious."

Eli appeared at Faith's side, his satellite phone pressed to his ear, barking orders at dispatch to send two ambulances.

"Where are they?" he asked.

"In the cottage," Jenny answered.

Eli yelled across the yard to his officers, "We're going to the cottage. Wait here for the buses."

With Jenny in the lead, they sprinted a hundred yards to the tunnel of undergrowth. As they entered the clearing, Faith saw two figures, dimly illuminated and huddled together on the floor inside the cottage. Paula, a butcher knife dangling from her hand at her side, stood over a man's motionless body on the ground just outside the front door. Eli rushed to the man's aid while Faith continued up the steps, stopping in the doorway at the sight of Bridget sprawled out on the floor and Molly holding a bundle in her arms.

Molly looked up at her. "She's tiny, but she appears to be in good health. I tied the umbilical cord, and delivered the placenta. I cleaned it up with my top."

Faith noticed that Molly was naked from the waist up except for her bra. She entered the cottage and knelt down beside Bridget who was shivering uncontrollably, her teeth chattering and face covered in perspiration. "She's going into shock."

"Caroline and Tilda have gone to the house for blankets,"

Molly said. "I'm surprised you didn't see them. They should be back any minute. We need to get her to the hospital."

"An ambulance is already on the way."

Caroline and Tilda arrived with stacks of blankets. Caroline tucked one around Bridget's trembling body while Tilda draped another around Molly's bare shoulders.

Faith took a blanket from Caroline and draped it over her arms, holding them out to Molly. "Let me hold the baby while you tend to Bridget."

When Molly placed the newborn in her blanketed arms, Faith was overcome with mixed emotions. Joy over the baby, so tiny and vulnerable, the true miracle of life. And admiration for her residents, these broken women, who during the past few hours had bonded together to overcome great hardships. Molly, a homeless woman, who'd delivered a newborn baby. And Paula, the victim of an armed robbery, who'd conquered her fears by fighting back against her attacker.

Faith walked the baby to the doorway. "Bridget's going into shock, Eli. We need to get her to the hospital. Maybe we should drive her ourselves instead of waiting for the ambulance."

At that instant, Elmer appeared in the clearing followed by a single-file line of paramedics. Faith counted six of them. The paramedics split into two groups, one attending to Bridget and the other to the evil stepfather. Within minutes, they'd lifted Bridget onto a stretcher and carried her out of the cottage and through the tunnel.

One of the two female paramedics took the baby from Faith. "Can I ride with you in the ambulance?" Faith asked. "I don't want Bridget to be alone."

"You'll have to ride in the front with the driver," the paramedic said over her shoulder on the way out.

Faith stopped to speak to Eli who was hovering near the paramedics as they worked on Bridget's stepfather. "I'm going to the hospital in the ambulance. I'll come back in Mike's car once she's settled. Could one of your officers stay with the other residents until I get back?"

"I'll do better than that," Eli said with one eye on his prisoner. "I'll stay here with them and send Porter and Pittman to the hospital with this deadbeat."

"Bless you, Eli." She gave his cheek a peck and turned toward the tunnel.

When she exited the other side, the paramedics were loading Bridget into the back of the ambulance. "Will you please radio ahead to Dr. Mike Neilson in the ER? He's my husband, and he's familiar with this woman's case."

In the front passenger seat beside the driver, Faith stared out the window as they drove across the lawn to the gravel driveway. Aside from a few downed tree limbs, there didn't appear to be any major storm damage on the property. But there was no telling what kind of emotional toll the events of the night would have on the residents.

The short ride to the hospital was made longer by the same detours she'd encountered earlier with Eli. Mike was waiting for them when they arrived. As the paramedics unloaded the teenager from the ambulance, he said, "This explains why Bridget refused treatment. I suspected she was hiding something, but a baby?"

"I'll give her credit," Faith said. "She did a fine job of it. Poor thing. She must've been terrified."

As they followed the gurney down the hall, Faith gave her husband the rundown of everything that'd happened that evening.

"How does Bridget feel about the baby?" Mike asked.

"According to the other residents, she doesn't want anything to do with it," Faith said. "But I'd like to hear her say it herself."

They dodged a frenzied nurse scurrying into one of the examining rooms with a bag of IV fluids. "Looks like your night has been chaotic as well."

"You have no idea," Mike said, shaking his head. "It's been one of the craziest I ever remember. If I wasn't ready to leave this job before, I am now."

When the orderlies wheeled the gurney into an examining room, Faith and Mike entered behind them. Faith tugged on the sleeve of her husband's white coat. "I'll be out in the waiting room. I don't want to leave until I know she's okay."

"You should stay back here with her," Mike said. "She's young and scared, and I know she'll appreciate the friendly face."

"If you think so," Faith said, taking a position in the corner of the cubicle, out of the way, while Mike and the nurses worked on Bridget. The obstetrician on call, who came in to examine her, pronounced everything intact. "Whoever performed the delivery did a good job."

Faith thought, *If only you knew.*

Bridget was semiconscious and incoherent at first, but over time, as they pumped fluids into her and the medications began to work their magic, she became more lucid. Faith didn't speak, just stroked her arm every so often to remind Bridget of her presence. Bridget eventually drifted off to sleep, as did Faith, shortly thereafter, sitting straight up in a chair.

When Mike woke Faith sometime later, the mayhem in the hallway outside the cubicle had quieted down.

"She'll sleep for a while," Mike said, checking Bridget's vitals. "As soon as we have a vacancy upstairs, we'll get her into a room."

Faith stood and stretched. "Where's the baby?"

"In the nursery. I checked on her a little while ago. She's on the small size, but by all indications, she's full term."

"What happens now? With the baby, I mean." Faith thought about how she'd always longed to have more children, but the doctors had warned her against it after a difficult pregnancy with Bitsy. And adoption had been out of the question considering all the younger couples waiting in line to adopt healthy babies. But what about now?

"Robin should counsel Bridget, to help her decide if giving up the baby is really the right choice," Mike said, finally breaking her reverie. "If Bridget decides to go through with it, we'll help her identify an agency to facilitate the adoption." He glanced at the clock on the wall. "It's almost morning. Why don't we go to Lovie's and check on the other residents? I'm worried about them. I'd feel better seeing for myself that everyone is okay. We'll come back to the hospital later. I'll leave word that no one is to speak to Bridget without one of us present."

29

FAITH

*D*espite the early hour, the day's activities were already in full swing when Faith and Mike arrived at the home. She looked a rumpled mess in her day-old clothes and unkempt hair, but Mike look as handsome as ever in his scrubs. She would miss seeing him in his scrubs when he retired in three days.

Molly greeted them in the kitchen. "We haven't been to bed yet," she said with a snicker. "We were so keyed up, we talked all night, long after Eli finished asking all his questions and zonked out on the sofa. He's still there now, dead to the world. He's a hunky one, that Eli. Sam's a lucky gal."

Faith had never seen Molly so vibrant and full of herself. Delivering Bridget's baby had given her the final boost of confidence she needed to go out into the real world.

"She is that," Tilda said from the stove where she stood stirring a pot. "Not only is he handsome, he's patient and kind."

"I'm so proud of the two of you," Faith said, giving each of them a hug in turn. "You performed a miracle last night. You delivered a baby and saved Bridget's life."

Tilda pointed at Molly. "She's the real hero."

Molly's face beamed red. "I only did what I'd seen done on the streets a few times."

Mike squeezed her shoulder. "Well, you done good. I've delivered many a baby in my day. It's no small task in the emergency room where I have all the equipment I need. But in a cottage with a violet man beating down the door . . ."

Faith smiled. "You were all very brave. You deserve medals of honor."

Mike moved over to the stove and investigated the contents of Tilda's pot. "I love grits. And I'm starving. I hope you made extra for me."

"I made plenty," Tilda said, looking up at him. "The power's still out, though. Thank goodness we've got a gas stove. I've got the kettle on for instant coffee. Should be boiling any second."

"Cook called to say she's running late," Molly explained. "Her roof leaked during the storm. Sounds like she's got a mess on her hands. Tilda got all the eggs out of the henhouse. Do you think it's okay to open the fridge? I'd like to get some bacon, but I don't wanna let all the cold air out."

"Open it once and grab everything you need," Mike said. "But make it quick."

Molly nodded. "Good thinking."

Faith peeked into the empty dining room. "Where're the other residents?"

Molly tossed a hand in the air. "Around here somewhere, unless they gave up and went to bed."

When the kettle whistled, Faith poured boiling water into two of the mugs Tilda had prepared with instant coffee granules. Adding raw sugar and dry creamer to both, she handed one of the mugs to Mike. "Let's go see if we can find them," she said and led the way out of the kitchen.

They passed through the empty dining room to the parlor where Eli was sound asleep on the sofa with his mouth wide open. Through the windows, Faith could see Jenny and Caroline in the rockers on the porch with their heads close together and serious expressions on their faces. They moved on to the solarium where Paula sat perfectly still, with her body draped in a nylon cape, while Rosalie danced around her, clipping at her hair like a true professional.

"Well now," Faith said. "Isn't this a sight for sore eyes?"

"I know, right?" Rosalie said, looking up and smiling. "Can you believe she's actually letting me cut her hair? I'm trying to convince her to color it. I'm thinking a mixture of highlights and lowlights to get a tone in between blonde and brunette."

Paula gave Faith a sheepish grin. "Do you think I should let her do it?"

"Absolutely! A new hairdo to celebrate the new you." Faith held Paula's gaze. "Last night . . . what you did . . . you are one brave woman. I hope you're proud of yourself."

Paula lifted her chin. "I don't know what came over me. Anger, I guess. And outrage that the same thing could be happening all over again, that I was once again vulnerable to a vicious attacker. When I thought about all the pain I'd suffered, something inside of me snapped. My adrenaline kicked in, and I went after him."

Mike gave her a fist bump. "And you saved the lives of six other people as a result."

"I just hope I never have to do it again," Paula said.

"I hope not either," Faith said. "You've certainly encountered your share of dangerous men to last a lifetime. But if you do, I have no doubt but what you'll handle it with the same courage you showed last night."

Paula's eyes glistened with unshed tears. "Your faith in me means a lot."

Mike turned to Faith. "I want to see this cottage. Will you show it to me?"

"Sure. Why not? But I'm warning you there's not much to see."

They left the solarium, retracing their steps through the

parlor, and exited the house via the front door, waving at Jenny and Caroline as they crossed the porch to the lawn.

When they reached the tunnel, Mike eyed the opening with skepticism. "You mean it's in there?" he asked and she nodded. "No wonder I never noticed it before."

They were careful not to spill their coffee as they ducked through the tunnel to the clearing. "According to the survey, this once belonged to the caretaker," Faith said as they stood sipping coffee and staring at the cottage.

"Why doesn't anyone live here now?"

Faith cut her eyes at him. "Like who?"

"Like us."

Her mouth fell open. "Are you serious? I've thought about living on the grounds. A lot, actually. Not necessarily in this cottage, because it's way too small. It would make our lives so much easier."

"The idea makes perfect sense." Mike turned to her. "You've been running yourself ragged, wanting to be two places at once. And I've grown increasingly more attached the estate. Especially after last night. I couldn't wait to get here this morning to check on the residents."

When Faith's phone rang, she removed it from her back pocket and read the screen. "This is Emilee. I need to talk to her. Why don't you have a look around inside."

She waited for Mike to push open the splintered door and enter the cottage before accepting the call. "How's your mother?"

"Not great," Emilee said. "She survived the stroke, but she has considerable paralysis on her left side. The risk is high that she'll have another one."

The sadness in Emilee's voice broke Faith's heart. The pain of her own mother's illness and death was still fresh, but Faith had been too preoccupied since the ribbon-cutting ceremony to dwell on her loss.

"I'm so sorry, Emilee. I'll be praying for her. And for you. Is there anything I can do to help?"

"Thanks, but no," Emilee said with a sigh. "She has a long recovery ahead of her. I know this is inconvenient, and I hate to do this to you, Faith, but I have to quit my job. I need to be with her. She has no one else."

Faith tightened her grip on the phone. "Of course. I understand. Your mother comes first."

"I'll come by later this afternoon for my things," Emilee said and ended the call.

Faith dropped to the front steps, burying her face in her hands as she considered the repercussions of losing her live-in caregiver. Mike found her there five minutes later when he emerged from the cabin.

He sat down next to her, setting his empty mug on the brick steps. "What's wrong?"

"Emilee just quit her job. Her mother's in bad shape, and she needs to take care of her."

"That's not good," he said. "And it leaves you in a bit of a bind."

"That's an understatement. Especially after last night. I'd already decided to add additional security. A live-in caregiver is a must. I'll have to fill in until I can find someone to replace Emilee. I'm sorry, Mike." She rested her head on his shoulder. "You didn't bargain for all this when you married me."

"When I married you, I made a commitment to support you in every way. I told you not ten minutes ago that I'd grown attached to this place. You may not want to hear this, and this may not be the right time to say it, but I take Emilee's leaving as yet another sign for us to make a move."

She lifted her head to look at him. "You can't seriously mean for us to move into the cabin?"

"Only while our house is under construction."

"What house, Mike?" Faith asked, frustrated with trying to

read his mind. "What are you talking about? Just come right out and say it."

"I'm talking about clearing an area of forest a little closer to the house and building a proper caretaker's cottage with three bedrooms, a large living area, adjacent kitchen, and a huge screened porch with a bench swing, picnic table, and lots of rocking chairs."

Faith shook her head. "That's a beautiful dream, honey. But it won't work. Lovie's is already struggling financially. Last night's storm proved how much we need a generator. I don't know why we didn't think of installing one when we were doing renovations. No telling how much one will cost. We simply can't afford to build a caretaker's house."

"No, sweetheart, you don't understand. I'm talking about selling our house and using the proceeds to buy the lot from the estate and build the cottage. When, and if, we ever decide to leave here, we'll sell the cottage back to the estate." He stood and pulled Faith to her feet. "Just think about it. This would solve all our problems."

"You're right about that. A lot of them, anyway." Jumping to her feet, Faith paced in circles, with her mug dangling from her thumb, as she formulated a plan. "If I hired a cleaning crew to clean the cottage, we could move in as early as this weekend. I could pay a tree service to clear out the trees and undergrowth so we'd be in plain sight from the main house. Bitsy would certainly love it." She slapped her thigh as another thought came to mind. "You know what's even better? I could hire Molly to take over the Salt Life program from Jamie. She could work at Sweeney's in the mornings and here in the afternoons. Instead of paying her, I could let her live in Emilee's room for free."

Mike rose off the steps to face her. "Which would give you a live-in caretaker inside the actual house in case of immediate emergencies. She certainly proved herself last night."

Faith leaped into his arms, spilling the remaining drops of her coffee down the front of his scrubs. "You're brilliant, you know that?"

"You may have mentioned it before," he said, brushing the dribble of coffee off his scrubs.

"Let's go tell Molly. She'll be so excited. And relieved."

She turned to leave but he grabbed her by the arm. "Wait! There's something else we should discuss. We always suspected an opportunity to adopt a baby might present itself through my association with the emergency room. That very thing has happened with Bridget's baby. Are you interested in pursuing it?"

She looked up at her husband, her eyes wide. "Are you?"

He shrugged. "I'm pretty content with the way things are now. But it's now or never."

With a decisiveness she'd never known before, Faith said no. "A year ago, I would have jumped at the opportunity. But so much has changed. Like you, I'm satisfied with my life the way it is now. I consider the residents my family. My grown children."

Mike scooped her off her feet. "You mean *our* grown children."

She wrapped her arms tight around his neck, smothering his face with kisses. "Mike Neilson, you are an angel from above. I promise you, we'll have a meaningful life here."

"I have no doubt about it. We are blessed to have the opportunity to make a difference in the lives of others."

With Faith swatting away errant tree branches, Mike carried her back through the tunnel and all the way up to the porch. When they entered the house, the residents were gathered around the dining table with Eli at the head. Molly and Tilda presented bowls of sliced cantaloupe and steaming hot grits and platters of scrambled eggs, hickory-smoked bacon, and whole grain bread slathered with homemade orange marmalade.

"This is delicious," Eli said, breaking a slice of crispy bacon in half and stuffing it into his mouth.

"Tilda did all the cooking," Molly said. "I only sliced the cantaloupe."

"You've been holding out on us, Tilda," Faith said. "Why didn't you tell us you had such talents in the kitchen?"

Tilda's face turned bright red. "I'm far from talented, but I enjoy cooking. Unfortunately, I never had much practice. When Frank was in office, we either ate out or our cook prepared our meals."

Faith tore off a piece of bread. "Are you familiar with a gourmet market in Charleston called Tasty Provisions?"

Tilda nodded. "I know it well."

"My friend Heidi Butler owns it. If you ever want a part-time job, Tasty Provisions would be a fun place for you to work."

Tilda's face brightened. "I'll keep that in mind."

"Guess what, Faith?" Without waiting for a response, Rosalie continued, "Tilda is letting me live in her carriage house for free while I attend cosmetology school."

Faith clapped her hands together as if the thought had never occurred to her. "That's wonderful news."

Jenny said, "And I'm moving with Caroline to her farm. I'm going to help get her business started. At least I hope I am. If my parents don't freak out when I tell them."

This unexpected news delighted Faith. "That is also exciting. Give your parents a chance, Jenny. They might surprise you."

"You don't know my parents," Jenny said under her breath.

Faith noticed the smile disappear from Molly's face at the same time Paula lowered her head. "Don't worry, Molly. We'll talk more after breakfast, but I've come up with a solution to your housing problem that I think you're going to like." She shifted her gaze to Paula. "Just think how far you've come in twenty-four hours. With Robin's help, you'll be out of here and on your way home in no time."

Molly and Paula perked right up, and for the rest of breakfast, the talk centered on Bridget, her baby, and the vile stepfather.

Eli cleaned his plate of three helpings. "My wife fancies herself the best cook in Prospect. But that was one of the best meals I've ever eaten." He pushed back from the table, rubbing his belly. "Nothing better than simple cooking when the ingredients are fresh."

Molly batted her lashes at him and Tilda smiled sweetly.

"I best be getting home. I need to shower before heading to the hospital to check on Vern."

"Speaking of Vern, assuming he doesn't die, what will happen to him now?" Jenny asked.

"According to my sources, his injuries were not life-threatening," Eli said. "He'll remain in the hospital with guards at his door until he's well enough to be transferred to prison."

"How did he even find Bridget?" Rosalie asked.

"As far as we can tell, he used the family tracker on her iPhone to ping her phone," Eli said.

There were arguments on both sides as to whether residents should be allowed to have cell phones. At the next board meeting, Faith would revisit the issue. Perhaps they would implement detailed rules regarding usage.

Eli stood to go. "Faith, may I have a word with you and Mike before I leave."

"Sure." Faith rose from the table. "Ladies, I'll be back to help clean up in a minute."

Faith and Mike walked Eli down the hall and out the back door to his cruiser.

"You need to prepare yourself," Eli said. "The press has gotten word of what went on here last night. They'll be beating your door down before long."

Faith fell back against the side of his car. "But they can't do that. My residents have a right to their privacy."

"Obviously, you'll want to keep Bridget and the baby out of the limelight. But I get the impression they're more interested in Molly and Paula and the way the residents worked together as a team. If you want, I can station patrol cars at the street to prevent the press from trespassing, but I would think about the human-interest side of the story before you make that decision."

"What do you mean?" Faith asked.

"I mean, this story, if you spin the right light on it, could bring you positive publicity."

A light bulb went off inside Faith's head. "Which could bring Lovie's the financial support we so desperately need."

30

MOLLY

*o electricity meant no air-conditioning. And by the time they'd finished eating breakfast, the heat had begun to build inside the house. Molly went from room to room opening windows. As she was opening the last window in the solarium, the power blinked on and recycled air blasted from the vents. She chuckled to herself. *Go figure.* Then she decided to ask Faith to turn off the air-conditioning so they could enjoy the cool fresh air brought in by the storm.

When she tapped lightly on her office door, Faith's muffled voice called for her to come in.

"The power's back on," Molly said, entering the office.

"I can see that." Faith gestured at her computer that was in the process of powering back on.

"I opened all the windows. The weather is so nice, I was wondering if you would turn off the air-conditioning for a while."

"Good idea. It'll save on the electricity bill." Faith reached for her cell. "I'll text Mike to do it. Have a seat. I was going to send for you, anyway. We have a few things to discuss."

221

Molly experienced what Robin called a flight or fright response. Faith had mentioned during breakfast something about a possible solution to her housing problem. She'd thought she was ready to leave Lovie's. But she wasn't so sure anymore. Her legs felt weak as she stumbled to one of two chairs opposite Faith's desk.

"I have bad news, good news, and interesting news," Faith said. "Let's start with the bad news, which is also the good news. Emilee is leaving us to take care of her sick mother."

"Oh no!" Molly said. "What will we do without Emilee?"

"Well." Faith placed her hands on her desk. "Mike and I have decided to move to the estate. We feel this is the best scenario for everyone, for the residents as well as for us. We'll live in the cottage until we can build a bigger caretaker's cottage closer to the house. I plan to hire a part-time receptionist to take over Emilee's daytime duties, which leaves her room above the kitchen vacant. I thought you might be interested in living there."

Molly felt a rush of adrenaline. "Do you mean it, really? That would be a dream come true for me." Her shoulders slumped. "But I can't afford to pay you rent and it ain't right for me to live here for free."

"That's the catch," Faith said. "You wouldn't be living here for free."

Molly's heart sank. She knew it was too good to be true.

"I'd like for you to take over the Salt Life program in exchange for room and board." Faith leaned forward and lowered her voice. "I can't afford to pay you. We're experiencing some . . . let's just say we're struggling to get our feet on the ground financially."

Molly remembered what Rosalie had told them about money being tight at the home. More than anything, she wanted to stay at Lovie's. But, as much as she would like to help Faith, she would never get ahead in life if she didn't earn some money. "But what about Sam? I'm supposed to start work at Sweeney's on Monday."

"Timewise, the Salt Life program shouldn't interfere with your job at Sweeney's. Unless you feel you can't do both."

She moved to the edge of her chair. "I can do both, all right. The Salt Life program isn't work. It's fun."

"Then it's settled," Faith said as a smile spread across her face. "All we have to do now is figure out your transportation to work. You'll need to update your driver's license at some point."

She'd once had a driver's license, back in the day when she worked for Ed at the diner and he needed her to make occasional deliveries in his van. But that had been a long time ago and she wasn't too keen on the idea of driving a car. "Are there any old bicycles lying around here that I could use? If not, I'll buy one with my first paycheck."

"Why didn't I think of that? A bicycle is a great idea! I have one at home that I haven't ridden in years. I'll have Mike pump up the tires and bring it over for you. But I'm going to insist you wear a helmet."

"You won't have to twist my arm. I'd rather not have my brains smashed all over the pavement if some crazy driver runs me down."

Faith came around the desk and pulled up a chair next to Molly. "Now for the interesting news. I want you to be honest with me about this. Because I'm not sure how I feel about it myself. The events of last night have leaked to the press. I had a call from a reporter at the local network a few minutes ago. She's interested in interviewing you for the six o'clock news."

"Me?" Molly said, her hand flying to her chest. "But I wouldn't know what to say."

"They'll ask all the questions. You just have to be your genuine self. They may want to speak with Paula as well. They know a success story when they see one. The two of you are heroes, Molly. You saved lives last night."

She cringed at the thought of having cameras and microphones shoved in her face. But then what Rosalie had told them about the home's financial problems popped into her mind. The publicity would be good for Lovie's. It might even bring in some donations. And Faith had been so good to her, she wanted to do something nice in return.

"I'll do it!" she said, suddenly excited at the idea of being on TV.

"Are you sure?" Faith asked, and Molly nodded.

"Then I'll give the reporter a call back," Faith said, reaching for the phone.

Molly listened to the brief conversation. When Faith hung up, she said, "she'll be here in an hour."

"Lordy be. I'd better get myself upstairs to the shower," Molly said, sniffing her armpits. "I reckon I should wear a dress, but I don't have none."

Faith stood and offered Molly a hand. "Your shower will have to wait. Let's go down to the thrift closet and pick out something fitting for your television debut."

Word of the interview spread like wildfire among the residents, who were eager to help Molly prepare for the interview. Rosalie styled her hair, Jenny smeared makeup on her face, and Tilda loaned her the right accessories, a simple strand of pearls at the neck and studs in her ears to accent the blue linen sleeveless dress Faith had discovered at the back of the clothes rack.

Molly had never felt prettier. She almost didn't recognize herself in the mirror. She entered the solarium for the interview with a confidence she'd never known. Kimberly, the reporter, had a special way of posing her questions that made Molly feel at ease, and she barely noticed the cameramen. Without mentioning Bridget's name—because Faith had made it clear they needed to protect the girl's privacy—Molly repeated the events of the previous night.

When she finished with Molly, Kimberly interviewed a reluctant Paula who presented herself beautifully to the camera. Lastly, she spoke with the remaining residents as a group, with each contributing her own version of the story.

Faith and Robin left for the hospital immediately following the interview while the residents turned their attention to their afternoon chores. It took all six of them the whole afternoon to clean up the yard from the storm. By the time Faith and Robin returned at five thirty, they'd all showered and, barely able to contain their excitement, were waiting in the parlor in anticipation of the six o'clock news.

"Bridget is recovering nicely," Faith announced.

"Is she keeping the baby?" Rosalie asked.

"No," Faith said in a solemn tone. "She decided to put her up for adoption. Considering the circumstances, Dr. Robin and I feel she's making the right decision."

"Damn straight," Jenny said. "She was raped. Why would she want to keep that man's baby?"

The other residents bobbed their heads in agreement.

"Bridget and her mother will both be released from the hospital tomorrow," Faith said. "They'll stay here for a while before they go home."

Molly was glad she'd get the chance to see Bridget again. At five minutes till six, Faith turned on the television and tuned in the local news channel. Their story led the rest of the day's events. Molly thought her face looked fat on camera, but the other residents assured her she looked beautiful.

After the segment ended, Faith turned off the television and stood before the group. "You all did an amazing job with the interview. I can't tell you how proud I am of what you've achieved during your time here, both individually and as a group. I'll always hold a special place in my heart for you, my first group of residents. You're always welcome here." She smiled. "Although my hope is you'll come back for a visit and not as a resident." Her eyes traveled the group, pausing for a few seconds on each of the women.

Faith ordered pizza for dinner to celebrate. Cook had gotten tied up with her roof repair and never made it to work. They ate outside at the table on the porch and, knowing their time together was limited, they lingered a while afterward, enjoying one another's company. Having been up for more than thirty-six hours straight, the residents retired to their rooms early that night.

———

Molly woke early the next day feeling refreshed. When she went downstairs for breakfast, she found Faith glued to the television in the parlor sipping coffee. Molly stared dumbstruck at the sight of herself on *Good Morning America*.

"You're an overnight celebrity," Faith said. "Your story has gone viral. The phone has been ringing off the hook with requests for interviews and offers of donations. Thanks to you and the others, Lovie's Home has survived our first financial crisis."

Molly collapsed on the sofa next to Faith. "I didn't do anything anybody else wouldn't have done in the same shoes."

"That's not true, Molly. Some would've fainted. Some would've freaked out. But you remained calm. And you handled the interview with that humble charm of yours that wins people over. I'm not surprised that America loves you."

For the first time since her parents died, Molly actually believed she was lovable.

The cordless phone that was the house line rang on the coffee table in front of them. When Faith answered it, her face turned to stone. "Just a minute, please," she said, placing the caller on hold.

She held the phone out to Molly. "It's Penny. She wants to speak to you."

Remembering the hurtful way her sister had treated her, she pushed the phone away. "Tell her I'm busy. And to have a nice life."

31

JENNY

*L*ovie's was a flurry of activity on Thursday morning with the phone ringing off the hook and two security men at the end of the driveway keeping the press at bay. A frenzied Faith fielded calls, interviewed candidates for the receptionist position, and met with the man from the tree service about removing the stand of pines at the edge of the forest in front of the cottage. Business continued as usual for the residents, although they took breaks from their chores to enjoy one another's company, savoring their last days together. As of yet, no one had made definite plans to leave, but they all knew—it was the elephant in the room nobody dared to mention—that their time at Lovie's was coming to an end. With the exception of Paula of course, who was gaining the strength to finally embrace her recovery.

Cook, having heard the news on television, arrived early to work that morning, eager to be a part of the celebration. She served a delicious lunch of open-faced crab sandwiches—crab salad sprinkled with pepper jack cheese and toasted on a kaiser roll—and a fruit salad with fresh pineapple, kiwi, strawberries, oranges, and grapes. When the residents raved about the presentation, Cook said, "You think this is good, wait until you see what I'm cooking up for your supper."

Faith offered the blessing, thanking God not only for the food but for granting the residents the courage to endure their hardships and for giving her the opportunity to play a role in their recovery.

After they'd said amen, Faith lifted her glass of sweet tea in a toast. "Here's to you. At this moment in time, all eyes in this country are watching you. You have shown your fellow Americans about fortitude and friendship and teamwork. I hope you're proud of yourselves, because I'm extremely proud of you."

The women clinked glasses, and Tilda held hers up to Faith. "And here's to you, Miss Faith. Without you, we would never have gotten this far. *You* are responsible for the progress we've made during our time at Lovie's."

After more clinking and sipping, Faith instructed them to start eating. "I've been flooded with requests for more interviews this morning from all the major morning shows and twenty-four-hour news networks as well as *The View, 60 Minutes,* and *Entertainment Tonight.* But I've turned them all down. You've told your story. No good will come from telling it again and again. And I'd hate for the press to encroach on your privacy any more than they already have."

Around the table, heads nodded in agreement.

"When you leave here, if you decide as individuals that you'd like to grant an interview, I will support you."

The note of finality in Faith's voice came not as a surprise to Jenny but as a reminder that her departure from Lovie's was imminent.

"So." Faith planted her hands on the table. "I have big news. I've just gotten off the phone with the governor. Not only did he approve our grant request, he personally guaranteed the funding to build our annex."

The residents erupted in cheers.

Faith went on, "Exactly seventeen days ago, I cut the ribbon, declaring Lovie's Home for Wounded Hearts open to women in need of a safe place to heal from whatever abuse or hardship or grief they were experiencing in their lives. I knew firsthand how tremendous the need was for such a place, but I was terrified I would let you down. The six of you have shown me the way. The path is so much clearer for me now. There's a job to be done, and thanks to you, I know how to do it." She lifted her fork. "Enough lecture for one day."

At the sound of sniffling, Jenny risked a glance around the table, and aside from her own, there was not a dry eye in the room, including Cook who'd been eavesdropping from the kitchen doorway. She suspected the others were sad at the prospect of leaving the home. But Jenny didn't feel sad. She felt ready, excited even, to move to the next phase in her life, although there was one hurdle she'd yet to overcome. Somehow, she would have to find a way to break the news to her parents that she wouldn't be going home to Sumter.

The residents had been covering the reception desk in shifts after lunch, answering calls and logging messages. Jenny was taking her turn around three that afternoon when the front door burst open and her parents stormed in.

Jenny shot out of her chair. "Mom, Dad, what're you doing here?"

Her father pointed at the staircase. "Get your things, we're taking you home."

Her mother elbowed her father out of the way. "That woman . . . that Faith whatshername is making a fool out of you. Now everyone in the whole country knows you're locked up in some insane asylum. You'll never be able to show your face in Sumter again."

"Good, because I'm not going back to Sumter. And need I remind you, Mother, that you're the one who insisted I come here."

The phone rang and Jenny sat back down to answer it, scribbling yet another message for Faith while her parents glared down at her. She hung up the phone and leaned back in the chair. She had the upper hand for a change, not because of the situation but because she'd become an adult. She was no longer their little girl. She was her own person. She'd proven to herself that she didn't need her parents to survive.

The pilot planted a hand on her hip. "You're trying my patience, young lady. Now get up out of that chair, march yourself upstairs, and pack your things."

She twisted the ink pen around her fingers, a habit that had always irritated the pilot. "I'm not a child, Mother. You can't order me around anymore."

Faith emerged from her office. "What's all the commotion?" When she saw Jenny's parents, she said, "Catherine, Carl, how nice to see you."

"I wish I could say the same to you," her father said. "We are appalled at the way you're exploiting our daughter with this media circus."

Her mother jabbed a finger at Faith. "You've brainwashed Jenny. She says she's not coming home with us."

Faith opened her office door wider. "Why don't we talk in private," she said, stepping out of the way for Jenny and her parents to enter her office.

"Have a seat." Closing the door behind her, Faith walked over to her desk, picked up the phone, and summoned Dr. Robin to her office. "We have a situation. Jenny's parents are here."

Dr. Robin arrived less than a minute later, pulling up a chair to complete their circle. "Your daughter has made great progress over the past few days. She's addressing her anger management issues and making a lot of new friends."

Her father said, "You make Jenny sound like a disobedient ch—"

The pilot shot him a death stare that silenced him. "If that's the case, she's ready to go home."

"She's ready to leave Lovie's," Robin said. "Where she goes from here is up to her."

Jenny took a deep breath for courage. "And I'm moving with Caroline to her farm. I'm going to help her start a plant nursery."

Her father humphed. "You most certainly are not. You're coming home to run the lumber company. You have an obligation to your family."

Anger pulsed through Jenny's veins, and she was hit by a strong urge to scream at her father. Instead, she crossed her legs and inspected her fingernails as though bored. "That's the thing though, Daddy. I don't have an obligation to anyone but myself. Until now, I've lived my life according to you. I went to business school instead of NYC to study art. I've been managing *your* lumber company, even though I have to drag myself to work every morning because I hate it so much. I even married Derek, despite that gnawing feeling that warned me not to, because you thought him the perfect man for me. He was the perfect man for you, as a son-in-law, but not for me as a husband."

Her father's face turned red with either anger or shame—Jenny wasn't sure which. "I had no way of knowing Derek would turn out to be such a deadbeat."

"That Derek business is all behind you now." The pilot gave Jenny the once-over. "I can see how much you've improved. You've even stopped humming. You'll find a new husband in no time."

Jenny's feet hit the floor. "I don't want a new husband. Not now. Maybe not ever." She crossed the room and swung open the door. "You can leave now. I'm not going home with you and that's final."

A bewildered expression crossed her mother's face. "Are you saying you don't want us to be a part of your life?"

"Not if I have to live that life on your terms."

"Everyone calm down, please," Dr. Robin said, standing. "Let's talk this through and see if we can come to an understanding."

"What am I supposed to do with the lumber company?" her father asked. "I built it for you."

"That's not true, Dad, and you know it. You built that company for yourself. And now that you're ready to retire, you're trying to pawn it off on me." Jenny threw her hands in the air. "Sell the company. Take that trip around the world that you're always talking about. Move to the beach or buy a house on Kiawah and live out your days playing golf. I don't care what you do as long as you let me make my own choices about my life."

Her parents softened as they looked at one another, and Jenny knew she'd won them over.

"Sit back down, honey." Her mother eyed her empty chair. "And tell us about this plant nursery."

Jenny sat back down, and for the next fifteen minutes, she told her parents about Caroline's plans for her nursery. "This would only be temporary for me. I need some time to myself, and this seems as good a way as any to get it. I'll work with her through the summer and fall and reassess my situation come December. I'm hoping to find a local artist who might be willing to mentor me. Caroline says there's plenty of wildlife and land-scapes to paint at her farm. Who knows? I may even decide to go back to school, to NYU this time."

Her father let out a sigh of annoyance. "Not that again."

"I told you," the pilot said, sending an elbow to her father's ribs. "If you'd listened to me when she was applying to colleges, we wouldn't be in this mess."

"And just how do you plan to support yourself with no income?" her father asked.

"I have plenty of money in my savings. And I'll earn free room and board working for Caroline. I think you'd feel better about the situation if you met her. I'm sure she's out in the garden." Jenny slowly rose to her feet. "Shall we go find her?"

"Sure," her mother said with an eager expression. "I'd like to meet her."

Her father rolled his eyes, but he followed them out of Faith's office, grumbling about meeting the girl with the ludicrous idea about starting a nursery on her own."

Jenny smirked. Her father was in for a big surprise. Caroline was no girl.

She led them down the hall, out the front door, and across the yard to the garden. She called to Caroline who was staking tomato plants. "My parents came for a visit. They want to meet you." She lowered her tone so only her parents could hear. "And be nice."

Caroline straightened and adjusted her sunhat. She smiled and waved as she made her way toward them.

"She's a looker," her father said, "for someone so old."

"Do you consider yourself old, Dad? Because she's younger than you are."

When she made the introductions, Caroline said, "I've heard so much about you," even though Jenny had told her very little about her parents. She wished she'd had a chance to warn Caroline that her parents might be rude.

"Jenny was just telling us about your business venture," her father said. "I have some concerns about allowing my daughter to live in the woods with a virtual stranger. Do you mind if I ask why you're here? I need to make certain you're emotionally stable before I offer my blessing."

"Dad!"

"It's fine, Jenny. I don't blame your parents for being concerned." Caroline drew in an unsteady breath. "The truth is, I lost my son several years ago in an ATV accident. Cory was only a few years younger than Jenny." She looked away from them, fixing her gaze on her garden. "I came here initially as a volunteer. When I went home at the end of my first day, my husband was waiting at the door with his bags packed. He'd taken a job on the West Coast without consulting me. Our marriage did not survive our tragedy."

Jenny's mother reached for Caroline's hand. "I'm so terribly sorry."

"Thank you," Caroline said with a warm smile. "Two weeks ago, I couldn't talk about Cory without tearing up. But Faith, and her nephew Jamie, who was my son's best friend, and Dr. Robin and all the wonderful women here like your daughter have helped me finally get my feet back on the ground. For the first time in years, I have some direction in my life. I can't guarantee the nursery will be a success, but I plan to have a good time finding out. I love to garden, as you can see." She spread her arms wide at the bountiful landscape of vegetables and flowers.

"Your garden is lovely, Caroline. I'm certain your nursery will be a success. I'd like to come visit sometime." Her mother turned to Jenny. "If you'll have me."

She smiled. "I'd like that very much."

Her father leaned over and pecked Jenny's cheek. "Stay in touch."

Jenny's eyes met Caroline's and they burst out laughing.

"What's so funny?" her father asked.

"Caroline and I destroyed our phones," Jenny explained. "Not at the same time. She threw hers in the creek on her first day here, and I smashed mine with a shovel when I saw Christy and Derek's engagement picture on Instagram."

A smile tugged at her father's lips. "I can't say I blame you. I'll have my secretary send a replacement from our cellular provider."

"Thanks, Dad, but it's time for me to pay for my own phone." She nudged Caroline. "We've already decided. The cell phone store will be our first stop when we leave here."

3 2

FAITH

aith worried that, after two decades on staff at the Creekside Regional Hospital, Mike would have a difficult time saying goodbye to the emergency room. But he worked his last graveyard shift on Friday night, bid adieu to his coworkers on Saturday morning, and drove off in his pickup truck without so much as a glance back. He went straight to U-Haul and rented a truck. He enlisted help from Eli and Jamie, and since late morning, the threesome had been moving furniture from their house to the cottage. By three o'clock, they'd already made three trips and were nearly finished moving the necessities. They would store whatever furniture remained in the house until construction on their new home was complete. Once the decision had been made, Faith had become increasingly more eager to move. She would miss the view of the inlet, but she wouldn't miss the memories of the bad things that had happened to her in that house. She would no longer have to walk around the spot in the hall where her ex-husband had bled to death.

The tree service had already removed the stand of pines in front of the cottage, offering them a different view of a different part of the inlet, a more serene vista, a quiet creek without the constant boat traffic and a large expanse of marsh grass.

They'd found plans online for a simple Lowcountry cottage with a wide front porch, three bedrooms—two up with a first-floor master—and one common living area with kitchen, great room, and dining area. Mike had already scheduled meetings for early in the week with three different builders to begin the process of getting bids.

The residents had decided as a group that making a mass exodus from the home would be easier than departing one at a time. Cook had planned an impromptu farewell party for them on the porch that Saturday afternoon. She'd made blueberry pound cake and was churning homemade peach ice cream. Bitsy, who'd been helping the men in her life with the move, was keeping one eye on the back door, waiting with anticipation for Cook to emerge from the kitchen with her bucket of ice cream. When the cook finally made her appearance, Bitsy dashed across the yard and rang the dinner bell, announcing the party had begun.

The residents exited the house as one, with the exception of Paula who had sequestered herself to her darkened bedroom with a migraine. Bridget and her mother had been released from the hospital the day before, and they'd mostly kept to themselves since arriving at the home. Faith was allowing them the weekend to settle in. The process of healing would begin for them on Monday. Faith predicted they'd be staying at Lovie's for a good long time. Five new residents were already lined up to arrive on Monday from different parts of the state. And based on the number of inquiries she'd received, she anticipated having all of her beds filled by the end of next week. Not that long ago, the thought of having a full house had terrified Faith, but having Mike at her side and money in the bank instilled a new confidence in her.

Faith made the point of speaking with each of the residents in turn as they stood on the lawn, eating ice cream and cake and chatting with the men and Bitsy. Tilda pressed a check into her hand and Faith did a double take at the amount.

"This is so very generous of you, Tilda. I don't know how to thank you."

Tilda placed a hand on Faith's forearm. "I'm the one who should be thanking you, dear. And there's more where that came from. Sometime in the fall, if you're interested, I'd like to host a cocktail reception in your honor with the goal of garnering support for Lovie's Home."

"That would be wonderful. I'd like that very much," Faith said, making a mental note to talk to Moses about appointing Tilda to the board of directors. Her perspective as a past resident would be invaluable to them in making decisions. "What're your plans for the summer?"

"My intention is to stay busy. I'm hoping to reconnect with some of my old friends, but I'm also going to take your advice and talk to Heidi Butler about a part-time job. I've shopped at Tasty Provisions many times, and I think I'd enjoy interacting with their type of clientele."

"You'd be perfect for the job. I'll put in a good word for you with Heidi."

Tilda surprised Faith when she burst into tears. "These are happy tears. I'm just so grateful to you for all you've done for me."

Faith handed her a napkin to wipe her eyes. "Something tells me our relationship has just begun."

When Faith moved on to Rosalie, the young woman's face was aglow and she talked a mile a minute. "I have an interview at the cosmetology school on Tuesday. As soon as I get settled, I'm going to look for a job for the summer. I hope one of the salons will hire me as a receptionist or shampoo girl. Then again, I'd make good tip money waitressing. What do you think, Faith?"

"I think you'll know the right job when you find it," Faith said. "And I know you'll take good care of Tilda."

"We'll take good care of each other."

Faith gave Rosalie a hug. "Study hard. I have a feeling I'll be driving to Charleston to have my hair done from now on."

That landed a big smile on Rosalie's face, and she went off in search of a second helping of ice cream.

Jenny and Caroline were standing together when she approached them. "I'm really going to miss you two."

"No, you won't," Caroline said with a wide grin. "Because we're not going anywhere. Jenny's parents are bringing her car to her this week. We've already talked about it, and one of us will come by every few days to check on our garden."

"Really?" Faith said, placing her hand on her chest. "That would be so wonderful."

Jamie joined their circle, giving Caroline a half hug. "Let me know as soon as you have some vegetables to sell."

"We've decided to try our hand at beekeeping," Jenny said. "With any luck, we'll have some honey for you by summer's end."

Caroline eyed the moving truck. "Faith, do you know how long Mike will have the truck?"

"He has to return it Monday morning. Why?"

"Do you think he'll let me borrow it to move a few things from my house to the farm?"

"Sure," Faith said. "I don't see why not."

Caroline looked at Jamie. "Are your services for hire?"

Jamie winked at her. "For you, Mama Caroline, my services are free."

Faith smiled to herself. Having Jamie back in her life had done more good for Caroline than the hours she'd spent in counseling with Robin. Out of their love and grief for Cory, a new relationship had begun to develop between them. Faith had no doubt that Caroline would love him like her second son, and Jamie would be as loyal to his Mama Caroline as he was to Sam.

When the time came for them to go, the residents migrated through the house to the driveway. Tilda had hired a car service to drive her and Rosalie to Charleston. The driver had already loaded their luggage into the trunk of the black sedan and was waiting for them alongside Caroline's SUV under the porte cochère. Faith blew kisses and waved at them as they drove off together—Jenny and Caroline, Tilda and Rosalie.

"I'm going to miss them," Molly said, sniffling.

Now that Tilda was gone, Molly would be moving into Emilee's room, and Faith, who'd been sleeping in one of the vacant resident rooms, would be spending her first night in the cottage with Mike and Bitsy.

Faith leaned in close to Molly. "Me too. But while we won't see them every day, I have a feeling that our friendship with those four is just beginning."

Faith felt a lump in her throat. Her journey had been long, but she was finally able to bury the past and move toward the future. Not since her childhood, growing up in the little yellow cottage on the inlet with her parents and two sisters, had she felt such joy and peace as she felt at that moment standing with her loved ones in front of Lovie's Home. She would always miss her mother terribly, but Faith took great pride in knowing that Lovie's memory would live on through the lives of the women who crossed the threshold of her Home for Wounded Hearts.

A NOTE FROM THE AUTHOR

I wrote this novel with a heavy heart knowing so many of my reader friends face life-threatening challenges every day. The lighthearted tone of *Home for Wounded Hearts* is intended to uplift and not in any way diminish the difficult situations many of you are enduring.

You are not alone if you're suffering from domestic violence. Call The National Domestic Violence Hotline today.

Homeless and need help? Reach out to the National Coalition for the Homeless.

ACKNOWLEDGMENTS

I'm grateful to the many people who helped make this novel possible. First and foremost, to my editor, Patricia Peters, for her patience and advice and for making my work stronger without changing my voice. To my literary agent, Andrea Hurst, for her guidance and expertise in the publishing industry and for believing in my work. A great big heartfelt thank-you to Kathy Sinclair, criminal investigator with the Bartow County Sherriff's Office, and good friend Alison Fauls for giving me honest and construct feedback on my works in progress. To Stella Schindler for sharing her adorable chickens with me. To Karen Stephens for information regarding real estate. And to my behind-the-scenes team, Geneva Agnos and Kate Rock, for all the many things you do to manage my social media so effectively.

I am blessed to have many supportive people in my life who offer the encouragement I need to continue the pursuit of my writing career. I owe a huge debt of gratitude to my advanced review team, the lovely ladies of Georgia's Porch, for their enthusiasm for and commitment to my work. To Leslie at Levy's and the staff at Grove Avenue Pharmacy for helping my books make it into the hands of local readers. Love and thanks to my family—

my mother, Joanne; my husband, Ted; and the best children in the world, Cameron and Ned.

Most of all, I'm grateful to my wonderful readers for their love of women's fiction. I love hearing from you. Feel free to shoot me an email at ashleyhfarley@gmail.com or stop by my website at ashleyfarley.com for more information about my characters and upcoming releases. Don't forget to sign up for my newsletter. Your subscription will grant you exclusive content, sneak previews, and special giveaways.

ABOUT THE AUTHOR

Ashley writes books about women for women. Her characters are mothers, daughters, sisters, and wives facing real-life issues. Her goal is to keep you turning the pages until the wee hours of the morning. If her story stays with you long after you've read the last word, then she's done her job.

Ashley is a wife and mother of two young adult children. She grew up in the salty marshes of South Carolina, but now lives in Richmond, Virginia, a city she loves for its history and traditions.

Ashley loves to hear from her readers. Feel free to visit her website or shoot her an email. For more information about upcoming releases, don't forget to sign up for her newsletter at ashleyfarley.com/newsletter-signup/. Your subscription will grant you exclusive content, sneak previews, and special giveaways.

ashleyfarley.com
ashleyhfarley@gmail.com